An Interview with President Custer


Author: Joe Plegge
PresidentCuster.com

Plegge Enterprises
Dickinson, North Dakota 58601

First Edition
ISBN: 978-0-98-822662-3

# Table of Contents

# Preface

Have you ever wondered how changing one historical turning point could reshape the future? In this speculative history, I explore the hypothetical scenario: What if George Armstrong Custer had survived the Battle of the Little Bighorn? This story imagines his unexpected rise to the presidency, becoming the 19th President of the United States. While I believe pivotal events such as World War I, the Great Depression, and World War II would still occur, this narrative explores the alternative political and personal landscape that Custer's survival creates.

The central part of the story is set in 1926, when young journalist Ethan Thorne visits the mansion of former President Custer in Laurel, Maryland. Ethan's task is significant: to conduct a frank interview with the General, urging him to reveal his achievements and the darker truths of his past, including the crucial events at the Little Bighorn. As Ethan is led into the library, his career-defining quest to understand Custer, the man, with all his complexities, begins.

My journey into Custer's world began as a young child, sparked by stories at Fort Sheridan, Illinois. My father was in the Army and stationed there for a few years before his next assignment. On the base, a 227-foot-tall tower was visible from a great distance in any direction, and everyone knew the rumor that Sitting Bull had been held prisoner there for a short time. This event fueled the imagination of a young boy. I did not realize the rumor was false until I researched historical facts for this novel. The tower turned out to be a water tower with a brick exterior, not a detention facility. Sitting Bull was never held at Fort Sheridan.

It's fascinating how a small, seemingly insignificant phrase can spark a wide range of ideas, and that's precisely what happened to me. I remember studying Elizabeth B. Custer's books, getting lost in her life on the American frontier, when a particular phrase jumped out at me: "back in the States." The phrase struck a chord with me; as a kid, I often used it while living with my family in Bangkok, Thailand, where my dad was stationed. "Back in the States" was our shorthand for home, for everything familiar and distant. Reading Elizabeth Custer's stories about living in the harsh Dakota Territory in the 1800s and seeing that exact phrase created an unexpected and powerful link across time, softening the stiff historical image of her husband, George, and deepening my long-lasting fascination with the legendary and tragic Battle of the Little Bighorn.

My interest in such pivotal conflicts is longstanding. As a civilian instructor at the U.S. Army Armor School at Fort Knox, Kentucky, I spent years grading battle analysis papers, scrutinizing decisions and outcomes, and constantly pondering the numerous "what-ifs" of history. The armor lieutenants studied many battles, from ancient times to the present. One of their assignments was to write about how they could apply the lessons from these battles to improve their leadership skills. Through their writings, I learned about the tactics—both the strengths and weaknesses—used by military leaders.

My visit to the Little Bighorn Battlefield National Monument in 2000 deepened my interest in this story. Standing on Last Stand Hill, I could feel the weight of history, which made me wonder: What if Custer had survived? This book explores that alternate history, considering the possible ripple effects and different paths his survival might have set into motion.

A note on terminology: I intentionally use "Indians" throughout this book instead of "Native Americans" solely to preserve historical accuracy and reflect the language of the period.

After researching Custer's life, I incorporated real events and figures from 1876 to 1926 into the story. Sitting Bull, for example, participated in the July 4th parade in Bismarck, Dakota Territory, in 1889. For narrative purposes, I deliberately created new events, including details of the Battle of the Little Bighorn and Elizabeth B. Custer's life.

Join me as we examine the life of former President George Armstrong Custer, who defied death at the Battle of the Little Bighorn and finally shares his story, revealing not just his history but the complex heart of a living legend.

## Chapter 1: The Assignment

The air in the office was thick and blue, and Walter Bennett, the editor-in-chief of the *Washington Sentinel*, sat behind his desk smoking a cigar. He was a true newspaperman, with ink running through his veins. The ever-present cloud of smoke lingered in his office, a silent sign of his love for Cuban cigars. The constant haze was as much a part of his office as he was.

He had just secured the story of a lifetime.

As he hung up the phone, he sprang to his feet, his eyes blazing with fiery enthusiasm. His persistent efforts finally paid off; he secured the interview he had been working on for years. Feeling the need for immediate action, he started his plan. He stepped to his doorway. “Nora, send Thorne to my office the moment he gets back,” he instructed.

Nora’s reply was crisp, “Yes, sir. Will do.”

Bennett leaned back into his old leather office chair, which creaked and groaned under his weight. He was a stout man, with a ruddy complexion and eyes that missed nothing. He had worked his way from the mailroom to the top office, gaining a wealth of knowledge and insight into the business from the inside out. Guided by a strong moral compass and tireless dedication, he led by example, always inspiring his team to give their best.

When Nora handed Ethan the message, he headed directly to Bennett’s office. Normally, his conversations with the editor and fellow reporters were casual and straightforward, but this urgent call was unusual and unsettling. He knocked on the open door and asked, “You wanted to see me, Boss?”

“Yes, Ethan. Come in and close the door,” Bennett stated as he gestured toward the chair in front of his desk.

Ethan took a deep breath, shut the door, and sat down.

“We're preparing a special feature for the anniversary of Custer's presidential election. It’s been 50 years since he was elected in 1876. I’m assigning this story to you. Now, I’m taking a pretty big risk by putting you on this report,” Bennett puffed on his cigar. “You’re young and not very experienced, but you proved yourself with that piece you wrote about the Sinclair Oil leases.”

Bennett continued, "It was good work. Sharp. You didn’t just report the facts from the Senate hearing; you dug up land deeds and followed the money. You've uncovered the story behind the story, and those extra details are what separate a good story from a great one. Your personality encourages people to speak openly, resulting in more candid responses.”

“I’ve been working for years to secure this interview, so don’t let me down on this project. Your goal is to make the former president speak honestly. Question him about the war, his political campaign, the extraordinary events at the Little Bighorn, and his life after politics. Remember, he’s quite the performer. He’ll enjoy the challenge if you give him a chance. And don't be fooled by his age. He's still clever and has a trick or two up his sleeve."

Ethan nodded, feeling the burden of responsibility settle on his shoulders, with a heavy mix of excitement and nervousness flowing through him.

Bennett leaned forward, his eyes small and sharp, locking onto Ethan. "Every paper from here to San Francisco will run a retrospective. They'll print the same tired photos and rehash the same old speeches about Manifest Destiny and national pride. It's boilerplate. It's filler. It's not a story. I want the man himself."

Ethan's mind raced. "An interview? Sir, he hasn't given a substantial one in twenty years."

"Correct. He has spent half a century shaping his own legend, turning his life into a statue. He's refused every request we've sent for the past decade." Bennett paused, taking a long drag from his cigar and exhaling a cloud of blue smoke. "But his aide called this morning. The General is ready to talk. For the anniversary, he wants to tell his story one last time. And he's granted exclusive access to the *Sentinel.* And it's not just any interview. I had been pitching the idea, reminding him of his life before he was president, when a reporter traveled with him during military campaigns, allowing him to present the real Custer. It must have appealed to him because he agreed to an interview spanning several days."

A surge of raw, unfiltered ambition surged through Ethan. This was the kind of assignment that could define a career.

"I want you to have it, Thorne. I believe you're the right man for the job."

Ethan was stunned into silence. He looked at Bennett, searching for a joke, but the editor's gaze was serious. "Me, sir? With all due respect, shouldn't it go to a senior correspondent?"

"A senior correspondent will go in thinking they already know the story," Bennett interrupted sharply. "They'll ask about Gettysburg, the election deadlock, and the end of Reconstruction. They'll get the same canned speeches Custer's been giving since 1880. You, on the other hand, are young, and I'm depending on you to ask real questions."

Bennett leaned back. "Look, kid, I know you're green. But that Sinclair business showed me you have instincts. You aren't afraid to dig. I don't want a puff piece. I want the truth. I want the mud and blood of the Civil War, not just the parades. I want to know what his presidency cost him and what it cost the country. I want to know what a man who has outlived his legend thinks about when the lights go out."

He pointed a thick finger at Ethan. "Your first session with him starts next Thursday. Go to his estate. Spend as much time as he'll give you. Get his story. The whole thing: from Appomattox to the Little Bighorn to the White House to wherever he is now. This series will commemorate the anniversary on the front page for a week. It's the biggest story of the year. I don't want you working on anything else but this project, starting right now."

Ethan's mind was a whirlwind of names, dates, and battlefields. He felt a tremor of fear mixed with excitement. He was asked to interview a monument. Ethan understood that this opportunity could potentially shape his career path in profound ways, either elevating it to new heights of success or plunging it into uncertainty.

"He's so experienced at controlling his public image. What if I can't get past the legend, Sir?" Ethan asked sincerely.

Bennett's expression softened for a moment. "Custer's a vain man, Thorne. Always has been. He wants this story told. He thinks he can control the narrative and shape it one last time for the history books. Your job is to listen, to let him talk, but to find the cracks. Find the details he doesn't want to discuss. That's where the real man is. The man inside the statue."

He stood up, signaling the end of the meeting. "Oh, here is our file with everything we have on the General, and here are your train tickets and vouchers to and from Laurel, Maryland," Bennett said as he handed Ethan an envelope from his cluttered desk. "It leaves Union Station at 7:45 a.m. and begins the return trip at 6:15 p.m. If you're late, you'll have to provide your own transportation. Custer's driver will meet you at the station. All you need to do is concentrate on getting this story."

Ethan stood up and grabbed the envelope, his legs feeling unsteady. He left the office in a daze, with the familiar noise of the newsroom sounding distant and muffled.

He had a week to prepare to meet the man whose very existence had become folklore. Seven days to figure out how a young reporter with just one good story could uncover the truth in the memory of a living hero. He sat at his desk and pulled a fresh sheet of paper into his Underwood typewriter. At the top, he typed a single name.

CUSTER

The single name stared back at him, stark and imposing on the bright white page. It felt less like a subject and more like a challenge, a wall to climb. The newsroom, usually a lively chorus of clicking keys, shouted conversations, and ringing phones, now seemed to hum with an almost suffocating silence around his small corner. The magnitude of Custer's half-century lore, the hero of the Civil War, and the architect of a controversial but undeniable presidency pressed down on him.

Ethan spent the remainder of that day and the long evening hunched over Bennett's thick file. It was not just a collection of clippings; it was an archive. Yellowed telegraphs detailing troop movements, faded political cartoons showing Custer with his iconic long, flowing hair and flamboyant uniforms, transcripts of Senate speeches, reports from the Reconstruction era, and a surprisingly detailed account of the Little Bighorn incident from various, often conflicting, perspectives. There were photographs too: a dashing young cavalry officer, a triumphant general accepting surrender from his enemies, a stern-faced candidate on the campaign trail, and more recently, an aged statesmanlike figure still holding a glint of the old fire in his eyes.

Warm coffee and a growing sense of awe and dread kept him working late into the night. The legend was undeniable, crafted with meticulous care over fifty years. Custer had been a master of public perception even before the term existed. However, as Ethan cross-checked dates and events, he began to see faint outlines of the "cracks" Bennett mentioned: gaps in the story, sudden shifts in political alliances, and an ongoing controversy surrounding the decisive battle that made him famous and eventually led to the presidency. The Civil War section, especially around Appomattox, was surprisingly light on personal reflection, focusing primarily on military strategy and public praise. And the Little Bighorn? A victory, of course, but the details were vague; the "extraordinary events" Bennett discussed were left tantalizingly unclear.

The following six days blurred into a relentless cycle of research. Ethan almost lived in the public library, poring over old newspaper archives, examining dusty historical texts, and scanning through the Congressional Record. He read both complimentary and critical biographies, trying to piece together a detailed, honest portrait of the man. He filled notebook after notebook with questions, organizing them into categories: early life, military career, the

Little Bighorn, the campaign, the presidency, post-political life, and personal reflections. He practiced his phrasing, looking for ways to ask about painful or controversial topics without sounding accusatory but genuinely seeking comprehension.

His small apartment had turned into a war room, with papers scattered across all surfaces and a timeline of Custer's life pinned to the wall. He underlined key phrases, circled inconsistencies, and drew connections that were not immediately obvious. Bennett's words echoed: "Don't be fooled by his age. He's still clever and has a trick or two up his sleeve." And, "I want the mud and blood of the Civil War, not just the parades."

By Wednesday evening, Ethan felt both exhausted and oddly prepared. He had immersed himself so completely in Custer's world that he started to feel like he knew the man, or at least his public persona. He anticipated the story Custer would probably share and, more importantly, the awkward silences he would need to handle with skill. He had crafted his "real questions," designed to pierce through the polished exterior and reveal the man underneath.

He packed a small satchel with his notebooks, a freshly sharpened pencil, and a few extras. He dressed in his best: a dark, well-pressed wool suit. He spent extra time polishing his boots, hoping to impress the General. The train tickets and vouchers sat on his bedside table, serving as a tangible reminder of the monumental task ahead.

Ethan sat at a table to write a letter to his fiancée, Julia. He had received two letters from her the previous week, but he had not responded because he had been working long hours on research.

He wanted to share the incredible opportunity he'd received and express his excitement about it. He hoped to explain how his name would always be associated with this monumental series of articles and the pressure he felt to do well. He recognized that success could lead to more opportunities and potential achievements for both his future and theirs.

However, seeing the time, he realized it was too late to send a detailed letter. Instead, he decided to write a short note. He planned to mail it to Julia on his way to the train station the next morning.

He apologized for not writing sooner and explained that Mr. Bennett had assigned him a significant story to cover, which kept him busy with research. He said he was eager to share all the details with her as soon as possible and noted he would be fully immersed in the project for the next two weeks. He probably would not be able to send many letters during that time, but he promised to make it up to her later.

It was late, and he knew he needed to stay clear-headed for the next day. He reminded himself that he was prepared and ready for what lay ahead, trying to calm his nerves. As he finally drifted off to sleep, he dreamed of the train's rhythmic movement and low rumble, taking him toward Laurel, a living legend, and the biggest story of his emerging career.

## Chapter 2: The First Session

Union Station was chilly the morning Ethan prepared to board the train to Laurel, marking the start of a journey to a remote estate in Maryland. As the train started to move, he paused to adjust his tie, reflecting the mix of nervousness and excitement he felt about the trip ahead. The steady clatter of the train wheels against the iron tracks provided a calming backdrop for his racing thoughts as he pondered the importance of this venture.

The crisp, earthy October breeze slipped through the ill-fitting windows of the old passenger car, swirling around him and softly rustling the pages of his well-worn notebook. The gentle breeze whispered the season's secrets, carrying the nostalgic aroma of fallen leaves and a touch of winter coming.

He looked out at the expanding view. The trees along the tracks swayed in a captivating dance of colors. The steady oaks clung to only a few of their dark, shiny leaves, while the dazzling maples displayed a spectacular show of fiery reds and golds. The stunning landscape stirred a mix of excitement and hesitation within him. This trip marked his first visit to Laurel, and he felt the heft of the day's significance pressing down on him, like the well-worn pencil behind his ear, ready to record the key moments ahead.

Taking a deep breath, he tried to calm his nerves as he looked at the other passengers in the car. Every face he saw seemed to hide a mystery, hinting at stories waiting to be uncovered, and fueling his strong desire to record them.

He focused on his project interviewing General Custer, a renowned military figure and former U.S. president, known for his bold leadership, unconventional behavior, disregard for social norms, and unique interactions.

As the train began to slow, Ethan felt his heartbeat match the rhythmic screeching of the brakes on the metal tracks. He leaned closer to the window and watched the outside scenery transform into something lively and vivid. A large peach orchard, nestled in the suburban landscape, came into view. The trees were arranged in long rows, with their lower branches bare, while the higher branches stubbornly held on to the last leaves, resisting the approaching winter chill. To Ethan, those trees symbolized a slow, poignant retreat, a visual sign of autumn surrendering to the inevitable cold.

"Next stop: Laurel," announced the conductor, briefly breaking the silence and pulling Ethan out of his thoughts. As the train smoothly came to a stop at the station, he took a breath, readying himself for what lay ahead. The importance of the challenge felt like a comfortable coat, wrapping around him with purpose. Ethan saw this job as a rare opportunity to learn about history and maybe add a new chapter to the inspiring story of a man who greatly influenced the nation.

Ethan stood with determination, adjusting his overcoat as he stepped down. His satchel swayed gently, and his trusted notebook stayed securely under his arm. The train station buzzed with activity and noise, but his heartbeat was louder than everything else as he focused on his surroundings. A sleek black car sat quietly beside the platform, a silent guardian amidst the chaos. As he approached the vehicle, the driver, a tall, thin man in a sharply tailored dark coat, tipped his hat politely. The man radiated professionalism and anticipation. "Mr. Thorne?" the driver asked, his voice smooth yet commanding, cutting through the ambient noise and drawing Ethan's full attention.

"Yes," Ethan replied with confidence, locking eyes with the driver, his gaze steady and deliberate, hoping to show he was ready for the task ahead.

"General Custer is expecting you," the driver told him, pointing toward the open back door of the vehicle. Those words sank into Ethan's mind, heightening the importance of what was about to happen.

As they drove through the charming town, where friendly faces greeted them and lovely shops lined the streets with colorful displays, Ethan let the calming scenery surround him like a warm, reassuring hug. In the distance, he saw fields of ripened corn swaying gently in the breeze and vast meadows passing by, creating a beautiful backdrop against the calm sky above.

Traveling along the winding gravel path that led to the grand estate, Ethan felt a rush of excitement and anticipation, imagining the splendor awaiting him. Still, his focus stayed on the high-stakes interview that was now just moments away. To his right, a fenced area held several well-groomed horses, their majestic bodies grazing peacefully, with sleek coats shining brightly in the sunlight, showing shades of rich caramel and dark ebony. Beyond that captivating scene, he could see the outlines of sturdy stables and training pens—practical structures that were also decorative and meant to make a good impression.

The grand house loomed majestically ahead, a regal blend of neoclassical design adorned with tall white columns framed by expansive porches, ideal for captivating summer nights lit by the flickering glow of fireflies. Large, shiny windows reflected the sky above, forming a mirror-like surface that changed with the weather. An American flag hung from its pole, its colors muted in the calm of that beautiful day, fluttering softly as if silently greeting.

When the car smoothly came to a stop, the driver skillfully exited and approached Ethan's door with a professional demeanor.

As Ethan stepped outside, the driver signaled for him to come to the front door and said, "The General is waiting for you inside." Ethan's eyes were attracted to the view of the mansion, brightly lit by the sunlight but partly hidden by a large apple orchard on its left. The branches of the trees were almost bare, and the fallen leaves drifted gently around the trunks, swirling gracefully.

Determined, Ethan's hand hovered near the heavy, ornately carved door, ready to knock. Before he could tap, the door swung open, revealing a direct view into the inner realm of the mansion.

At the entrance, a commanding man in a sleek black coat that suggested sophistication stood tall, his confident stance radiating strength and poise. His face bore a professional, stoic expression, hiding any inner thoughts and maintaining a calm, composed demeanor.

"Mr. Thorne," the man said in a low, commanding voice that carried a sense of importance. "Welcome. I am Harold," he introduced himself, his tone warm but formal, setting the tone with seriousness.

Ethan nodded in acknowledgment, feeling a complex mix of pride and nervous anticipation. "Thank you. It's an honor to be here," he said sincerely, stepping inside and crossing the threshold, ready to begin a journey that might change his life.

"Follow me," Harold instructed, motioning with an inviting gesture, leading Ethan into the grand home, a world where each step promised discoveries waiting to be revealed.

As they walked through the grand and imposing entrance, Ethan was immersed in a soft, soothing blend of aged leather, shiny polished wood, and the gentle, lingering scent of pipe smoke that subtly drifted through the air, creating a warm, inviting atmosphere. Harold, acting as a gracious host, led him through a series of rooms that resembled museum exhibits more than ordinary living spaces, each filled with fascinating artifacts. The inviting seating areas that Ethan glimpsed featured plush, comfy chairs that invited passersby to sink in and stay a while, losing themselves in conversation or reflection. Meanwhile, gentle lamps flickered warmly in their corners, casting a cozy glow that illuminated walls adorned with a captivating collection of old portraits. Among these striking images were depictions of a younger Custer, who exuded determination and ambition; his moments of victory were captured beautifully, each picture showing the unmistakable sparkle of ambition in his eyes.

Eventually, the carefully curated rooms led them to the library, a haven of knowledge and imagination that Ethan yearned to explore. The sight of the library shelves surpassed his expectations. Harold paused at the door, returning to offer one last reassuring remark.

“The General will be with you shortly,” Harold confidently stated. "In the meantime, please make yourself completely at home, and you are welcome to explore the surroundings.” He graciously stepped aside, allowing Ethan to enter the library and immerse himself in its rich atmosphere.

A wave of excitement and reverence swept through Ethan as he entered the room, his eyes drawn immediately to the tall shelves filled with a wide array of books, each a gateway to different worlds and limitless ideas. This space was more than just a room; it was alive with the promise of knowledge and the potential for personal growth. He settled into a plush armchair that supported him comfortably, mentally preparing for the critical conversation ahead.

Suddenly, he heard the sharp creak of the heavy wooden door opening, resounding in the previously quiet space like a rallying cry, signaling the entry of a figure steeped in history and renown.

Custer entered the room with deliberate grace, each step measured and purposeful, his progress supported by a finely crafted cane etched with intricate patterns that whispered tales of masterful artistry and storied history. His stoic face softened into a faint smile, in contrast to his tall, upright posture, which radiated an undeniable presence. His stature was commanding, emanating power and authority, showing no signs of the years that had sculpted his face and body into a map of experiences. Long, silver hair flowed down to his shoulders in waves, reminiscent of a noble warhorse's mane, symbolizing a man who had faced countless adversities with unyielding resolve and perseverance. The sharp blue eyes that met Ethan's gaze were as keen as ever; they held the wisdom of experience, remaining alert and watchful, as if still searching the horizon for allies and foes.

"You're younger than I expected," he commented, his voice resonating strongly as he fully entered the room.

Startled by the commanding figure before him, Ethan rose instinctively to greet him, his heart pounding with anticipation and nervousness at the significant encounter, his pulse matching the moment's intensity. "Mr. President... General, sir," he stammered, the formal titles slipping from his lips as he tried to conceal his awe.

Custer waved, as if dismissing convention and projecting an air of relaxed confidence. "Forget the formalities," Custer said, his voice low but firm. "Only one title ever mattered, and I earned it in blood. Call me General." He spoke with authority, reflecting a man who had fought tirelessly for every honor he had earned throughout his distinguished career.

With deliberate grace, he moved smoothly toward his desk. Each movement exuded an elegant ease that belied his age and looked effortless, a mastery refined through years of public service. Slowly, he settled into the chair, the cane placed beside him like a trusted companion at rest, symbolizing the challenges he had overcome.

Seemingly without thought, he reached for his pipe, a familiar ritual showing relaxation and contemplation. However, as he grasped it, the pipe unexpectedly slipped from his fingers, softly landing near Ethan's feet, causing a brief distraction in the heavy conversation.

Ethan eagerly bent down to pick up the pipe, showing genuine respect and noble intentions.

"Leave it," Custer ordered sharply, his tone cutting like a knife. He stared intensely at Ethan, his gaze steady and penetrating, a challenge in his demeanor that conveyed the moment's importance.

Ethan hesitated, his hand stopping mid-movement, ready to pick up the fallen pipe, caught in a moment of doubt. The change in the room's atmosphere was instantaneous and chilling, as if nature held its breath.

Custer let the silence linger, letting the moment's influence hang between them. Then, with a practiced move and a slight flex of his cane, he retrieved the pipe with the ease of someone used to overcoming habitual challenges, placing it back on the desk with an air of confidence that showed both assertiveness and self-reliance.

“People must learn from their mistakes,” he emphasized, drawing on a lifetime of experiences to highlight the value of personal growth. "True awareness is only gained by observing and acknowledging lessons from one's past.”

A sense of humility overcame Ethan, his solemn nod silently confirming the encounter's significance. He realized this meeting would go beyond simple pleasantries, igniting a stronger resolve to take personal responsibility and be authentic.

"Now,” Custer began, his voice softening to a more relaxed tone that suggested a welcoming openness and marked a notable shift in their conversation. "I'm curious how your interview will differ from all the others I have done over the years.”

Ethan opened his notebook with purpose and a wave of determination, ready to engage in a meaningful dialogue. "I'd like to hear your story, General, in your words. The fiftieth anniversary of your election is a major achievement that deserves thorough recognition and exploration."

Custer raised an eyebrow, genuine curiosity shining as he talked about those years. "True, fifty years have elapsed. No man can halt the relentless march of time." The thought seemed to evoke a range of memories, from the triumphant moments he had celebrated to the many challenges he had faced.

"I want to tell your story in your words, to capture the essence of your experiences and perspectives truly, and I believe that doing so will give readers an authentic view of your incredible journey," Ethan said. He spoke with conviction, his determination a counterweight to the gravity of the moment. "So please, don't hold back or sugarcoat anything."

As Custer considered the reporter's words and the legacy he intended to leave, a slow and mysterious smile spread across his face. He lit his pipe and said, "Then let's ensure the words are worth it." The smoke between them curled like a veil. "Remember, Mr. Thorne, every story has two versions: the one told in public and the one buried with the dead. I'll share both with you if you're ready to hear them."

# Chapter 3: West Point

The bright morning sunlight poured through the tall, dusty windows of the library, casting warm golden beams that twinkled across the room. The towering shelves, carefully lined with a diverse collection of books, stood tall and proud. The gentle light cascaded like liquid gold onto the polished wooden floor, filling the space with a peaceful and tranquil atmosphere.

As Harold entered, he carried a carefully arranged tray with a steaming hot teapot, two delicate porcelain cups on saucers, and a plate piled high with freshly buttered toast, each slice aromatic and appealing. With deliberate grace, he set the tray down on a polished side table, the faint clink of the delicate china in the quiet room before he silently left, vanishing like a shadow into the vastness of the library.

Custer's actions were careful and deliberate, showing a certain reverence for the act. However, a flicker of uneasiness crossed his face as he lifted the pot, indicating both a literal and a symbolic burden. As he filled both cups, the aroma rising before him seemed to evoke some distant memories.

An air of curiosity filled the room as they sipped their tea. Beneath the surface of polite conversation, a quiet assessment of character was underway, with each man trying to gauge the other.

“I have read that you once mentioned that West Point felt like a kind of prison,” Ethan began, eager to perceive Custer's complex history and learn about the pivotal moments that shaped him into the man he became.

Leaning back comfortably in his chair, Custer adopted a relaxed posture, holding the hot cup of tea in one hand while gripping his pipe in the other. The rich scent of tobacco slowly filled the room, blending nicely with the fragrant steam of the tea. "A prison? No, my friend. West Point was more like a furnace. It challenged me, trying to burn away the softness and laziness I might have had. However, it ultimately fell short," he replied thoughtfully, a small smile tugging at his lips, revealing the complexities of his feelings toward that formative experience.

He sipped hot tea, enjoying the comforting warmth as it flowed through him. He paused briefly, idly tapping the rim of his cup with his finger, letting the soft sound fade into the background of his thoughts. "Every time I showed even the slightest trace of independence, they made it a point to discipline me. My room was always chaotic, my boots shined with overly polished care that seemed to bother them, and my lively, spirited personality was clearly not to their taste. Secretly, I kept a frying pan hidden under my bed; it was my makeshift tool for making the eggs I had stolen. There was one time I even swung a stick at a sergeant who tried to humiliate me in front of my fellow soldiers. In winter, besides the cold, there were lively snowball fights, secret trips to nearby pubs, and my cheeky jokes about corporals being shared through the corridors. My actions were never meant to be hurtful; they were simply a bit of mischief. I was trying to pass the time and add a little spark to the dull routine."

As Custer's voice softened, he drifted into thought, staring into his cup; the swirling, steaming tea mirrored the turbulent memories of his past. "At times, I felt like I was pushing the limits of my identity, constantly questioning whether I would face serious consequences for daring to be my true self."

Ethan leaned forward, eagerly jotting down every detail in his notes, his curiosity burning like a flame as he explored the story's hidden layers. "Weren't there times you faced severe punishments for your actions?"

"They definitely tried to punish me," Custer replied, a mischievous spark lighting up his eyes as he spoke. "But I had a talent for connecting with others, even back then. I could easily charm an annoyed officer with a few clever remarks when needed. Even though my classmates sometimes muttered under their breath about my antics, they still chose to follow me on every adventure I planned. Some even said that I made the experience more worthwhile."

A chuckle escaped from his chest, a mix of joy and nostalgia softening his features with a touch of sentimentality.

"I believe the instructors saw the situation quite differently. They would pray earnestly for the day I finally quit or graduated. Given my various misdeeds, even I was quite surprised when graduation day arrived."

Ethan turned to another blank page in his notebook, feeling sorry for the instructors at West Point. His enthusiasm grew as he was about to ask another question: "Weren't you on the verge of expulsion for stealing exam questions?"

Custer waved his hand dismissively, a grin spreading across his face as he recalled the event fondly. "Oh, that was simply a case of getting mixed up with the wrong crowd. While others faced serious consequences, I somehow managed to slip away without a scratch. You could say it was pure luck or a twist of fate that saved me."

For a moment, a shadow of fatigue crossed his gaze, a complex mix of humor and life experiences that had shaped who he had become. He grew quiet, lost in thought.

Custer retrieved his now-cold pipe and found a moment of peace amid the turbulent thoughts and duties that consumed him, a quiet sanctuary in the storm. As he held his pipe, it unexpectedly slipped from his fingers. Whether it was merely an accident or a subtle reflection of his thoughts remained uncertain. The pipe softly landed near the hearth; the sound boomed through the room.

Ethan instinctively rose, sitting across from Custer with respect and readiness, and began to reach for the pipe.

"Leave it," Custer instructed firmly, his voice carrying enough weight to make Ethan stop mid-motion, halting him where he stood. He instantly realized that his quick reaction had been a mistake. He had momentarily forgotten the instruction Custer had given just hours earlier. Embarrassed and regretting the error, he pulled back his arm and sat down. Custer slowly leaned over to retrieve the pipe.

Custer paused briefly, taking a moment to collect his thoughts. His earlier confidence and lightheartedness had given way to intense reflection. Finally, he leaned slightly forward, a new sense of determination in his voice as he prepared for a more meaningful conversation with Ethan.

Fixing his gaze on him, Custer said, "Let me ask you something, Mr. Thorne. What do you believe true leadership entails? What traits should a leader possess to inspire and guide others effectively?"

"Leadership, to me, is about empathy, judgment, and the power to inspire," he replied sincerely. "A true leader must have vision and courage but also an innate compassion, knowing exactly when to lead with strength and when to listen attentively."

"And do you think this ability can be learned?" Custer asked, his eyes narrowing as he explored the philosophical side of the topic. "Or do you believe it is an innate trait, something a person is born with?"

Ethan found Custer's question challenging and carefully thought about his response. He had spent a week preparing questions for Custer and planning how to keep the conversation on track. He hadn't expected Custer to ask him questions, much less challenge him on his opinions or beliefs about serious topics. Custer's latest question tested Ethan's character. He knew that his answer would have a direct impact on the rest of the interview.

Ethan took a breath, looked Custer in the eye, and said, "Sir, I believe that experience and self-reflection can develop many key qualities of leadership, even if it's true that some people are naturally inclined to lead. In my view, the best leaders often learn just as much from their mistakes as their successes."

Custer nodded, a spark of admiration and respect lighting up his face, a silent acknowledgment of Ethan's insights. "Experience, indeed. It shapes and molds us in ways we seldom recognize," he affirmed, allowing the importance of his observations to linger. "I've encountered many leaders throughout my life, some were truly inspiring, while others have left much to be desired. The key difference between them usually lies in their ability to be honest, not just with others, but also with themselves and those who follow them."

Encouraged by the change in tone and the depth of their discussion, Ethan pressed on, eager to participate further. "Would you argue that honesty is the foundation of effective leadership?"

"Absolutely," Custer confirmed firmly, with urgency clear in his words. "Without honesty, trust begins to erode, and a leader's influence diminishes. It requires a delicate balance. True leaders must be open and transparent, even when facing difficult truths. That's the only way they can create an environment where others feel inspired and willing to follow."

In Ethan's eyes, Custer was a complex figure, embodying a captivating mix of contradictions that continually shaped his multifaceted character. At that moment, his stern, determined face seemed to form an impenetrable barrier, concealing the layers of his inner thoughts and turbulent experiences that had molded him. He deliberately took his pipe in hand, drawing a long, steady breath that seemed to symbolize his lifetime of struggles faced with unwavering resilience. As he leaned back into the comfort of his chair, Custer let his memories wash over him as urgent thoughts faded into the room's calm.

Masterful leadership involves a strategic assessment of when to intervene and when a hands-off approach is more effective. You don't need to fix every mistake, especially those made by others," he said softly, his voice gentler with each word. The wisdom in his statement carried a depth that Ethan found difficult to grasp fully.

As Ethan contemplated Custer's words, he stayed silent, allowing the realization to fill the air. This peaceful moment prompted both to reflect on the veracity of their life experiences.

Outside the library, as the sun rose higher and cast a golden glow through the tall windows, the room was filled with a warm, inviting light. The soft illumination created a peaceful atmosphere, with dust particles lazily drifting in the sunlight, enhancing a calm mood that contrasted with the intensity of their conversation.

As Ethan watched Custer intently, he became acutely aware of the intense pain and life stories reflected in the General's eyes, a testament to the battles fought and lives lost in his fierce devotion to duty.

"Very soon, I'll share the story of Bull Run with you. That's where the true narrative begins," Custer stated, shifting from a contemplative mood to one of serious intent. Ethan's curiosity was sparked at that moment, drawing him irresistibly into Custer's world, a realm defined by stubborn resolve, deep-rooted brotherhood, and the significant consequences of past choices.

As Ethan settled back into the high-backed chair, he placed his well-used notebook comfortably on his lap. The worn edges of the pages showed the many entries and reflections he had written over time. He rhythmically tapped his pencil against the page, lost in thought as he examined the story unfolding before him. Outside, an expansive field stretched proudly toward the horizon, where distant horses grazed quietly and peacefully, unaware of the subtle shifts in the cool October breeze. The clear autumn air surrounded them, but the horses remained undisturbed, fully immersed in their peaceful surroundings.

Harold arrived, a familiar figure, pushing a sturdy cart carrying a simple yet satisfying lunch designed to revive them after a long morning. The meal included delicious roast chicken sandwiches, carefully crafted and topped with crisp, pickled cucumbers that added a delightful crunch, along with steaming cups of hot cider. The rich aroma of the cider wafted through the air, filling the room with a warm, inviting scent. Next to the hearty sandwiches, a white bowl was artfully filled with bright, glossy apple slices, their vibrant colors contrasting with the richness of the other food. Ethan quickly devoured the meal, savoring each bite, his focus sharpened by the steady, rhythmic ticking of the grandfather clock that stood sentinel in the room.

After their meal, Custer glanced at Ethan briefly, a playful smirk spreading across his face as he jokingly said, "Walter Bennett sent a pup to question a wolf." His surprisingly friendly tone showed no sign of hostility, adding an unexpected warmth to the conversation. Curious, Ethan looked up from his notes, his brow slightly furrowed as he thought about the joke. "My editor believes the wolf might still have some bite," he replied, his voice softly challenging, suggesting the underlying tension in their interaction.

Custer let out a grunt that sounded like a laugh, his expression brightening with a flash of amusement that softened his usually serious demeanor. He walked over to his desk, the old wood creaking softly under his weight as he sank into his familiar, worn chair. Then he lit his pipe with steady hands, instantly changing the room's atmosphere, filling the air with fragrant smoke that lazily drifted upward like a ghostly apparition. A cozy feeling settled over them for a few moments, with Custer's gaze drifting to the orchard outside, perhaps searching for forgotten tales among the bare, twisted branches stark against the autumn sky.

When he shifted his focus back to Ethan, a wisp of a secret or a long-buried memory seemed to hover just out of reach, shadowed in his expression.

"I never really liked journalists," Custer admitted, his voice tinged with nostalgia and regret, as if he were revisiting a painful chapter of his past. "Not even when I was one myself."

Ethan's surprise was clear as his eyes widened when he heard the revelation. "When were you a journalist?" he asked, genuinely shocked and curious about this unexpected truth.

"Only for a brief period," Custer replied, leaning back in his chair with a wistful look crossing his face, as if reconnecting with an old memory. "After my time in Texas immediately following the Civil War, I left the Army and wrote for a newspaper in New York. I shared my stories of battles, thinking it was better to chronicle my experiences than to let someone unfamiliar with the fight distort the truth."

He paused, letting his words settle in. "Yet journalists... They have a knack for twisting stories. They can turn victories into scandals. There can be cowardice in ink, Mr. Thorne." His voice lowered, highlighting the seriousness of his experiences.

Ethan reflected on Custer's poignant words, sensing underlying frustration and bitterness shaping the general's outlook. He decided not to interrupt, letting the moment settle, and instead jotted down the phrase "cowardice in ink" in his notebook. His pencil moved swiftly as he captured Custer's complex thoughts and feelings.

Suddenly, Custer dropped his cold, smoking pipe. It hit the ground with a loud clang, landing dangerously close to Ethan's feet, as if a challenge was deliberately set before him, inviting a response or action.

Ethan's instincts kicked in almost immediately, and a wave of unease washed over him due to the unexpected disruption. He leaned forward slightly in his chair, preparing to pick up the pipe, but he remembered Custer's earlier warning and stopped. Instead, he respectfully asked, "Would you like me to retrieve your pipe, General?"

Custer responded, "Let a man reclaim his weapon, boy. That's the first rule of being a leader."

"You're making progress," Custer said, picking up the pipe and settling back into his chair. He effortlessly lit the pipe with a quick strike of the match, the flickering flame illuminating his features for a moment. His eyes twinkled with playfulness as the flame sparked to life, casting a warm glow that highlighted the camaraderie blooming between them.

Custer's sharp gaze carefully studied Ethan, searching for recognition in his eyes. "You write about conflicts, but there are lessons that go beyond those fought with weapons. A true leader knows when to step in and let others find their way. You must learn to see that balance, as it will shape your future."

Feeling the heft of this responsibility, a burden that seemed to run within him, Ethan slightly lifted his head, recognizing the importance of Custer's powerful advice. Their conversation was rich and layered, a complex blend of storytelling and guidance that transcended professional boundaries, revealing the intricacies of human interaction.

Custer stood confidently by the fireplace, balancing ease and authority in his posture. One hand rested lightly on the elaborately carved mantel, a sign of his stature, while his eyes remained fixed on Libbie's portrait hanging on the wall. The soft glow in the room cast gentle shadows that danced across Libbie's features as he was lost in a meaningful personal memory. Finally, as he turned to greet Ethan, Custer's voice was steady and prepared, ready for a conversation that promised to be both meaningful and engaging.

"She never enjoyed those tales of my antics," he said, breaking the peaceful silence that had wrapped the space like a cozy cocoon. "She worried that some stories may cast me in a foolish light, especially the one about the rooster and the feathers. She was concerned that others would see me as a boy laughing while the world fell apart around me. But, Ethan, mischief greatly influences who we are; it's a key part of life's recipe, a mix of experiences that shape our perception of happiness and sadness alike." The influence of this statement hung in the air, full of meaning and open to different interpretations, prompting further reflection on life's complexities.

Ethan adjusted his sharpened pencil, ready to jot down every word. His eyes shifted to the wisps of smoke curling up from Custer's pipe, each swirl telling its story and momentarily taking him elsewhere. As the hours passed, a genuine bond of mutual respect started to form between the two men.

"It was a night without a moon," Custer started, his voice lively as he settled back into his chair, looking eager to share a story. "The rooster insisted on crowing far too early, again and again. The relentless rude awakenings were enough to put us in a madhouse. I wasn't the only one annoyed by this early-morning racket; many cadets shared my frustration, and we reached our breaking point together. We devised a clever plan in a flash of inspiration, sneaking past the barracks guard like shadows slipping through the dark. After an hour, we had that irritating bird right in our hands, and before dawn, it was boiled and eaten, a tasty proof of our cleverness and daring."

A broad smile spread across Custer's face as he fondly recalled that rebellious prank, savoring the sweetness of their youthful defiance buried in his mind. "However, the real artistry was in the trail of feathers we left behind; each one proof of our mischief. That detail became the highlight of our adventure. Every successful prank, I believe, needs a bit of drama. That's what makes the memory even more vivid."

Ethan carefully took notes, glancing up occasionally to notice the subtle shifts in Custer's tone, which grew steadily more serious, making the moment's significance unmistakable.

"We should have faced the consequences for our actions that night. That would have been the fair outcome. Yet, somehow, we escaped unscathed. When I saw the feather trail, I seized the chance to turn things in our favor. With quick thinking and a spark of inspiration, I grabbed a feather and cleverly slipped it into the boot of another cadet, poor Jenkins. The chaos that followed was a joyful frenzy of laughter and shock. That one act led to a phrase that quickly caught on with my friends: 'You've been plumed.' That was my idea, and it's still told today, echoing through the halls of history and still relevant to newer generations."

Leaning forward in his chair, his eyes shining with mischief and insight, Custer continued, "That's the conundrum with reputation, my friend. Many people mistakenly believe reputation appears out of nowhere, like a reward for the deserving. But in reality, you build it carefully, piece by piece, trick by trick, and through each calculated risk you take. It's a journey, an ongoing exploration throughout life." Custer reclined slightly, letting his insights fill the room and encouraging Ethan to reflect on the subtle nuances of life, risk, and reputation, themes that Custer's diverse experiences had illuminated.

Their conversation touched on influence, mischief, and personal growth, effortlessly weaving together various topics. Custer, a man exuding undeniable charm and charisma, revealed layers of his character that Ethan had not yet fully encountered. Each captivating story combined history with personal reflection, forming a dynamic narrative of life lessons that grew richer and more meaningful over time.

The talks inspired Ethan, captivating him with Custer's insights into how resilience, honor, and duty shape character. The stories of youthful rebellion conveyed more than just playfulness; they offered essential life lessons, showing that success and respect are often earned through a blend of bold action and careful planning.

As the afternoon progressed, Ethan realized he was experiencing something more significant than simply being an inquirer and student of Custer's life; he started to feel the natural growth of a partnership rooted in mutual respect and a shared journey to understand life's complexities. He wasn't merely recording stories; he was actively connecting with a mentor who embodied curiosity, exploration, and courage.

Ethan said, "Thank you for sharing your stories, General. I truly appreciate the wisdom and insight you've offered today. Your words are certainly thought-provoking, and I look forward to hearing more."

Custer nodded in agreement, a slight smile on his lips, his expression showing heartfelt approval and thoughtful awareness of the moment they had just shared. "What is storytelling if not a path to realization and enlightenment? Ethan, every story carries lessons. The key is listening carefully and absorbing those lessons."

"Walk with me," he said firmly but kindly, his tone blending warmth with a commanding presence that could not be ignored.

Ethan paused, briefly confused by the unexpected command. "Sir?" he asked, a clear note of surprise in his voice.

"To the back window," Custer explained, nodding sincerely, a look of determination crossing his face. "I want you to see the field."

Curious, Ethan followed Custer as they moved through the spacious room, the plush rug softly muffling their steps. Reaching the back window, the outside scene spread out beautifully before them, like a painting coming alive. The wide field extended in front of them, with horses moving gracefully, embodying the wild spirit of nature. In the distance, the busy stables bustled with activity; handlers skillfully guided mares while a spirited young colt galloped happily, playfully chasing shadows that danced on the lush grass, fully displaying the freedom and joy of youth.

"Here is what we create," Custer stated, his eyes affectionately fixed on the diverse landscape stretching before them, a tapestry of rolling hills and green meadows. "Heritage. Aspiration." He gestured toward a pen within the expansive grounds and pointed decisively at a magnificent stallion in the enclosure. "See that horse there?" Custer pointed out a particular one in the paddock. In a tone full of pride and confidence, he said, "His grandsire had narrowly missed winning the coveted Derby. He's swift and slender, and he'll be noticed." He spoke extensively about the horses, as if giving Ethan an exclusive look into the rich equestrian tradition they carefully cultivated.

Ethan was absorbing Custer's passionate words and their meaning when a firm knock suddenly interrupted the moment. Harold entered the room with careful deliberation. His voice was calm and controlled. "Excuse me, General. A foal's leg needs immediate care." The urgency in his tone underscored the heavy responsibilities they were all carrying, duties that went far beyond simply breeding horses.

Custer sighed, and in that moment, a complex mix of reluctance and pride crossed his face, highlighting the importance of the situation. "It's time to attend to business." The words hung in the air, clearly showing their commitments.

Custer turned toward Ethan and softened his expression, showing a hint of warmth beneath his stern exterior. "Use this interval wisely. Explore the surroundings." He pointed to the portrait on the wall, elegantly framed with intricate yet subtle details, embodying the essence of history. "My Libbie," he said with a note of reverence. "She always loved this room more than any other."

With that, the aging general, a figure shaped by countless conflicts, intense experiences, and buried emotions, walked away, leaving Ethan to reflect on the gravity of history and the importance of the moment alone.

Ethan took a breath, letting the cozy atmosphere of the room and the beautiful view outside wash over him.

The fire flickered gently, its flames dancing in the stone fireplace and casting playful shadows on the walls. Aside from the clock's ticking, a palpable silence filled the room, mingling with the rich smell of smoldering cedar and the wisps of smoke drifting leisurely around the space.

After some time, Harold arrived and carefully arranged everything, leaving no detail overlooked. "The General will be here shortly," he said as he set two steaming cups of dark, rich coffee on the polished oak table, the warmth of the mugs sharply contrasting with the cool, brisk air that had come in with the late October breeze.

Once Harold confirmed the room was prepared and suitable for their continued conversation, he quietly left. Ethan took advantage of the quiet in the library to think about Custer's words. He organized his thoughts and prepared his following questions. He was excited about the prospect of a lively discussion and was ready to adapt to any unexpected turns it might take.

# Chapter 4: The Civil War

Custer entered with a determined look. He returned to his chair, his silhouette blending with the dimming daylight filtering through the windows, casting a faint outline against the background. He lifted his steaming coffee to his lips, and his gaze wandered, lost in thought as he watched a few mares gracefully trotting across the sprawling pasture. The peaceful scene contrasted with the visible signs of concern on his face. Ethan sensed a heavy silence would settle over them before more conversation began. He drank his coffee quietly, knowing that Custer often takes his time to ponder the complex layers of his thoughts before speaking, weighing his words carefully. Only when Ethan settled back into his chair did Custer finally break the silence; his voice had a slightly raspy yet commanding tone.

"And now we'll focus on my military service after graduating from West Point," Custer remarked, steadily tapping his polished pipe against a brass ashtray, the sound reverberating faintly in the library's quiet. A flicker of longing appeared in his eyes, revealing the memory's warmth and importance. "The Battle of Bull Run is where my journey truly began, where the seeds of my future were planted within the ashes of that first conflict."

"At that time, you were still a lieutenant, correct?" Ethan asked, his voice suggesting eagerness as he leaned slightly forward, eager to learn every detail of the history that shaped the man before him.

Custer replied, his tone carrying a touch of bitterness that was hard to miss. "It was a temporary rank. We were all just temporary. The Army at that moment was nothing but a name, a young idea struggling to find its place amid chaos and uncertainty, trying to establish its identity on the battlefield."

He leaned back in his chair, his eyes drifting far beyond the library's walls, lost in a daydream of memories and reflections, with each moment from the past playing out before him. Memories flickered inside him, intense and raw. "We were a diverse group, gathered under General McDowell, made up of inexperienced soldiers and even greener officers, young men who had barely understood the realities of military life. Eager and fresh from training, we charged into battle, confident in our knowledge of warfare, naively believing that our classroom lessons would translate easily into the chaotic theater of war. But when the artillery fired, our training faced a brutal reality that no one could have prepared us for."

He paused, tightening his grip on the pipe until his knuckles turned white against the dark briar. The clarity of his memories became sharper, as real as the smoke curling around him, and the intensity in his eyes grew. "In that chaotic moment, some men were frozen by fear, standing as still as statues, unable to find their footing amid the swirling mayhem. Others, overcome with panic, fled as instinct took over, leaving no impression of bravery they might have had.

However, adrenaline coursed through my body, pushing me to move swiftly, driven by youthful ambition and a primal desire to survive."

Ethan leaned in, fully immersed in Custer's words, as if hearing a treasured story. The air around them grew tense as the historical tale unfolded, allowing him to picture himself back in time with the soldier. He quickly finished writing Custer's account in his leather-bound notebook, the pencil scratching clearly across the page.

Custer leaned forward, resting his elbows on his knees, signaling that his memories were becoming clearer. "At the First Battle of Bull Run, I was just a boy, a second lieutenant driven more by ambition than experience. I was with the 2nd U.S. Cavalry, sent to help during the Union's retreat, and bedlam erupted around us like a fierce storm. Confusion, disorder, and despair characterized those early war days, and each second on the battlefield felt like an eternity weighed down by uncertainty," he said.

His tone grew more forceful, as if he were plunging back into the battle, re-experiencing those crucial moments. "The retreat had fallen into total disarray. People from Washington, curious onlookers unaware of the harsh reality of war that awaited them, clogged the narrow dirt roads meant for the army's withdrawal, blissfully ignorant of the danger beyond the horizon. They arrived with picnic baskets and umbrellas, intending to witness a spectacle, only to unwittingly plunge into the ensuing disorder. Carriages overturned, wagons became entangled, and horses reared, further worsening the upheaval and increasing the confusion. When soldiers saw their officers hesitate, the pallor on their faces and the lack of control struck fear into the men's hearts, causing some regiments to fall apart completely. But despite the overwhelming disorder, not all did; some stood firm, showing unshakeable courage that proved their resolve and training."

He drew on his pipe, letting the rich tobacco scent fill his lungs, and paused briefly as the glowing ember highlighted his determined expression. "I found myself standing at a pivotal crossing, a critical point of tension that demanded every ounce of strength I could summon. Horses reared in pure terror, their hooves pounding the ground with an almost deafening rhythm as men shouted urgent cries into the chaos around us, and the thunderous roars of the enemy grew closer, threatening to break our remaining courage. There was no time to wait for orders or consider my next move; the seconds slipped away too fast. I pushed my horse into the crowd, maneuvering through the confusion like a skilled surgeon guiding a complex operation, giving commands instinctively, though I can't quite remember the details. Still, it worked. A spark of order appeared, igniting a flicker of hope. We didn't scatter; instead, we regrouped as perhaps battered soldiers united by our unwavering discipline and purpose."

An intense silence filled the room, broken only by the crackling of the fire as Custer puffed on his pipe. Ethan stared at him intently, imagining the young lieutenant he described, a man facing the intense challenges of battle with determination and uncertainty swirling around him.

"General Kearny saw my potential when others only considered me reckless and bold; he was truly surprised by my actions at that bridge. He noticed something in me that others overlooked, so he arranged for me to transfer from the cavalry to his staff. His gesture marked my first internal promotion, if not officially, but his steadfast belief in my abilities signaled a significant turning point in my military career."

Custer stood up and walked thoughtfully to the tall window at the back of the room, his gaze drifting out toward the vast field. "From that pivotal moment, I became an essential part of McClellan's forces in the Peninsula Campaign. Although I had yet to prove myself in battle, a restless feeling grew inside me. I longed for action and constantly felt held back by the military command's slow and careful pace. And then, there came the balloons."

Ethan blinked briefly in confusion, his mind scrambling to grasp the sudden shift in the conversation. "Balloons?" he repeated, a mix of skepticism and curiosity in his tone.

With a lively sparkle lighting up his eyes, Custer turned to face Ethan, a youthful brightness illuminating his expression as he spoke enthusiastically. "Yes, hot-air balloons! They were tethered to the ground like oversized kites, seemingly whimsical yet crucial to our strategy. There was a pressing need for an officer to ascend into the skies above, conquer the heights, and provide vital reports on enemy movements. McClellan sought a strategic vantage point above the treetops, aiming to gain a broader perspective on the battlefield's complexities. I was more than eager to accept this unique challenge and opportunity."

"What was it like being so high and exposed to the enemy?" Ethan asked with genuine excitement, captivated by the thrilling story of Custer and eager to learn every detail.

"Frightening and chilly, but rousing," Custer replied without hesitation, the memories flooding back as he recounted his experiences. "The basket rocked violently with each gust of wind; the ropes groaned ominously under the strain, and the landscape below transformed into a vague, distorted map. From that high vantage point, I saw detailed enemy camp layouts, artillery positions, and supply trains moving along distant roads. McClellan was very impressed with the intelligence I gathered from those heights and quickly promoted me to his aide-de-camp. That was when my name began to resonate in important circles, a whisper of promise carrying the hope of even greater achievements."

Custer's accounts vividly described his early military years, emphasizing the key events that shaped his character and career. His stories outlined what happened and conveyed the essential lessons and personal growth from those moments. Each carefully chosen word captured the essence of a soldier forged in the fire of combat, grounded in the harsh realities of leadership under the relentless pressures of war.

Ethan eagerly took notes, aiming to capture the essence of a remarkable individual whose influence extended beyond the bounds of time. As he listened to Custer's story, he realized he had shifted from merely observing quietly in the library to actively participating in a lively, vital historical conversation. The combination of personal stories and military strategies offered insights that went beyond the present and resonated throughout history.

Custer returned to his chair with relaxed confidence, as if he still commanded a clear view of the world. "Then came the Battle of Aldie," he proclaimed sharply, adding vigor and intensity to his voice. "It was June of 1863. Troops converged in a dramatic tableau, a striking display of steel and smoke. Jeb Stuart's forces confronted us, trying to defend Lee's maneuvers as they advanced northward toward Pennsylvania. On that fateful day, I led numerous cavalry charges, surrounded by thick clouds of dust kicked up by pounding hooves, the fierce battle cries of my comrades, and the clang of swinging sabers. It was awe-inspiring how the saber's gleam blended with the hooves' thunderous sound, creating an exhilarating rush in the middle of battle. It sparked a raw, primal excitement within me. On the battlefield where I claimed victory, I earned my general's star, attaching it to my uniform with immense pride that day."

Ethan blinked, surprised by the intensity of Custer's experience. "That quickly? How is that possible?" Ethan could not hide the disbelief coloring his tone.

Custer answered with a yes, a flicker of pride lighting his eyes as he remembered the moment. "The War Department sought bold, brave leaders willing to take risks and seize fleeting opportunities. I was one of them. And then came Gettysburg."

The name alone served as a solemn statement that linked past tragedy to a lasting national purpose. Immediately, the atmosphere was filled with a mix of sacrifice, patriotism, and resilience, though the predominant feeling was an acknowledgment of the enormous human toll.

After some time, Custer said, "I shouldn't have ended up in that dangerous position. The orders clearly instructed me to guard a flank and stay in place. But a strange feeling in my gut warned me that trouble was approaching. Stuart's entire cavalry was moving to surround us, preparing to attack the Union forces from behind, a move that could have had serious consequences. I trusted my instincts over the slow-moving bureaucratic orders, strategically repositioning my troops where they were least likely to face an attack."

"And it succeeded?" Ethan murmured, his voice barely audible, hovering on the edge of anticipation.

Custer smiled, but behind the corners of his mouth was a tension, an underlying strain that never quite reached his eyes. "We stood firm in the face of adversity. We pushed Stuart back, successfully breaking his renowned cavalry, and many historians argue that it was crucial in saving the capital that fateful day. Maybe we did play that pivotal role. However, what resonates most within me is that it was during that moment that I first truly felt the burden of leadership. It was no longer just an honor; it became an immense burden of responsibility. Every soldier beneath my command depended on me to make wise decisions, often needing to discern between timing dictated by my leadership and that guided by a higher power. The cost of our hard-won victory left an imprint on my soul."

He leaned back comfortably in his chair, his gaze drifting to the embers flickering in the fireplace. "At the tender age of twenty-three, I found myself in the position of general, a title that carried with it an incredible level of responsibility, especially for someone so young. This rapid rise fundamentally changes a person; it requires accelerated maturity and demands that one either grows and adapts or risks collapse under the pressures faced."

Diligently writing in his notepad, Ethan looked up and softly asked, "Do you think you were too young to bear such a heavy mantle of command?" He realized too late that his words could be taken as an offense.

Custer met Ethan's gaze with a penetrating look, a complex spark flashing in his eyes that softened as a smirk played on his lips. "No, perhaps it was the speed of my ascent that felt overwhelming. The rise itself was undeniably remarkable. However, I wouldn't say I was too young. In fact, youth often brings a vibrant perspective, free from past failures and full of eagerness to innovate, explore new territories, and seize opportunities. Ironically, it's often those who are older who forget the importance of taking calculated risks."

Drawing again from his pipe, he let the rich, fragrant smoke fill the air, creating a comforting atmosphere. He set it down with a sense of finality, feeling content in the moment. "The war transformed every aspect of who I was. It was a grueling trial of fire and blood, but my identity was carefully shaped amid its aftermath. It would serve you well to keep that in mind as we continue."

As silence filled the room, an almost tangible thickening settled over them, with only the crackling fire and the steady ticking of the grandfather clock breaking it. This rhythmic sound created a subtle connection between Custer's memories and Ethan's careful note-taking, as each tick drew them further into their shared focus.

After Gettysburg, the nature of the war changed dramatically," he continued, his tone turning more serious. "The fight became fiercer; it shifted from strategy to the harsh reality of attrition. Grant understood these conditions better than most of his peers. He always preferred bold commanders who acted decisively and were willing to accept the costs of war. Without hesitation, I took on that demanding role. It was early 1864 when I received my second star."

With a firm grip, he seized the heavy iron poker from beside him and nudged the smoldering coals, igniting a quick burst of bright sparks that shot up the dark chimney above. "In the war's final months, I joined forces with Sheridan in a fierce campaign, charging relentlessly through the Shenandoah Valley, leading a purposeful campaign of destruction. Our troops engaged not only in confrontations; we carefully dismantled the vital supply lines to the Confederate forces. We burned barns and mills intentionally, effectively starving the opposing army and cutting off their access to crucial resources. It was a grim but necessary strategy."

Ethan's pencil moved carefully across the paper, each word written with the precision of a historian dedicated to capturing every detail, while also reflecting a serious commitment to recording the intense, honest memories shared by Custer, who understood the importance of this exchange in the broader story of war and leadership.

"Then came Appomattox," Custer remarked, the name slipping from his lips like a soft sigh. "In April 1865, the Confederacy was taking its last breaths, surrendering its final, desperate gasps as the realization of defeat settled heavily upon them. General Robert E. Lee was desperately trying to maneuver his army westward, hoping against hope to evade our advancing forces and regroup to delay the inevitable end of this long conflict. Meanwhile, my commanding officer, General Philip Sheridan, ordered me to lead the cavalry, an unstoppable force forged in the smoke of battle, determined to intercept Lee's retreating forces and bring this conflict to an end."

As Custer spoke, the soft crackle of the fire filled the room, casting a warm and comforting glow on the study's walls. Ethan shifted in his seat, the leather creaking softly under his movement, but he chose to stay silent as he focused on the imposing figure seated opposite him.

Custer sank further into the worn leather of his chair, the flickering flames illuminating his narrowed gaze, which reflected a mix of curiosity and fascination. The lingering aroma of old tobacco and wood smoke filled the air, creating an atmosphere rich with memories and the heavy significance of past events.

"We intercepted them near the village," Custer recounted in a low, clear voice, his tone resonant with forceful command. "Their positions were poorly defended, open to attacks from all sides, indicating their weakened forces. My men struck with precision and accuracy, capturing their artillery and seizing three batteries before many had even woken for breakfast. It wasn't a grand cavalry charge to celebrate but a quick, fiercely fought battle amid mud and chaos. The thick smoke choked us, forming an acrid fog that blinded us, clawed at our throats, and filled our lungs. During the battle, two horses were shot from under me in the fight, each a harsh reminder of the turmoil and violence around us. Yet, despite the carnage, that morning felt uniquely significant. We fought valiantly, advancing relentlessly until we finally claimed the high ground, taking the ridge with our flags fluttering high in the wind, proud symbols of our victory."

His fingers tapped rhythmically against the worn armrest, surprisingly soft for a man used to wielding a saber in combat, conveying a quiet but clear sense of intensity. "From that high point, Mr. Thorne, the view stretched like a vast, grim chessboard. Lee's army lay below, weary and thin. Even from a distance, their banners appeared dull and their faces haggard. They were trapped in an impossible situation, like animals caught in a cruel and inescapable snare. Behind them, the Union soldiers surged forward like a relentless tide, a cohesive force pushing steadily toward their goal. The Confederates had no escape; their position was dire and desperate."

Custer's voice softened, filled with admiration. "I didn't need to give a command for a final attack. Lee, a true soldier, recognized the futility of what lay ahead. He understood the trap we had set and decided to surrender to Grant that afternoon, acknowledging the futility of further resistance."

Ethan let out a quiet sigh, breaking the tense silence. "And where were you?" he asked softly, his voice filled with genuine curiosity, trying to fathom the details of that moment. "What were you doing then?"

A bittersweet look crossed Custer's face, a fleeting glimpse into his thoughts. "I was waiting in the saddle, Mr. Thorne. Just waiting. I watched history unfold on that dusty, blood-soaked field. Sheridan had sent me to witness the Confederate cavalry's surrender. My sword rested sheathed at my side, its leather hilt warm in my hand, a reminder of the battles fought and the many lives that had been sacrificed. There was no thirst for revenge that day. Instead, we were engulfed in a thick, somber silence, a solemn knowledge of what had happened. And with that came a disorienting awareness that we had somehow survived."

Custer stopped speaking, and a somber silence filled the room. For several minutes, not a word was spoken. It was as if Ethan were witnessing the quiet reverence and hushed respect shown when a funeral procession passes. Ethan patiently waited but struggled to ask an important question. Finally, he gently inquired, "Did it feel like a victory?"

Custer's eyes met Thorne's almost hesitantly, his gaze distant and unfocused, as if he were lost in memories of a long-ago time, perhaps recalling the field where the events had occurred. "It seemed like a conclusion, Mr. Thorne," he stated, his tone plain and unembellished. "This ending left us confused, trying to determine the meaning of what had just happened. Some men celebrated loudly, their cheers sounding harshly across the field like an unsettling refrain; others sobbed openly, their bodies trembling with grief. As for myself, I stood there, covered in dust and surrounded by the pungent, sharp smell of gunpowder lingering in the air, the silence wrapping around me completely as I wrestled with the heavy thought of what was coming next."

He then shifted his gaze back to the fire, which softly crackled, the once-bright flames now dimmed to a gentle yet comforting glow, accompanied by the image of a pipe resting quietly on the side table, its presence unobtrusive yet significant.

“That day marked the end of conflicts, Mr. Thorne,” he remarked quietly, nearly drowned out by the crackling sounds coming from the hearth, which created a gentle backdrop for their conversation. "Yet, even as the skirmishes stopped, the war remained strong inside us. It carved itself into the very fabric of our lives. We carried it into every room we entered for the rest of our days, an unyielding, quiet, invisible force that influenced our thoughts and actions, shaping who we were.”

Ethan shifted slightly, causing a faint rustling of his clothing to be the only sound breaking the silence around them. He stayed quiet, listening carefully. The atmosphere grew heavy with tacit emotion and tension until Custer spoke again, his voice stripped of its earlier boldness, revealing a raw, vulnerable honesty that had been hidden before.

They rarely discuss what comes after,” he said, his eyes fixed on the dying embers, as if searching for meaning in their faint glow. "You achieve success. The newspapers loudly proclaim it, and parades erupt in celebration, but you come back completely changed. You return with pieces of yourself forever lost, fragments of a reality that once made sense but now is unraveled.”

Grasping the cool pipe again, he held it not to smoke but to find comfort in its familiar presence. "I lost men in every battle,” he continued, his voice lowering to barely above a whisper. "Courageous young fighters, driven by fierce and unshakable loyalty, followed me without question. Some held letters from home close to their hearts, hopeful reminders of lives they longed for; others wore wedding bands around their necks on strings, treasured remnants of love waiting for them. I sent them into combat, Mr. Thorne, and they never returned. That harsh and painful reality is rarely recorded in history books; it is forever etched in the hearts and minds of those left behind, forever changed."

Once eager to capture their dialogue with excitement moments earlier, Ethan's pencil now lay still on the surface, silently bearing witness to the intensity and gravity of Custer's heartfelt words. For the first time during their conversations, he felt a sense of doubt and moral conflict. He struggled with the tormenting question of whether these honest, raw experiences should belong to the eager audience craving tales of heroism and bravery or stay hidden in the somber, haunted corners of this intimate space, protected from the curiosity of the outside world.

The General continued, exploring the effects of war and the burden of survival, always remembering those who didn't return, and engaging Ethan with heartfelt words. Discussions about such experiences often emphasize bravery and victory, painting a powerful picture of glory amid suffering. But they usually overlook the scars and shadows that linger long after the battles.

As if summarizing his thoughts, Custer said, "We returned to parades and festivities, yes, shining examples of national pride and celebration, but we also came back to a country that was forever transformed, just like us, shaped in countless ways by the profound shifts that war instigated. This reality had a strong, lasting effect on our spirits, embedding a complexity in our emotions that can be challenging to articulate."

Custer's story uncovered a surprising depth that went beyond the well-known heroism often emphasized in popular accounts, revealing the emotional and mental struggles of war that are seldom recognized. In that heartfelt moment, both men felt the stark contrast between the romanticized public image of warfare and the brutal reality the soldiers had personally faced, a journey marked by loss, pain, and reflection.

Ethan felt a pain as he realized that history often ignores the serious human toll of conflict, despite its grand stories of heroism and victory. He understood there was another story, a voice waiting to break the silence, one that would resonate deeply with those willing to listen, a tale rooted in the fight for survival and the heavy burdens carried long after the fires went out, smoldering in the corners of their minds.

As evening approached, the room was filled with the cozy, warm glow of the fire, creating a small sanctuary amid the heavy discussion swirling around them. The analysis of battle, a mix of its grandeur and terrors, quietly lingered in the late afternoon. They reflected on the lasting impact of survival and loss on their own lives and on the lives of others.

Custer's voice, barely above a whisper, resonated with a sorrowful intensity, almost as if he were confiding in himself rather than speaking to someone else. "Tom, my brother, rode with me from the very beginning. You must have read about him in the chronicles of our endeavors. He was the first person ever to receive two Medals of Honor for his bravery, and he possessed a courageous spirit that inspired those around him. Then there was Boston, our youngest brother, whose laughter was a light in the darkness.

I kept them both close, always under my direct control, thinking I could protect them. Other family members, too: my sister and brother-in-law, my nephew, and several childhood friends. We lived at the same posts, traveled together, shared meals, and engaged in lively conversations. My commitment to my family drove my actions, and I felt a strong duty to ensure their well-being and safety. In hindsight, I might have kept them too close. I falsely believed that physical proximity equaled security, that maintaining family within arm's reach would shield them from harm. But war, Mr. Thorne, cares nothing for closeness. It is solely driven by its insatiable hunger, consuming everything in its wake without mercy."

He let the silence settle around them, heavy with grief and sorrow, before speaking again in a voice filled with pain, almost ethereal. "Both Tom and Boston fell at the Little Bighorn," he murmured, mostly to himself, as intense memories whirled in his mind like ghostly shapes from long ago, shadows of shared laughter and brotherly camaraderie. "But I sensed Tom's loss much earlier, during our last offensive in Virginia. He rushed forward, taking reckless risks, trying to match my passion." The rough, uneven revelation uncovered vulnerabilities beneath his battle-hardened exterior, exposing the soft underbelly of a man forged in the fires of war.

Custer paused from his whirlwind of thoughts, pressing his hands firmly on the chair's arms, fingers spread wide as if anchoring himself in the present. Intense emotions briefly pulled him back to the past, reminding him of the bonds he had formed and the burdens he had endured.

"We were a family of warriors," he said, his tone steady but still shaded with melancholy, haunted by memories of fallen comrades who fought bravely. "Yet, fighting diminishes a part of your identity. The chance to sleep peacefully at night became a distant dream, a memory from the past." His honesty revealed that each victory came at a cost: a part of one's humanity sacrificed to the relentless demands of war.

Ethan finally summoned the courage to speak, his voice slightly trembling with curiosity and concern about Custer's experiences. "Did you ever consider leaving the Army after the war?" he asked, trying to sense the mind of a soldier whose life had been driven by duty and loyalty.

"I did," Custer answered, nodding slowly, an almost imperceptible motion weighed down by fatigue and the burden of countless memories. "For a short while, but I realized I couldn't. Despite what some may say, I didn't have romantic notions about war. That's a lie, a story told by those who have never faced the real terrors of the battlefield. I stayed because I couldn't imagine what else I could be. You fight long enough, and it becomes part of you, embedded in your thoughts, shaping your worldview, influencing your self-presentation, and even your breathing."

His eyes shifted to a framed photograph of Libbie on his desk, her smile frozen in a moment of happiness. A brief flicker of emotion flashed across his face, suggesting hurt or remorse, softening his features. "She tried to remind me of who I was before it all," he whispered, his voice catching slightly. "Before the battles, before the carnage of war consumed us. Some days, especially in those early years, she succeeded. On other days..." His voice faded, lost in the shared memories that lingered between them like a thick fog, heavy with emotion and rising tears.

Ethan, genuinely touched by Custer's stories, gently asked, "Do you think the burden ever eases or becomes less noticeable over time?"

He abruptly answered, his voice steady and determined, "No," as if the word had fallen into a bottomless abyss. "No, Mr. Thorne. It never truly disappears. But if you're fortunate and resilient enough to withstand it, you learn to live with it. It feels like a ghost lingering in a nearby room, a constant presence you sense at the edges of your consciousness. Occasionally, you might hear the door creak open, a fleeting whisper, or a chill, but you don't seek it out. You don't invite it in; you let it pass, hoping it doesn't stay too long, praying it doesn't become a permanent part of your heart."

He leaned forward with intense focus, gently setting his cold, intricately carved pipe on the edge of the ashtray, as if it bore a heavy weight on his mind. "The war brought me honor, Mr. Thorne," he said firmly, keeping his eyes on the glowing ashes that flickered softly in the dim room light, "or what society considers honor. Yet, it demanded an insurmountable price, a quiet loss that echoes in the depths of my mind. Something even more precious: peace. The simple, carefree peace of a man who hasn't faced too much, who the harsh realities of conflict haven't scarred."

Ethan swallowed hard, feeling the act dry and painfully laborious, before cautiously picking up his pencil, mindful of the moment's heaviness. He moved slowly and carefully, as if he weren't just recording a fleeting memory or recounting a historical event but rather inscribing an emotional open wound, one that still bled, remained tender to the touch, and resisted any form of healing.

The conversation hung in the air. Custer's stories were not just tales of bravery; they were part of a life forever shaped by war's harsh, unforgiving realities. The courage and sacrifices of those he cared about resonated intensely through his words, revealing a haunting reality that defined the very core of his existence.

"Experience can be a bitter teacher. Major events impact you and leave a lasting impression. With that hard-won wisdom, you slowly realize that the battlefield is bigger than what you can see," Custer shared, his voice softly shifting as he expressed these thoughts. "It seeps into your everyday life, shaping how you interact, influencing relationships, and altering moments of silence. It changes everything."

Ethan listened carefully, recognizing the meaning of Custer's reflections. Awareness became a central theme in their talk, including the victories and losses on the battlefield and the complexities of human connections, which often carried unseen burdens. It was a heartfelt reflection on losses that far exceeded what any battlefield could measure.

"That's why I ride every morning," Custer continued, his voice steadying and filled with renewed purpose. "I ride every morning to make sure grief doesn't settle inside me like an unwelcome guest. I might not ride far or fast anymore, but as long as I keep moving forward, I can stay ahead of it, avoiding those shadows that threaten to consume me." His words carried conviction, shaped by years of experience, showing the ongoing struggle with inner battles. "Each day, I ride past the orchard and head toward Libbie," he said, his gaze drifting toward the window, lost in thought.

Custer's thoughtful pause intensified as he gazed at the scenery before him, momentarily captivated by nearly bare trees gently swaying in the breeze. "Something is soothing about the routine," he said reflectively, almost to himself. "The familiar surroundings give a sense of grounding. When the sun rises and spreads its golden rays across the landscape, I can almost feel her presence beside me, savoring the peace we once shared in those simpler times."

Ethan watched Custer with keen awareness of the strong and intricate link between love and grief.

"The experience of riding offers unparalleled clarity," Custer stated, his tone softening as if he were about to reveal a treasured secret. "The sound of hoofbeats thudding rhythmically against the ground and the cool, invigorating air softly brushing against my skin helps enhance each unforgettable moment. It serves as a reminder that life continues to move forward despite hardships and challenges. Every ride I take reflects my cherished memories and pays heartfelt tribute to the beautiful life we once shared."

Even amid the weariness that filled their conversation, a flicker of hope remained: the legacy of those who fought bravely for their beliefs is not only about sadness or despair but also reflects the incredible strength and resilience of the human spirit.

"I also see it as a tribute to my brothers," Custer continued, his voice growing stronger with each word. "Although they have long since passed, their spirits ride with me, genuinely connected to my very core. Every ride I take weaves their presence into mine, forming an unbreakable bond. Whenever I feel the sun's warmth breaking through the morning's lingering chill, I am reminded of their lasting presence; their laughter and lively friendships ring in my heart, inspiring me to face life head-on."

At that moment, Ethan realized that grappling with the spirits of the past was an essential process for Custer and a valuable experience for anyone facing the overwhelming burden of loss and sacrifice. Drawing meaningful lessons from suffering and finding significance amid pervasive pain formed a key, common thread that connected their lives. This narrative thread highlights resilience, demonstrating that while one cannot simply erase the scars left by conflict and trauma, one can learn to live with them, enriching the journey of life instead of letting them define one's existence solely.

"I have business to attend to tomorrow, but when you return on Monday, I'll speak about life after the war, living in the territories, and feeling isolated from what was happening back in the States," said Custer.

As the day slowly ended, the sincerity and impact of Custer's heartfelt words resonated in the room. Ethan felt a strong urge to share the meaningful truths from their conversation. Moments like these, filled with mutual understanding and connection, didn't happen often. He solemnly promised to cherish these times, honor the complex stories of the past and the lives they touched, and keep them alive for future generations to learn from and value.

# Chapter 5: After the Smoke

Before dawn, Ethan awoke in a boarding house on H Street in Washington, D.C. The radiator beside his bed hissed out more air than heat, making his breath visible in the thin moonlight filtering through the curtains. He lay there for a moment, staring at the cracked ceiling and listening to the muffled footsteps of the waking city downstairs.

He had a restless night, constantly replaying the conversations from the previous day and analyzing the General's words. Ethan's promise to himself weighed heavily on him. Still, his first feeling of the day was relief. They had agreed to meet again in a few days, and Ethan looked forward to reviewing and organizing his notes. He knew he needed to guide Custer so his storytelling would stay on track.

On the small bedside table sat his notepad, its edges worn from use, with three fresh pencils lined up like soldiers ready for inspection. He ran a thumb along the grain of one, wondering if its lead was sharp enough to catch any lie Custer might tell.

The break during the interview was expected to be very busy. Throughout the day, Ethan carefully reviewed his many pages of notes, examining each word. He began compiling Custer's various stories, which he later turned into a historical timeline of Custer's life. After all the sessions, he would need to condense them into a series of clear, engaging, and enjoyable newspaper articles that still met his editor's standards.

Ethan approached this opportunity with seriousness and urgency, driven by a strong need to absorb as much information as possible. His goal was clear: to scrutinize the complex nuances of Custer's discourse, which were essential for accurately quoting him in future discussions and preserving his insights. This period of solitude provided Ethan with the necessary space to prepare for the upcoming talks and became a meaningful time for reflection. As he worked, he felt the full weight of his responsibilities to the newspaper and to himself.

He organized his thoughts and prepared questions for the upcoming meetings. The tumultuous period after the Civil War could steer the discussion in different directions, requiring careful planning and readiness on his part.

After the weekend ended, Ethan woke up on Monday morning, eager to hear the news waiting for him. When he stepped onto H Street, streetcars clanged their iron frames as they moved through the city. Newsboys shouted the day's headlines while Ethan headed out to catch a northbound train once again to see the legendary Custer.

At Union Station, the smell of coal smoke and hot oil mixed in the winter air. Ethan held his satchel tighter, feeling the shape of the pencil tin as he headed for the platform to catch the train to Laurel. He boarded and saw that most of the people from the previous ride were in their usual seats, so he took his seat again near the front of the car.

After arriving in Laurel, Custer's driver took Ethan back to the estate, where he saw Harold waiting. Harold greeted him with a subtle nod and signaled for Ethan to follow him to the library. Inside, the room felt peaceful, filled with the quiet ticking of the clock and the gentle crackle of the fire, carrying the faint scent of burning wood. The flickering light cast shadows across the polished dark wood of the bookshelves. Each carefully arranged volume held a treasure of knowledge and stories waiting to be discovered.

Custer stood by the window next to his desk, lost in thought, gazing at the trees outside. Today, he looked older than Ethan remembered; the deepening lines around his eyes, shaped by time and a mix of demanding and rewarding experiences, told the story of his journey.

Custer turned to Ethan and greeted him warmly. "Good morning, Ethan. I hope you had a chance to rest, refresh, and prepare for today's discussions." Ethan nodded and sat in his designated chair, ready to take notes.

As the General settled into his chair, his expression grew more serious and introspective. His voice softened to a tone appropriate for confidential disclosures. "In 1865, very soon after the war ended, I was dispatched to Texas. While the Southern border states had divided loyalties between the two sides of the conflict, Texas had very few Union sympathizers.

No one wanted us there, and the men sensed that. The situation was grim," he admitted softly, a hint of sorrow in his voice as he reflected on the past. "The majority of soldiers I led were volunteers eager for battle. They felt drained, discouraged, and bitter, their morale worn down by long months or even years of trials. Many had not seen home in a very long time." A distant look crossed his face, as if he were imagining the young dreamers who had become tired shadows from relentless fighting and the harsh conditions of military life.

Custer kept explaining how the enthusiasm that once united them and gave them purpose faded away, like sand slipping through fingers. "Payment was often late," he said, sounding irritated. "Food supplies were limited, hardly enough to keep a soldier going for a day." He described how the local people were hostile, and their faces showed the same anger that weighed on the soldiers' hearts.

His expression sharpened as he leaned in, fully aware of the importance of his following words. "Some of the troops turned to heavy drinking, masking their pain with whiskey, disregarding orders as their discipline fell apart." The vivid memory sparked anger, reminding him how quickly control could slip away, especially under pressure.

"There was one special night," he recalled slowly, feeling the heaviness of the memory, "when I lay down with a loaded Colt under my pillow. I had caught wind of conversations about mutiny," said

Custer. His tone dropped to a secretive whisper, as if the ghosts of that night still hovered around him.

While Custer paused, Ethan watched his face, trying to figure out what dangerous situation might have caused such caution. He leaned forward, eyes full of curiosity, gripping his pencil tightly. "What did you do in response to such a risky situation?"

Custer straightened up, regaining the confident demeanor of a strong leader known throughout history. "I woke them at daybreak," he declared firmly. "I issued an alert and ordered them to assemble for a roll call. The men hurried to get ready. After the count was taken, I walked out alone in front of the men. They focused on me, oblivious to the armed guards approaching from behind. The guards stood around the ringleader and ordered him to come with them. He gave no resistance."

"I joined that morning's patrol and led it myself. They followed, just." A heavy sigh escaped him. "But they realized I was ready to fight in front of them instead of from behind," he added, his voice filled with determination. "That realization made a significant difference."

"As we traveled across the sunlit landscape, I was acutely aware of the contradictions in our situation. These men showed courage at times but also experienced fear, disillusioned by the harsh realities of war and its effects on them. Still, the one lesson I learned was that revealing my vulnerability could be a strength. My willingness to stand with them marked a crucial moment."

Custer's tone briefly softened, becoming more reflective and sincere. "The reality is that true leadership is more than just having power or giving orders. It can also mean dropping pretenses and showing our humanity. My willingness to endure pain alongside them changed the atmosphere that day."

He leaned back in his chair, soaking in the mood of the moment, a silence filled with unspoken stories and experiences just beneath the surface.

In that quiet moment, Custer's story lingered with them, reminding them of the complexities of leadership, the importance of unity during challenging times, and the enduring resilience of people who persevere even in the darkest hours.

He looked out the window again, briefly lost in thought. "Discipline isn't an act of cruelty; it's essential for survival," he said confidently, with a truth that reverberated in the room. These words carried the wisdom of someone who had successfully led through the chaos of war. Outside, life went on, but in that moment, Custer stayed still, a steady symbol of the struggles soldiers and their leaders faced.

Preceded by the aroma of freshly brewed tea, Harold carried a tray of tea and warm pastries straight out of the oven. The cozy setting naturally encouraged open and relaxed conversation.

Custer took the opportunity to stand up and stretch his legs, which slightly protested at the sudden movement. The fatigue from years of challenges showed on his face. His eyes looked toward the distant stable, a large, weathered building where horses were kept.

"Do you know what kept my men together more than just the meals we shared?" he asked, his voice quiet and reflective, with a subtle tone of thoughtfulness, showing that their stronger bonds came from the hardships they faced together.

Pausing in his note-taking, Ethan's eyes sparkled with curiosity, eager to hear Custer's stories for valuable insights. "What was it?" he asked, fully aware of the importance of the anticipated response, hoping to grasp the core of camaraderie alluded to by Custer.

Custer, with a touch of nostalgia, recalled a song that held deep emotional meaning and a strong link to his past and his men.

"Is that the song 'Garry Owen'?" Ethan asked, somewhat confident in the answer he had prepared beforehand.

Custer's grin widened, warming the mood as he nodded. "Yes, it's a traditional Irish tune. One of my sergeants used to play it on his fife while we marched westward. Its lively rhythm energizes the horses, almost inspiring them to move in time with the pulse of the music."

As wistfulness wrapped around him like a familiar hug, Custer moved to the window, the light tracing his slim figure as he hummed a few notes of the uplifting tune, the sound gently filling the room, reminiscent of brighter days long gone.

"The song became our rallying cry," he shared proudly. "The 7th Cavalry would sing it before charging into battle. It made them feel invincible, as if they carried a piece of home with them on the battlefield, a sweet reminder of their true purpose amid the chaos. I felt immense pride as I inspected the four straight lines of mounted troops on the parade ground. I like to think they recognized how I genuinely felt."

As Custer returned to his seat, Ethan carefully took notes, scratching his pencil on the paper, and deliberately broke the silence; Custer's heartfelt remarks wove a beautiful quilt of friendship, strength, and unity that went beyond the many challenges he and his men had faced together.

"Men don't fight solely on orders," Custer continued with conviction, his voice firm yet filled with sensitivity. "They fight for melodies that repeat in their hearts, for cherished memories that motivate them, and for the honor that comes with their sacrifices. It's not just orders from above that inspire acts of bravery and valor. I gave them those three vital elements: the song that rallied us, the treasured memories of those we care about, and a lasting pride in their abilities and the noble service they provided."

He continued, "In 1866, I left the volunteer service and joined the regular military after receiving my commission. I was stationed on the frontier for a few years at Fort Riley, Kansas, but I'll talk about that later."

In early 1871, I received orders to move to Kentucky," Custer explained. "The war had been over for quite a while, and the Army needed us there. Have you ever seen Kentucky in the spring?" Custer asked, turning slightly to face Ethan, his tone thoughtful and filled with longing.

Ethan shook his head in response, his blunt answer showing his inexperience. "No, I've only seen it through photographs and stories told by others."

Custer leaned forward, his eyes filled with wistfulness and a touch of recall as he focused intently on a distant memory. "You would be amazed; it felt less like a posting and more like entering paradise. The clean, sweet air hummed with peaceful, rural energy. The lush green hills rolled like velvet under a clear blue sky. The land radiated happiness. Bright rivers meandered through the scene, reflecting sunlight like scattered diamonds. Red and black barns stood as symbols of human effort, each a testament to the local people's strength. Every detail, from sturdy oaks to fresh air, spoke of resilience and a spirit worth protecting."

"They sent me to a small town in Kentucky called Elizabethtown," Custer said. "Nestled among the hills, it initially felt like an untouched haven. But even paradise has its shadows. Early in the war, a peculiar skirmish took place in the town. General Morgan's Raiders quickly targeted the nearby railroad lines, which were vital to our supply lines. Firing cannons from a strategic hill on the south side of town produced loud booms and whistling sounds as the projectiles flew. Cannonballs tearing through buildings caused minor damage and rattled both windows and nerves. Fearing for their lives and property, residents climbed onto their roofs, waving white tablecloths and bedsheets in a united plea for peace. The civilian-led surrender caught the Union troops off guard, as most of them were inexperienced recruits. Confused, they eventually laid down their arms. Morgan's men continued their destructive work, tearing up the tracks and temporarily disrupting our logistics. Having achieved their goal, they left Elizabethtown to recover from its shattered peace."

Ethan’s brow furrowed as he tilted his head slightly. "Since Elizabethtown wasn’t a very strategic place, why would the Army send you there?”

Custer paused briefly, a surprised smile spreading across his face as he reminisced. "Can you imagine it? I, who had been present at the surrender at Appomattox, was given the strange task of checking hooves and negotiating horse prices.” A trace of disbelief remained in his voice, highlighting his astonishment at the almost comical nature of his situation.

Ethan carefully opened his notebook to a new page, eager to jot down every comment and detail from the conversation. "Did people see it as a demotion?” he asked, curious about the unexpected nature of the duty.

Custer dismissed the question, seeing it as a minor annoyance rather than a serious inquiry. "No, it was simply the Army's way of creating a semblance of order amid chaos. At that point in my life, I was a lieutenant colonel already adorned with command stars but astonishingly unaware of what 'normal' even meant."

Custer stood and thoughtfully paced in front of the fireplace, the flickering flames casting shadows on the walls and bringing recollections to the surface. Ethan noticed a mix of desire and pressure in Custer, recognizing that these memories were not just about past duties; they also revealed the formidable challenges and heavy responsibilities that came with leadership.

"However, Kentucky was anything but tranquil," said Custer. "It grappled with many challenges. Reconstruction became a highly contentious battleground. Men and women freed just months earlier stood at crossroads, some holding deeds to land, others facing night riders with torches. At the same time, a large part of the white population struggled with bitterness as they came to terms with the consequences of their losses. The Ku Klux Klan went from just a story to a real and threatening presence. Cloaked figures roamed the towns under the cover of darkness, spreading fear and chaos among residents. They set fires that turned peaceful neighborhoods into scenes of terror, causing great distress and anxiety for families adjusting to new circumstances. Even after defeat, the South stubbornly refused to accept the terms imposed on it, allowing anger and hostility to grow and spread in response to what they saw as injustice. This resentment towards the North continued to fuel tensions for years."

"But General, weren't you enforcing Union rule when Kentucky clearly had the responsibility?" asked Ethan, challenging Custer's recollection.

Custer watched Ethan intently, surprised by his boldness in asking that question but impressed by his courage. He paused to gather his thoughts and chose his words carefully. He wanted to convey the importance of the memories he was about to share in a heartfelt and sincere manner.

"I was told to keep a low profile, exercise patience, and focus on buying horses," he explained, "but I found it almost impossible to follow those directives," he added, with slight defiance in his tone. "Kentucky wasn't yet able to regulate itself. I concentrated on maintaining order and purchasing horses."

Ethan leaned in closer, captivated by the unfolding story. "Can you describe what actions you took?" he asked, eager for more details on Custer's recounting of the events.

"I reflected on the war, the grandeur, and the spectacle that had captivated the entire nation's attention," Custer replied, drifting into a daydream full of nostalgia. "I brought that same spirit with me to Kentucky. Each horse I acquired was proudly displayed along the town's main street, with me dressed in my sharp military uniform and my saber gleaming at my side. We trained cavalrymen to perform flawless formations and fostered in them a strong sense of pride and purpose. I made it a point to station guards at key intersections, insisting that passersby show us the respect and acknowledgment we deserved. We often instructed the soldiers to read the Constitution aloud to anyone passing by. This served as a powerful reminder of the rights and freedoms often forgotten or ignored."

A faint smile crossed Custer's face as he thought about his bold and defiant moments from the past, remembering the challenges he had faced.

"Our message was clear and powerful: We are still here. The Union remains strong, and we are dedicated to upholding our principles."

As he spoke, Ethan carefully took detailed notes on Custer's remarks, maintaining steady eye contact and trying to fully appreciate the significance of what was being shared. "What was the local response to your presence and activities?" he asked, eager to discover how such bold actions affected a region still dealing with its recent history.

Custer's expression shifted, showing a mix of pride and concern. "The reactions were quite varied. Some people saw us as a threat, clinging tightly to their old prejudices and grievances. Sometimes, clashes erupted, and the air was thick with tension. Meanwhile, many newly freed slaves saw us as a source of hope. They celebrated the unity of the Union, which gave them a sense of purpose and resolve."

Ethan stopped writing mid-sentence; his mind swirling with thoughts. "Did you ever fear for your safety?" he asked, showing a mix of curiosity and genuine concern.

Custer nodded slowly, contemplating the many dangers that constantly lurked nearby, unseen but close. "Definitely," he responded with conviction. "There were many nights when uncertainty hung heavily in the air, those haunting times when I felt the tangible tension of possible violence creeping in from all directions. Still, I couldn't surrender to fear, no matter how overwhelming it sometimes felt. The risks were high, not only for my safety but also for the many people who depended on our help and support. Every day, I reminded myself of our larger goal, which went beyond my safety concerns. We weren't just holding ground; we were building something. Fragile, yes, but real."

As Custer's thoughts hung in the air, silence surrounded them. It was a moment that highlighted the resilience needed to overcome such formidable challenges while fighting for justice and equality.

"What was it like to keep that energy going?" Ethan asked eagerly, eager to find out how those ambitious initiatives maintained their strength over time.

Custer took a breath, gathering his thoughts and preparing to articulate what was undeniably complex. "We needed to maintain a careful balance. Each small success, no matter how minor it seemed at the time, fueled an insatiable desire for further progress. However, we constantly faced fierce resistance from those who tried to sabotage our efforts, making our journey more dangerous. Whenever we organized an effort, shadows would always lurk, ready to extinguish the small flame of hope we had kindled. It required unwavering loyalty and a flexible mindset. We had to be strategic, always aware of threats while nurturing that spirit of defiance that had fueled our movement from the beginning."

As Ethan carefully took notes on Custer's reflections, he appreciated that these weren't just stories from the past but enduring lessons about the subtle complexities of leadership and the responsibilities that come with such roles.

Custer's eyes sparkled with excitement as he continued to explain. "Despite those tough obstacles, the victories we had were inspiring. Every parade we held and every show of unity we created sparked a strong sense of pride and hope that filled the air like a sweet promise. It was a movement that stood for hope rather than despair, resilience rather than defeat. I stood in the town square every Sunday, saber at my side, while a freedman read the Emancipation Proclamation. That was our act of defiance."

Their conversation continued to explore the rich history and numerous challenges he had faced, fostering a timeless and meaningful dialogue. This exchange gave them valuable insights into the core of leadership, the impact of responsibility, and the struggles with identity, reminding both men of their vital roles in an ongoing story that could affect their lives and those of many others.

"Some appreciated it," Custer stated, his expression contemplative as he reflected on the varied responses their efforts prompted. "Unfortunately, most harbored buried resentment and unease. It reopened long-standing grievances and old wounds that had never fully healed. Despite their strong feelings, they kept a sense of etiquette. For a while, the mere threat of our presence acted as a deterrent, as they struggled with the uncomfortable reality of the changes we aimed to implement."

The door creaked ominously as it swung open, letting Harold enter the dimly lit room. He carefully carried a small, elegantly made tray filled with an inviting variety of food: tender, warm roast beef sandwiches; bright slices of crisp apple; and a frosty pitcher of cool tea, its surface shimmering invitingly in the soft light filtering through the room. The rich, savory aroma of roast beef filled the air, blending with the sweet crispness of the apples to create an inviting atmosphere that beckoned for a shared meal. Walking purposefully toward the corner table, Harold gently set down the tray, ensuring everything was perfectly arranged for a presentation that showed attention to detail. He then silently nodded to Custer and Ethan, a quiet signal that their meal was ready.

Balancing an impressive yet approachable demeanor, Custer gestured toward the food spread invitingly before them. "Let's partake of this food while it's warm. We have more urgent matters to address this afternoon," he instructed, his tone tinged with a sense of urgency that underscored the seriousness of their upcoming discussion and the limited time they had to enjoy this brief break before they turned to heavier topics.

Ethan, fully immersed in their conversation, reached for a roast beef sandwich. As he gently lifted it from the tray, the soft, warm crust of the freshly baked bread responded under his touch, serving as a tactile reminder of the meal's preparation. He suppressed his curiosity and excitement, quietly preparing for the afternoon ahead. He was eager to learn more about the forceful, often hidden stories behind the man's rugged exterior and the many experiences that had shaped him.

# Chapter 6: Beyond the Mississippi

After finishing their lunch, Custer slowly rose from his seat and stood beside his desk, his lean figure clearly outlined against the window, which framed the breathtaking view beyond. He placed his hands casually behind his back, reflecting as he kept his gaze fixed on the vast backfield stretching endlessly before him, a muted expanse that gradually blended into the morning mist. A thick, glistening fog clung to the far tree line, gently softening the sharp edges of a landscape. Across the obscured ground, a beautiful chestnut mare ambled gracefully, her movements smooth and serene, her breath visible in large, cloud-like puffs in the cool afternoon air, each exhale a fleeting reminder of the unpredictable early winter weather.

"That mare is thirteen hands tall," Custer said softly, his voice unexpectedly gentle as he watched her with a keen eye. He studied her graceful movements intently, admiring how she carried herself with natural finesse. "Although she might not be tall enough to win the Derby, lacking the impressive stride of the legendary horses known to dominate the racetracks, she possesses an agility that is admirable and quick, moving with a nimbleness that reminds me of the brave scouts we once had, long before the cavalry overshadowed their quiet yet invaluable talents."

Ethan leaned in slightly, captivated by Custer's reflections, his full attention now on Custer. "Do you still cling to your dreams of a Derby champion after all these years?" he asked, genuinely wanting to comprehend Custer's emotional state and acknowledge his innate determination, which remains steadfast despite the years.

Custer stepped in front of the fireplace and let out a quiet, almost wistful laugh as he briefly looked at the fire, its flickering light warming his face and revealing the lines carved by many experiences. His sunken eyes reflected countless untold stories from his past. "Always," he responded, a single word capturing his unbreakable spirit, full of resilience and defiance. He paused momentarily, letting the crackling flames fill the silence and invite reflection. "Hope," he continued, his voice softening with each word, "is what you hold on to when the world cruelly tries to forget you. It's the last spark in a dying fire, the flicker you protect when all warmth is gone, an ember that refuses to go out within the cold."

Ethan settled into his comfortable chair and opened his notebook. He ran his fingers over the smooth leather cover, feeling its coolness against his skin as he pulled a fresh pencil from his satchel. He quickly jotted down a note, the sharp scratch of the pencil on paper piercing the quiet. "I read an article where you said that, after the Civil War, the West was basically different from the South. What, in your opinion, makes those two regions different?" he asked, eager to hear Custer's insights.

Custer turned entirely away from the warm glow of the flames, seeking a brief moment of relief from the flickering light as a thoughtful expression settled on his face. He approached his chair slowly, gathering his thoughts with each step. "The difference between the western territories and the southern states was significant in the 1860s through the 1890s," he began, his tone adopting a seriousness that matched the importance of his thoughts. "Early on, the South, despite its rich traditions and cultural heritage, had long struggled with its complex past; its economy remained closely tied to the effects of the Civil War and the hardships that followed. This complicated situation had fostered a certain resilience among its people but had also created a degree of isolation that hung like a shadow."

As Custer spoke, he shifted slightly, his demeanor lively yet controlled, every gesture purposeful. "On the other hand, the West represented a vast, nearly free spirit," he continued, the passion clear in his voice. "Here, the spirit of opportunity aligned perfectly with the relentless call of adventure that beckoned at every turn. It was a place where societal limits were continually challenged, and creativity thrived in the lure of the open frontier. The challenges faced here weren't just about survival; they centered on creating a meaningful presence in a constantly changing landscape, a blank canvas filled with endless possibilities waiting to be shaped by those who dare to dream. Well," he coughed, "the canvas wasn't completely blank because so many

Indians lived there. With enough room for everyone, we aimed to find a way to coexist."

Ethan listened carefully to Custer's perspectives, shaped by a lifetime of navigating complex matters and influenced by both regional and contemporary realities.

Custer sank into his familiar armchair, feeling its comforting embrace. "Living on the plains in the early 1870s was like moving from a carefully organized play to the wild chaos of a storm, Ethan. I shifted from a world where everyone knew their lines, costumes, and roles to one of pure turmoil and unpredictability. Out there, the enemy had no uniforms to identify them, no bright banners waving in the wind, nor the steady drumbeats announcing their presence. Their movements and tactics were unpredictable; you only realized they were near when an arrow just missed your ear or a loud battle cry shattered the silence. When they attacked, it was quick, fierce, and all-consuming. This force was unstoppable, ruthless, and unavoidable. Yet, strangely enough, there was a kind of beauty in it. It was the raw beauty of survival, a world stripped down to its simplest, most primal form. Horrible, but breathtaking in a way that's hard to explain."

He picked up his well-worn briar pipe from the table, tapping it lightly on the smooth wooden surface, and briefly paused their conversation.

"I was assigned to Fort Abraham Lincoln in the rugged terrain of Dakota Territory in early 1873. The freezing conditions we faced there were as relentless and unforgiving as death itself. I thought I had grown used to winter storms living in Michigan, but I was unprepared for the storms in Dakota. The winds howled mercilessly from the northwest, each gust a cruel reminder of the severe environment we had to endure. Every day felt like a demanding, strenuous test of our endurance, made worse by the constant marches that pushed us to the limit. The air was thick with the tension of an impending storm, heightened by the threat of conflict with the Sioux and Cheyenne tribes. In stark contrast to groups like the Klan, which operated in secrecy and spread fear through their elusive tactics, these Indians stood tall and proud, embodying great strength and steadfast loyalty. They carried a spirit that demanded respect and recognition, even as we prepared for the inevitable clash of battle."

Custer rose from his high-backed chair, moving deliberately and briefly pacing across the wooden floor, his boots making a soft, rhythmic creak. He paused at the window, gazing out as if at distant horizons, before returning to his seat, a thoughtful expression on his face.

"In the summer of 1873," Custer began, his voice growing more solemn as he recounted the events, "my regiment, the Seventh Cavalry, took part in the Yellowstone Expedition. Our primary mission was to protect the Northern Pacific Railroad surveyors as they extended the line of Manifest Destiny further into uncharted lands. It was a vast, sprawling effort. For weeks, we traveled along the Yellowstone River, following its winding course through the wilderness, from the Dakota plains into what would soon be Montana. During this expedition, I first became aware of the formidable presence of the Lakota medicine man, Sitting Bull. Although I never met Sitting Bull face-to-face during that initial encounter, I met warriors influenced by him: men from his village fiercely defending their ancestral lands."

Custer leaned slightly forward, his eyes narrowing in concentration, embodying the tension of the moment. "Our first major clash took place at a spot we called Honsinger Bluff in the Montana Territory. Their Lakota forces were expertly concealed within the dense tree line, a silent, unseen threat. A small group of their braves, maybe two dozen or so, rode out openly, trying to lure us in, to bait us into a classic ambush. I recognized this tactic immediately; it was exactly the kind of move I had studied a lot, especially in connection with the tragic Fetterman Massacre from a few years earlier. My men were eager, ready to charge, but I held them back, sensing the trap. The ensuing battle was grueling, a relentless fight that lasted hours under the oppressive summer heat. The air was thick with dust from the horses, the crack of rifles, and shouts from men. It tested the skills and survival instincts of both sides, a brutal dance of attrition. Fortunately, I lost only one man and two horses that day. But it wasn't the last time we faced them. We encountered Sitting Bull's warriors several more times during that expedition, each encounter sharpening our recognition of their determination and tactical skill."

Ethan, completely absorbed, hunched over his notebook as his pencil scribbled furiously across the page while transcribing Custer's narrative. He found himself reflecting on the leadership displayed on both sides. The General's methodical approach, keen perception of the enemy's tactics, and flexibility in adjusting strategies had been undeniably crucial. This foresight, Ethan mused, and this disciplined command undoubtedly helped Custer avoid the kind of devastating ambush that had claimed so many lives in other, less fortunate campaigns.

Custer's voice grew stronger as he recalled additional details. "We were sent out in the summer of 1874 to explore the Black Hills. Our group included botanists, surveyors, four reporters, two gold miners, 1,000 men, 110 wagons, and 70 Indian scouts. You should have seen the size of our column! I was also tasked with finding a suitable site for a new fort. The recent gold discovery there had sparked fierce ambition in many men, leading them to brave the harsh landscape. The treaties made earlier meant little to the many miners who blatantly ignored their promises to the indigenous peoples. Our orders were clear: we were tasked with protecting those seeking wealth, and it was important to understand that these commands came from the highest levels of military leadership, underscoring the gravity of our duty."

Custer paused briefly to let his words sink in, his face turning serious and contemplative. "I followed these orders dutifully, but I must admit that I never fully supported them."

Outside, a sharp, spirited neigh from a horse cut through the crisp autumn air, reverberating against the walls like a rallying cry, awakening something intense and instinctive in both men, and stirring a sense of connection to the moment and the tumultuous road ahead.

Custer's mood began to shift slightly, becoming more serious and tense. Dazed, he absentmindedly rolled the stem of his unlit pipe between his fingers, an odd and ironic habit for a man who usually found comfort in smoking. His gaze seemed distant, as if he were lost in a realm where present worries faded, leaving him with the heavy burden of memories.

"It all started with gold," he said quietly, his voice thick and heavy with a sense of defeat and resignation. "Doesn't it always?" A wistful tone tinted his voice. "Men are forever drawn to the lure of wealth and the promise of opportunity, often turning a blind eye to the destruction they cause in their pursuit."

Ethan leaned in slightly, thoroughly captivated by the story of Custer. This wasn't just a dry history lesson; it was the core of a long-lasting conflict that shaped relationships and destinies across generations, resonating through the ages.

"Rumors ignited like a firestorm," Custer continued, his voice growing stronger, "feeding the insatiable dreams of the greedy. There were prospectors, driven by desire, murmuring about gold veins as thick as a man's wrist, buried just beneath the surface, ready to be claimed. Newspapers, eager for the story, loved spreading the tale, relishing the dramatic twists of fate. Soon, hopeful fortune seekers were heading west, eager to claim their share."

With deliberate slowness, Custer rose and moved toward the large wall map. Each step was careful and purposeful, as if he were inching closer to a truth he could no longer avoid facing. He gently traced his fingers over the areas carefully marked with bold lines and names, lands that represented both great opportunity and real danger, reflecting the complex history they held.

"We, the U.S. government, signed the Fort Laramie Treaty in '68," he continued, his tone showing bitterness and grievance. "The Black Hills were sacred to the Lakota people, rich with their heritage and history. Yet, when rumors of gold discovery reached Washington, they shamelessly ignored the treaty. They betrayed the very agreement meant to protect the Lakota's sacred way of life. The promise of wealth was too tempting for those in power to resist, corrupting their commitments."

Custer's words boomed through the room, highlighting the extent of past wrongs and injustices. It was clear why he was so passionate and troubled by these issues; he had witnessed firsthand the chaos of the battles fought, the ongoing injustices lurking in the shadows, and the suffering and struggles of many lives affected by these events.

Ethan paused to absorb the meaning of Custer's insights and reflections, allowing the significance of the information to sink in. This was no longer just a story of conflict; it had become a sorrowful tale of betrayal, woven with flickering hope and the complexities of fate. It depicted a situation where the ambitions of a few caused unbearable suffering for many others.

Both men understood they were more than passive witnesses; they were active participants in a developing story that demanded humility, wisdom, and, most importantly, a strong commitment to acknowledging the past while working toward a fairer, more just future. Custer moved his finger along the map, carefully tracing the outlines of culturally essential lands. Every movement seemed to send a shiver through him, the gentle scratch of his finger on the paper echoing the invasion and upheaval caused by those seeking wealth.

"My instructions were to conduct a geological assessment," he said with irony in his voice as he tried to hide the harsh truth of the situation with official language. "That was the formal version, the polite way we describe it among our ranks. However, we were practically acting as enforcement agents, making sure miners could move across the land freely and take properties that truly belonged to others, often ignoring the rights and histories of the legitimate owners."

"And what about the tribes?" Ethan interrupted, his fingers quickly skimming across the paper as he tried to convey the seriousness and urgency of the moment.

"They certainly resisted," Custer responded, his jaw tightening subtly as he spoke, the sharp contours of his face revealing the inner turmoil and conflict he grappled with. "They saw this as a betrayal. And indeed, it was. I led the charges. I gave the orders. I believed it was my duty. But duty to whom? Is it my duty to a nation building itself on unfulfilled promises? This loss was not only the physical displacement of their people but also an assault on their culture and existence. These lands were not merely plots of ground but a rich tapestry of history filled with sacred meanings and traditions passed down through countless generations. Taking these areas from them was an insult, an injustice they could not overlook or accept."

Ethan's pencil kept moving steadily across the notepad, carefully capturing every detail of Custer's expression, sensing the significance of the moment and the raw emotions beneath the surface of the story surrounding those past events.

Custer moved purposefully around the room, the significance of history and its wide-reaching effects almost tangible in the tense atmosphere. His steps revealed a restless inner conflict, as his thoughts swirled in a turbulent mix of regret, duty, and harsh truths from decisions made long ago. Every step seemed to reflect the anguished cries of those caught in the battle of manifest destiny, their voices longing for acknowledgment and awareness.

"Our gold miners confirmed that there was gold in the Black Hills," said Custer. "In fact, the precious metal was plentiful. The reporters were eager to send in their reports. I will admit several soldiers felt the siren's call to desert and search for gold, and my officers were quick to point out that the Indians would not tolerate intruders in their sacred lands."

"The journey into the Badlands of what is now South Dakota had been an exhausting and difficult ordeal, one of the toughest I had faced as a leader," said Custer. "Fierce winds howled across the barren landscape, whipping up swirling dust clouds that invaded our lungs with every ragged breath we took. Breathing became a slow, painful task, with each breath vividly illustrating the brutal, unforgiving land we were crossing. Water, an essential resource in such a harsh environment, was severely scarce, creating a strong sense of desperation. My men whispered among themselves, their voices filled with fatigue and hopelessness, their discontent rising like a faint, sorrowful song carried by the wind. Despite our hardships, I remained determined to keep us moving forward. I understood how exhausted they were. I saw the fading fire in their spirits, but inside, I believed that this was only the beginning of a much longer and darker journey, full of challenges we had yet to envision."

Custer slowly and carefully turned to face Ethan's searching eyes, his intense gaze steady on him. There was an apparent change in Custer's appearance, and Ethan saw how greatly this arduous journey had affected him and the others marching with him. It seemed to spark a strong desire in Custer to share what he had come to realize, a vital insight he believed was crucial for success.

"Keep these facts in mind, Ethan: the conflict begins long before the first shot is fired." His words lingered in the still air. Ethan needed to consider that Custer's struggle was not just about the inevitable physical battles; instead, it was about the complex web of choices, alliances, and hostilities that brought him to that dangerous point. Before gunfire shattered the fragile silence over the bleak landscape, real battles were already raging, fiercely fought within the hearts and minds of men destined to clash.

Harold quietly entered the room, carrying a tray with bowls of canned peaches and a pot of dark, rich coffee that filled the air with a delightful aroma.

While they ate, Custer sank into a meditative silence, his mind drifting in a sea of thoughts. Ethan was reviewing the discussion and concluded that Custer wasn't just recalling his past but shaping it with each word, guiding each revelation like a general planning a battle. Every response seemed to come from him with purpose, carefully thought out, while each story was chosen to make the most significant impact.

Ethan's imagination soared freely, exploring a landscape of inquiry and curiosity, asking questions that felt both urgent and vital to his appreciation. What did it truly mean to be part of this unfolding story? How could he hope to accurately portray the complexities of a situation so deeply rooted in historical importance and moral ambiguity?

Ethan remembered Custer's passionate description of the tribes' connection to the land, how their very identity was deeply linked to the natural world around them, their fierce resilience against an unstoppable wave of irreversible change, and the moral dilemmas woven into a mission aimed at dismantling a way of life that had lasted for generations. He felt a strong, almost undeniable duty to share these vital details, to honor the voices that the larger story had silenced, and to ensure their stories wouldn't be lost to the relentless march of time and history.

# Chapter 7: The Miracle of the Little Bighorn

General Custer was already seated at his desk. Custer's fingers skillfully sorted through a chaotic pile of worn telegrams, each stained with urgent messages detailing supply shortages, troop movements, and desperate pleas for reinforcements, remnants of battles fought not only on the ground but also in the political arena. The room felt tense, heavy with anticipation of upcoming revelations and frustrations.

"Before I begin recounting the Battle of the Little Bighorn and the miracle, I need to lay the groundwork. Following the disaster in the Black Hills region," he proceeded, his voice gradually shifting into a tone of reluctant scrutiny, "I began to examine closely what was being loaded into our supply wagons. The prices for basic necessities like flour and boots soared dramatically after that incident, and it was impossible to ignore the implications." He frowned, recalling the expensive realities he had faced and reflecting on the mismanagement that followed the dreadful events.

Leaning forward, he lowered his voice as if sharing confidential information with a trusted confidant. "I uncovered a heartbreaking reality beneath it all," he continued, his voice filled with a mix of sorrow and determination. "Corruption seeped through the quartermaster system like a concealed decay, an insidious rot that threatened the very integrity of our operations. Dishonest agents profited from both sides of the conflict, betraying their own in the process. Inflated invoices would make any trustworthy bookkeeper cry, while spoiled supplies were sold at full retail price, as though they were gourmet products from the most reputable sources."

He paused, carefully considering Ethan's reaction, wary of revealing personal grievances while exposing a systemic issue with far-reaching implications beyond their military missions. Could Ethan truly grasp the importance of these insights, or was he just another pawn caught in Custer's relentless plan to uncover the truth?

"I wrote countless letters to high-ranking officials, expressed my concerns in multiple meetings, and sought help from allies and colleagues, all in a relentless effort to highlight the seriousness of the situation. Instead of receiving the action or responses I hoped for, I faced overwhelming silence. This experience led me to a crucial decision: I chose to testify before Congress in the spring of 1876 to take a public stand."

Ethan leaned in closer, his curiosity piqued by Custer's brave resolve. He had hoped Custer would be willing to discuss his Congressional testimony and had planned to guide him to that subject at an appropriate time. He hadn't expected it to be the first topic after lunch, but he was ready. "That's when you dared to name the president's brother. Orvil, wasn't it?" Ethan asked, sensing the tension and seriousness of the moment. He realized this question could significantly change the direction of their conversation.

Custer gently nodded; his mind flooded with powerful memories as each word surfaced from his recollection. "Yes, that was certainly true," he confirmed, his tone steady but carrying the influence of his experiences. "Orvil Grant was involved in the contracts, intricately tangled in the elaborate web of deception I had painstakingly uncovered." He paused briefly, allowing the impact of his statement to settle. "When I presented the irrefutable proof to them—maps meticulously drawn, detailed accounts carefully documented, names and signatures that carried significant importance—it became glaringly clear just how widespread the corruption truly was. Instead of recognizing the seriousness of my discoveries and what they implied, their initial reaction was to try to silence me, dismissing my statements as the desperate cries of an unimportant blabbermouth, someone not worth listening to."

With a determined look, he got up from his chair, moving deliberately and confidently toward a tall shelf that held some of his most treasured possessions. There, he grasped a dusty leather folio, a once-proud symbol of his efforts that had, at times, also caused his fear and hesitation about his path.

"This," he said firmly, placing the folio on the table with great care and reverence, "contains my version of that testimony. It's not just a record; it's a dedicated effort to protect the truth, ensuring that history remembers everything that happened and the deception remains exposed."

Ethan remained still, his eyes fixed on the folio, which he instinctively recognized as a document of great importance. It symbolized not only Custer's personal struggle against overwhelming odds but also a crucial part of history, exposing innate political corruption in their society.

"Please tell me," Ethan whispered, his voice soft yet determined, barely disturbing the stillness in the room, "did standing up for the right thing concern you about your military career?"

"It shaped my reputation in ways I never anticipated," said Custer. "When the Democrats approached me, after extensive behind-the-scenes maneuvering, they weren't just seeking any politician to support. They specifically sought a fighter, a warrior in the political arena, someone known for their steadfast integrity and whose hands remained clean. They needed someone who wouldn't back down in the face of adversity and would always prioritize the people's interests first."

Custer smiled defiantly, radiating pride and fierce loyalty in his gaze. "I bravely engaged in challenging battles and confronted obstacles many others shied away from, all while upholding my integrity. I understood that such perilous endeavors sometimes come at great personal cost, a risk I gladly accepted."

With a renewed burst of intensity running through him, Custer slightly turned to face Ethan more directly. "Look, Ethan, this isn't just my fight. It symbolizes a larger battle against a widespread system that relies on exploitation, manipulation, and deceit. It demands individuals with the courage to confront the truth, no matter the personal costs." His voice was steady, filled with the urgency of his message.

"Politics," Custer scoffed, disdain clear in his words, his tone bitter enough to reveal he found the subject especially off-putting, something he could barely discuss without feeling disgust. The contempt in his statement was obvious, reflecting the years he had spent navigating the complicated world of government dealings and military politics, where alliances shifted like sand. His cynicism was unmistakable, a shield built through numerous betrayals and disappointments. "They'd follow you into a foxhole just to tax the bullets," he added, his voice dripping with scorn, emphasizing his aversion to the political games that constantly drained his resolve.

Custer then leaned back in his chair, letting out a sigh that revealed his fatigue and the burden he carried. The sound showed both physical exhaustion from battle and the mental strain of dealing with a corrupt system. With his fingers interlocked behind his head, he relaxed as if trying to clear his turbulent thoughts and carry the heavy burden of experiences and decisions that had shaped his views over the years.

"When you're a young lieutenant, you have no interest in politics. All you want to do is lead men. It's only when you rise in rank that you first see, and unfortunately get involved in, political maneuvers. I didn't enjoy being pulled into policy-making and deal-making. I wanted to expose dishonesty and protect soldiers," Custer added.

Ethan nodded, fully grasping the significance of Custer's words. The stories of his struggles and successes moved him, highlighting the ongoing battle against corruption in society. This conversation served as a poignant reminder that standing up for integrity and accountability in politics is a challenge that demands exceptional courage, unwavering perseverance, and a continued dedication to defending what is right and just.

The air in the quiet study, usually filled with the scent of old paper and polished wood, now buzzed with electric energy, sending a chill down one's spine. It was stirred by a man who seemed to challenge the very course of history.

"Let me give you some background before I reveal the details of the Battle of the Little Bighorn. In late 1875, President Grant issued a proclamation requiring all tribes to gather at their assigned forts for the winter. Those who disobeyed this order would be labeled as hostile and could face attacks. Any tribes that refused would then be considered enemies. Grant was putting pressure from all directions. I was to advance from the east with the Seventh Cavalry, a disciplined and aggressive force. General Terry and his infantry were to come from the north, and General Gibbon's forces were to move from the west with infantry and artillery. Lastly, Crook was to move from the south, aiming to cut off any escape routes." His long, surprisingly gentle fingers tapped the polished table in a complex rhythm, tracing their imagined movements across the vast Montana Territory, like a silent war drum mapping out its plan.

Already drawn in, Ethan felt a strange chill, as if witnessing something powerful and unsettling.

"On our march to the Little Bighorn in May of 1876, we had to delay for three days at the end of the month because of a sudden and severe blizzard," Custer explained. "We were camped in a valley just north of Square Butte in the Dakotas, where we had to contend with 6 to 12 inches of snow without any cold-weather gear. No one had expected such weather. We resumed our march on June 3rd and moved into position by late June."

With intense eyes and a sharp gaze, Custer leaned forward, explaining, "Army staff believed the tribes would flee, that our formations would enclose them like cattle in a pen. It was straightforward, brutal logic." A faint sneer brushed his lips. "They underestimated Crazy Horse. Sitting Bull. They underestimated me." His confidence wasn't just arrogance; it held a fierce, almost religious belief that stirred a mix of admiration and quiet fear in Ethan, who sensed Custer's complex reality.

Suddenly, Custer stood, breaking the silence of the library. It was as if a storm had erupted in the quiet room. He moved deliberately toward the tall map cabinet, his boots softly thudding on the rug. Ethan watched, pencil hovering over his notepad, eager for any new detail or real connection to the history they had discussed. With practiced ease, Custer pulled out a tightly rolled dispatch, its parchment yellowed with age. He unfurled it with flair, like a magician revealing a grand trick, then placed it on the table with such certainty that the crisp sound softly served as a quiet reminder of battles long past.

"This is the original," Custer said, his voice nearly reverent. "A copy of the movement orders, sent directly from Terry's headquarters. See here," he said confidently, pointing and tracing the fragile paper's faint, faded strategy lines. "Terry thought he'd be the anvil, and I the hammer. His forces would hold; he would give the signal, and I would strike." The creases and faint stains, possibly sweat or spilled coffee from over fifty years ago, seemed to pulse with the urgent, desperate need for command.

Ethan leaned in, eyes fixed on the document, fully immersed in the strategy and the gravity of the moment Custer was bringing to life.

"But Gibbon's scouts were ambushed before they could report, and his forces were slowed as they tried to move the artillery across the rough terrain. Crook got stuck miles away, with his troops harassed, disrupting their southern push. He finally turned his forces around. And by the time I, with the Seventh, reached the valley, the entire carefully planned attack was in ruins."

A long silence followed, broken only by the soft crackle of the fire. Custer's sharp and resolute eyes fixed on Ethan with fierce defiance, challenging the idea of certainty in history. "Terry attacked two hours early. I had orders to wait for Terry's signal, but it never came. I was supposed to stick to the abandoned plan and wait. I refused." The last two words were spoken quietly but firmly.

Feeling the impact of Custer's confession, which contradicted everything he had been taught, Ethan asked softly, "You disobeyed?"

Custer kept his gaze steady, with a steel-like sharpness in his eyes. His face revealed the struggles fought not on battlefields, but in silence.

"I adapted," he said, his voice sharp and confident like a freshly sharpened blade. "I've seen hesitation cost lives. I've seen waiting cause disorder, the enemy slipping away while we stood still. And," he lowered his voice to almost a whisper, as if sharing a secret, "the enemy wasn't standing still. Their war drums were beating. Their warriors were numerous and attacking. I sent Captain Benteen to scout the ridge line to secure our left flank. I sent Major Reno to cross the river and strike the southern camp to draw their fire. And I took the center column straight into the heart of their camp, where the main force was. Terry's forces were being decimated; I had no anvil to strike. I had my new plan, but I had no idea if it would work. If I did nothing, Terry's infantry would have been massacred."

Custer's words lingered in the air. An unforgettable display of defiance, bold leadership, and a strong belief that to leave a mark on history, sometimes you must act courageously, even amidst chaos and against the odds. Ethan's pencil raced across the pages, barely keeping up with the rush of words, the lead smudging on the creamy paper.

"Reno's forces bore the brunt of the Indian warriors' attack and were forced to retreat across the river. With their main force distracted, I led the charge into their sprawling camp. The Indians attacking Reno saw that their tepees and families were under attack, and they redirected their focus to my force instead."

"Yes, there were some women casualties, but when someone charges at you with a lance, you protect yourself regardless of gender," Custer said, emphasizing the comparison to the Battle of the Washita River. "We were outnumbered ten to one and should have been wiped out. They called it a miracle, and I still don't understand how we managed to accomplish it. We shouldn't have. Nine times out of ten, we would have been destroyed. I guess that's why they call it a 'miracle.'"

Custer's voice softened as he said, "I saw Tom get hit with a rifle bullet in the middle of his chest, and Boston dismounted to help him. An Indian bullet laid him to rest as well. I lost two brothers in a matter of seconds. That was fifty years ago, but I still remember Tom's vivacity and Boston's laughter from when we were children."

Visibly shaken, he paused briefly before continuing, "Somehow, we managed to reach the remnants of Terry's force, regroup, and attack again. This time, Reno, reinforced with Benteen's men, crossed the river toward the camp, with the main Indian forces between us. We didn't have enough men to fully surround the Indians, who panicked and quickly withdrew to the north. We suffered many casualties and decided to hold back on the pursuit. It was then I discovered that the battle had also claimed the lives of my brother-in-law, James Calhoun, and my nephew, Henry Reed, who was just 18 years old."

Custer took a long breath, as if reliving and absorbing the grief from long ago. "Family has always been very important to me, Ethan. I had always been surrounded by family. Libbie had been to every fort, and Tom had been with me since the early part of the Civil War. The staggering loss of four family members in a single battle was nearly unbearable, but I had no time to mourn. I met with General Terry to discuss pursuing the enemy. I gathered my forces and left General Terry to tend to his command," Custer recounted with a strong voice and a fierce look in his eyes.

Ethan paused from writing, moved by the boldness and strength of Custer's story. He looked at the man, a mix of realization and confusion crossing his face.

"So, you're saying," he asked, brow furrowed with curiosity and a desperate need to perceive, "you turned what should have been a disaster, a total rout, into a victory?"

Custer's expression sharpened as he stared at Ethan, his fierce spirit filling the space between them, daring the younger man to grasp it fully. "By my account, it was not only a victory," he said, his voice rising, "but an ascent! A rise to greatness! We broke their spirit, scattered their forces, and showed the strength of the United States."

After taking a breath, he continued, "We compelled Crazy Horse and Sitting Bull to flee north into the Canadian plains, broken and without many of their war ponies. But that's a story for another time." Sitting back, Custer took out his pipe and lit it slowly in a quiet ritual, the atmosphere filled with respect and nostalgia for the battles fought on that blood-stained land, battles he believed had ended very differently.

"And yet," he added, his voice heavy with a hard-to-explain sorrow. "The newspapers still got it wrong. They reported that I had died."

Ethan's head shot up, his pencil falling onto the table, shock and disbelief replacing his earlier admiration. "Died? That can't be true!"

Custer's lips curled into a hollow smile, one lacking genuine happiness, his laughter carrying a bitter edge, hinting at old wounds and enduring ironies. "The initial report was a disaster, really, setting the stage for what followed: a complete setback to the truth," he said, his voice low and rough. "A wounded courier had stumbled into camp, his uniform torn, eyes wide with shock and despair, whispering broken reports of total destruction. He said I had been killed in battle. A reporter overheard the report and quickly rode to a nearby town to telegraph the news to his paper. From there, the rumor spread."

"I was mourned as a fallen hero. My name was shrouded in tragedy, casting a shadow over the entire nation. Newspapers printed black-bordered obituaries; flags flew at half-staff; people even considered building monuments. Then, after the initial grief subsided and the truth spread quietly, then loudly, that I had survived and even triumphed, the whole country erupted. Almost overnight, wild admiration replaced the heavy cloak of grief. As I recount this story, I often think of Mark Twain's famous words: 'The rumors of my death have been greatly exaggerated.' By the time everyone knew I was alive, I wasn't just a general; I had become a legend, like a phoenix rising from the ashes of a supposed defeat."

He chuckled again, this time with a bitter cynicism. "The best lie ever told about me," he muttered, the irony thick in the air, mixing with the faint smell of pipe tobacco that lingered around the old leather and polished wood of the library. It served as a reminder of how fate can distort history, blurring the lines between reality and legend.

The soft amber firelight flickered, casting shadows across the room. Ethan sat on the edge of his chair, watching Custer. After a moment of silence, Ethan asked, "General, how did your wife react to the news of your death?"

Custer, focused on the embers with a troubled expression, gradually raised his gaze to the portrait above. He replied, his voice rough, "My dear Libbie was heartbroken. I later pieced together the details. A reporter from Bismarck traveled to Fort Abraham Lincoln to gather her reaction to the news, which had not yet been verified. She collapsed upon hearing the news and was comforted by the other wives in the fort. In an instant, her world shattered. She started mourning immediately, engulfed in silent sorrow."

He exhaled slowly, reminiscing. "Reporters swarmed our home like locusts. They created chaos, eager to capture a widow's grief for a sensational story. Yet Libbie..." Custer's lips tightened with pride. "Libbie showed extraordinary strength. She acted as a shield, refusing to give the newspapers what they wanted. She would not break for their cameras or cry for attention. Although she withdrew from the scene, her determination stayed strong against their greed."

"For three long days, Custer continued heavily, "she felt her world was shattered beyond repair. During that time, she lived as a widow, facing a future without me. A steady stream of condolence telegrams arrived every day. Across the nation, people sent cards and letters filled with sympathy for her, which Libbie received in the weeks that followed. The irony was cruel; the messages kept coming even after she learned, through slow communication, that I had survived. While she was elated, she also felt sorrow for the new widows in the fort and did her best to comfort them as they had comforted her. Remember, Ethan, we had lost four family members along with many officers and soldiers in that battle. Libbie always called my survival a miracle, a divine act that pulled me from death. From her perspective, having her life restored from grief's ruins was truly a miracle. She replaced her black mourning dress with a cavalry-blue dress."

Custer hesitated, gazing at the flames. The faint smile disappeared, replaced by a serious expression. In the room's stillness, he said, "I never called it a miracle," his tone calm and lacking cheer. "That day, too many men lost their lives." His words hung in the air, a harsh truth that overshadowed any victory and emphasized the sorrow of survival. The fire crackled softly, its warmth contrasting with the coldness in his words.

The library was silent, broken only by the ticking clock and the soft crackle of the dying fire. The flames had dimmed to glowing embers, casting flickering shadows on the tall walls and creating an atmosphere of quiet thought. Outside, the wind had grown stronger, howling through the bare, twisted trees surrounding the mansion. The leafless branches scraped against the windows like ghostly fingers reaching for something lost, a haunting sight in the purple-shaded dusk.

Ethan let the gravity of the situation settle in, feeling the impact of the lives lost fill the room. He looked up, searching for clarity in the pain etched on Custer's face. With a sense of sacrifice, consequences, and the enduring scars of war beyond just numbers or resources, he asked, "Do you see the results of their actions as a fitting legacy for their loss?"

Custer was silent for a long time. Still holding the stem of an unlit pipe he seemed to have forgotten, his fingers tapped against the arm of his chair in restless drumming that reflected his inner turmoil. His gaze drifted to the window near his desk.

He spoke again, this time softly, almost as a whisper to himself, as if contemplating an old, unchangeable truth. "In the aftermath, a nation often fails to acknowledge the toll of warfare fully." His gaze was fixed on a distant, unseen horizon. He reflected on the unbearable cost of war, murmuring, "The country has a short memory of the hardships, recalling only the banner raised afterward."

He moved with great difficulty, as if exposing the very marrow of his bones. His joints cracked in protest, producing a faint, dry sound like old timbers creaking in the wind. As he said, "We'll talk tomorrow about what came after, the chase, the capture, and the headlines that followed in the wake of this turmoil," a grim resolve settled over him, an unspoken vow to confront even more painful memories.

Ethan stood up, clutching his notebook tightly in his hands, its pages cool against his palms. From the discussion and Custer's raw vulnerability, he felt the human spirit's resilience and fragility.

Outside, as the final golden-brown, brittle, and pale leaves gently drifted to the ground, nature reflected the solemnity of the moment, a reminder of everything lost as time passed. The scent of damp earth and approaching winter wafted on a chilly wind that whispered through the branches.

The next morning, the estate's vast pastures were blanketed with crisp, clear frost, transforming them into a shimmering, almost magical surface that sparkled in the soft early-morning light. Every blade of dormant grass glistened as if dusted with tiny diamond particles. There was a sense of an approaching bright, sunny day, along with the sharp scent of frozen soil in the fresh, invigorating air. As the car carried Ethan up the winding gravel driveway toward the grand house, the crunch of the wheels blended perfectly with the sounds of nature awakening: the rustling of bare branches and the distant call of a crow.

When Harold led him into the grand home, he was eager for a new day of historical stories and insights. The library radiated warmth, with the latest fire in the stone hearth making it even cozier. Harold carefully set out a tray filled with a hearty breakfast. It included steaming coffee that filled the room with its rich, dark aroma; rye bread just out of the oven, still warm; and thick, savory slices of ham with a touch of grease.

Custer stood near one corner with his back to the room, gazing out the window at the expansive view. He appeared to be looking at something in the distance, but his eyes were fixed on the broad apple orchard beyond the estate. Despite the heavy frost, the scene held a certain stark beauty, showing how strong and resilient elements can flourish even in cold weather.

Custer's voice shattered the morning silence without turning. "Good morning, Ethan." His tone sounded stern, and as Custer crossed the room to pour himself a cup of coffee, Ethan noticed he seemed upset. He began speaking while sitting down. Urgently and angrily, he said, "Crazy Horse and Sitting Bull ran away to the north."

"Into the wilds. Toward the border with Canada."

Intrigued by the developing situation and the tension in Custer's voice, Ethan settled into his usual seat at the polished library table. He opened his notebook, the blank page ready for the story to unfold. His pencil was poised for careful note-taking, as was his habit, and his mind buzzed with questions.

"There were clear orders not to cross the border," Custer said, locking eyes with Ethan. It is evident that yesterday's conversation intensely troubled him and that he hadn't slept well the previous night. His serious, tired expression revealed an exhaustion that went beyond mere physical fatigue. "We were told by the Secretary of War himself to stay where we were and wait for the results of diplomatic negotiations without getting involved. It was a clear and simple order."

His eyes narrowed slightly as he sat in a high-backed armchair opposite Ethan. The lines on his face revealed the extent of his regret for his past choices. "But by then, I had seen the cost of waiting for myself. I had seen what doing nothing meant in blood and broken will. I couldn't just sit there and do nothing while they got away. So, I took action. I sent scouts across the river at night, and Bloody Knife was one of them. He was as skilled as ever. They returned with important information before dawn: the chiefs were hiding in a remote valley, resting, and thinking they were safe from us."

Ethan nodded, quickly jotting down every word Custer said with his pencil. He aimed to figure out the complex situation and how each strategic move was unfolding.

"Despite orders to the contrary, you crossed anyway," Ethan said, acknowledging Custer's bold defiance. It wasn't a question; it was a statement of fact.

"I did cross," Custer said firmly, a glint of the old fire returning to his eyes. "I wasn't going to let them get away again. We had been in pursuit since the southern part of the Montana Territory, and I wasn't going to let an invisible line stop me from capturing them," said Custer, his words resonating with forcefulness. "My men were quick riders who never gave up and knew how to talk to the wild. We moved quickly and quietly before dawn even broke. Bloody Knife was our guide, leading us through a narrow, dangerous ravine many Indians had never seen before. We managed to surround their camp, and we had the element of surprise on our side."

Ethan's pencil slowed and then came to a stop. It took a moment to grasp the gravity of Custer's actions, the boldness, and the significance of such a daring move. "Was the surprise enough, or did they fight back?" Ethan asked, his voice a bit lower and more strained than before. He leaned forward, eager to find out what happened after that fateful, defiant choice.

Custer leaned back in his old leather chair, and the glow from the fire in the hearth made the maps and military artifacts on the walls seem to shift. Despite his age, his eyes still held a sharp intensity as he recounted the story of this important event.

"Crazy Horse didn't give up easily," Custer said, his voice filled with admiration mixed with reluctant respect. He paused for a moment as that memory flickered across his face. "He fought bravely, like a true warrior, trying to break through our lines on horseback. It was a desperate, almost beautiful attempt to escape the inevitable. We could hear the loud hooves, the shouts, and the carbines firing. He was a windstorm of defiance, a blur of man and horse. But thanks to my scouts, we knew what he would do and could stop him at the pass, which was a choke point in the rough terrain. Our trap worked perfectly."

Custer's eyes sharpened as he shifted from a distant memory to a more immediate, visceral one. "Meanwhile, Sitting Bull stayed by the fire, with the smoldering embers of their camp all around him, his arms crossed defiantly over his chest. He didn't move or flinch. He had an air of royalty about him, even in defeat. His dark, unreadable eyes met mine across the space between us, full of a challenge that wasn't spoken. I had to summon all my self-control to resist striking him to stop that defiant look. The sheer pride, the unwillingness to bow. I was filled with a strong mix of anger and a strange, frustrated awe."

Custer paused again and exhaled sharply. The air rushed out of his lungs, releasing built-up tension and the raw emotion still tied to that memory. He instinctively reached across his body for the handle of his saber, even though he hadn't worn one in decades.

"Eventually, after the dust had settled and the last acts of resistance had faded, we managed to capture both leaders," he said, his voice steadying. It had become more of a story about what happened than a memory. "I quickly informed Washington about our success. The reports sparked a huge uproar in the newspapers, filled with sensational headlines and exaggerated stories. "Crazy Horse Captured by Cavalry Genius!" and "Custer Strikes Across the Border!" were among the headlines from every major city. They called me both a rogue and a savior, an interesting mix that stayed with me like a shadow. One minute, they praised my actions, calling me the country's brave protector. The next, they attacked them, questioning my methods and authority."

Ethan's pencil hovered over the page as he looked up from his notes. He was as interested in the political fallout as he was in the battle itself. "And what," he pressed, his voice matching Custer's intensity, "was the administration's response?"

Custer's face changed; his brow furrowed slightly, and a shadow that resembled one he'd seen before crossed his features. "President Grant was so angry with me. Outrage. I had gone against direct orders, which clearly warned against entering Canadian territory without permission. This open act of aggression on foreign soil, even against Indian tribes, was poorly received in the unstable politics of the time, especially since there was already a lot of ill will and tension between the United States and Great Britain. Grant faced a dilemma: would he punish me for disobeying orders, or would he hail me as a hero who captured Crazy Horse and Sitting Bull? I did not envy his decision."

"In response to my actions, Congress held hearings, a big show, to hold me accountable and set an example for others. However, amid all the controversy, public opinion appeared to be shifting heavily in my favor. My supporters and sympathetic media distorted the story around Sitting Bull's imprisonment, making it seem as if I had single-handedly ended the long and bloody Plains War. My ability to adapt to the circumstances then changed people's minds so much that even the president's anger couldn't fully overturn it."

Custer rose and moved toward the beautiful cherry wood bookshelf that covered most of one wall. He gently traced the spines of the leather-bound books, each documenting a campaign or treaty.

"When I testified before Congress, my loyal Arikara scout, Bloody Knife, quietly stood beside me. He served as a meaningful reminder of the hardships of frontier life, very different from the world of politicians dressed in tailored suits. Out of loyalty and bravery, I promised him, in the open Dakota Territory, that if I ever became president, he could live with us in the Executive Mansion. Of course, that's what we called it before Teddy Roosevelt officially named it the White House."

Ethan, curious about the personal connections revealed in the political drama, asked, "And did he ever get to experience that dream?"

Custer's lips curled into a knowing, almost mischievous smile, the kind that carried a complex meaning behind its silent curve. "He did. But I'll let you know about that later." He let out a soft, genuine laugh, adding a rare moment of lightness to the conversation.

Custer's pipe let out tendrils of fragrant smoke that drifted slowly in the golden light of the fire. He said, "They say war makes men gods." His voice was steady and deep, carrying echoes of countless battlefields. He settled into his chair, embodying a mix of authority and calm. "That's not true. War makes men either famous or not." His words hung in the air. Each syllable was a stark reminder of the harsh, dual nature of fame in turbulent times, a bitter reality forged in the heat of conflict.

"After the capture, a moment that will live on in history forever, stained with blood and glory, I was summoned to Washington. The dust of the frontier clung to my boots, while the scent of gunpowder and open plains lingered in my wool. I still wore my campaign uniform when I arrived. Crazy Horse was in a heavily guarded carriage not fifty yards behind me. He sat in chains, a king stripped of his sky. He was a prisoner brought to the heart of the capital."

He leaned forward, and his demeanor changed as if the memories were delicate and needed careful handling. "And then they cheered. Not just the politicians in their well-tailored suits, who had carefully planned expressions of approval on their faces, but also the everyday people, the crowds lining the streets, waving flags, and making a noise that shook the cobblestones. They wanted the soldier this time, not the speechmaker. They wanted a hero, someone who would show them victory, and for a brief, exciting moment, I was that person."

Ethan scribbled furiously in his notebook, the pencil scraping across the paper. Each word was a lifeline to the past, a desperate effort to save and preserve this rare revelation, this unfiltered glimpse of how a legend was made.

"Grant tried to censure me, of course, to publicly punish me for not following orders," Custer said, a faint, sarcastic smile on his lips. "But his efforts went horribly wrong. Instead of condemning me, the congressional hearings turned into a disaster for him and a huge success for me. They only made me more popular with the public and turned me into an idol. People thought I was brave because I wasn't afraid to speak up in front of a large audience. I was a man of action in a city of words. They called me "The Boy General" again, bringing back an old nickname. I had a certain charm, broad public appeal, and a sense of strength that people could recognize. They believed I could shoulder the weight of the West, a symbolic burden that struggling Democrats needed if they wanted to hold their ground and challenge the entrenched Republican power."

Ethan asked, "And you accepted their offer?" with a questioning look in his eye, sensing the shift from talking about the past to the verge of a big decision.

Custer's words were slow and deliberate, each syllable weighed down by the significance of that decision. "I saw it as a new kind of battlefield, Ethan, where people fought with words and policies instead of swords and guns. A chance to protect something valuable, not just to conquer it, but to help shape the future of a new nation. But don't be fooled; the nomination came from cold, calculated politics, not genuine admiration. Many of those who voted for me, as well as many who helped me rise to power, wanted to see me out of uniform, far from the bloody front lines, and never to ride into battle again. People wanted me to be a useful symbol but didn't want me to be a potential agitator. Once again, they underestimated me."

He looked out at the orchard, where the last stubborn leaves gently shook on nearly bare branches. This scene of seasonal change represented the end of one chapter and the start of a complex new reality, highlighting themes of transition and adaptation in their lives.

Ethan, who had been carefully transcribing what Custer said, with the sound of pencil lead on paper a familiar comfort, suddenly stopped. His heart, which had been beating steadily, now raced with a mix of professional curiosity and newfound excitement. A shiver ran down his spine, not from the cold but from the truth. "Do you regret it?" he asked, his voice barely above a whisper, as Custer's story drew him in.

Custer's gaze shifted from Ethan. He slowly rose from the worn leather armchair, which faintly smelled of old paper and wood smoke, and strolled over to the tall, leaded window. Soft light poured in, illuminating the study and making dust motes dance in the air. His eyes looked outside, across the well-maintained grounds, to the stables where the occasional low whinny of horses could be heard. He watched one of the younger horses, a beautiful bay, cantering in a training circle within its pen, moving around and around. Its movements were graceful, but it was unable to escape. It was a powerful symbol of the wild spirit that is now restrained.

A brief but intense darkness flickered across Custer's face. "I regret the men I lost," he said, his voice a low, gravelly rasp, as if each word were a stone dropped into a well. "Their faces are etched into the landscape of my memory, and the silence that follows their names now reverberates louder than any boastful cheer ever could, a constant, hollow ache." His gaze hardened like a blade; determination carved into every line of his face as he turned to face Ethan again. His eyes were fierce and piercing, like the last embers of a battle long forgotten. "But I don't wish I hadn't lived: not for a single breath."

The fire in the hearth behind them crackled. It was clear then that the power of the tales and the flicker of legend rekindled the atmosphere between them.

History, including Custer's, remained a living, evolving story. It was a living, breathing entity that constantly changed and was redefined by the stories of people who, like Custer, experienced it and, like Ethan, recounted it. A new chapter had begun, marking a significant shift in the tale.

In the silence that followed, Ethan felt a surge of determination awakening within him, prompting a growing awareness of the urgency to reveal the truth and the moral duty to oppose the widespread corruption that threatened to weaken the nation's very foundations. The valuable lessons he learned from Custer's experiences motivated him to keep moving forward, strengthening his resolve to fight passionately for the integrity that the political landscape desperately needs.

Outside, the wind tossed the last of the autumn leaves. Custer leaned back, the firelight catching the silver in his hair. "Remember this: peace is the hardest fight of all."

# Chapter 8: The Presidential Election

Custer's attitude changed noticeably, revealing a gentler, more nuanced side of his personality that offered insights into his emotions and thoughts. Setting aside a large, well-worn leather book dated 1876, he seemed to suggest, both physically and metaphorically, that he was leaving the burdens of the battles behind to focus on a new topic: the primary purpose of this interview.

"They arrived at dusk," Custer began. "Two Democratic delegates, fresh from an important meeting in New York City, wore suits that were far too fancy for the rough plains, and their shiny faces revealed an air of sophistication that made them difficult to trust."

Ethan's curiosity was piqued, and he leaned in eagerly, eager to learn more about the unfolding events. "And they offered you the nomination?"

Custer leaned back in his chair with his fingers steepled in thought. "They presented me with a significant risk disguised as a wonderful opportunity," he replied carefully, each word layered with sincere meaning. "The party was divided, burdened by recent electoral losses, and exhausted from a long struggle. They wanted a candidate who could do more than lead; they needed someone who could revitalize their energy, a person with charisma, resolve, a recognizable name that could draw attention, and someone whose very presence was full of compelling stories and broad appeal."

"Did you immediately find their proposal compelling?" Ethan asked, his voice firm yet tinged with keen curiosity.

"I aimed to shape the narrative," Custer declared, a spark of passion lighting his voice. "Emerging victorious from the Battle of the Little Bighorn lifted me to an almost untouchable status in the public eye. It marked a transcendence beyond my role as a general, transforming me into a living legend who defies death itself." Crossing his arms defensively, he exuded confidence that filled the room. "Assured of strong backing and the full machinery of the party, I was tasked with more than just smiling and giving speeches. The expectations included a strategic presence at parades and a nuanced approach to engaging with the public."

"What was Mrs. Custer's opinion on this?" Ethan seized the chance to learn more about the Custer family dynamics, comprehending that personal relationships often shape public decisions.

Custer's expression softened into a smile that showed his admiration for his wife. "Ah, Libbie. Ethan, please call her Libbie from now on. She would have insisted on it."

"She was a fighter in her own right, fiercely independent and headstrong. She wasn't opposed to the idea of the presidency at all. She reminded me that I had weathered much worse storms in my life.

Still, she had one unwavering condition: she wanted a cause worth supporting, not just an empty title. She insisted that I pledge my support for women's suffrage."

Outside, one of the elegant Thoroughbreds galloped across the vast meadow. Its powerful legs hit the ground with a smooth rhythm, showing strength and vitality. Custer moved to the back window, captivated by the sight of the horse, a surge of pride filling his chest as he watched the majestic creature roam freely. This inspiring scene brought back memories of past achievements and evoked the wild spirit of freedom he often associated with such noble animals.

Ethan carefully pondered the meaning of Custer's words and examined this crucial moment in Custer's life more intently. He leaned forward, his eyes shining with genuine curiosity. "How did you find the change... the experience of shifting from a general to a candidate?"

Custer sat down and relaxed comfortably in his chair; his posture was calm but reflective as he considered Ethan's question. "The shift from being a military leader to a politician felt quite unsettling to me. In the military, the chain of command is straightforward, and your orders prompt immediate action and responses from your subordinates. But politics is different; it involves making deals and compromises. Many layers of social dynamics, legal frameworks, and public opinions can obscure the real stakes, even though comprehending these details is crucial for success."

"At any time, did you regret getting into politics?" Ethan asked. He carefully jotted down his thoughts in the pages of his trusted notebook, his focus on Custer's inner world evident.

In that brief moment, the brightness in Custer's eyes faded, a flicker of doubt crossing his typically composed face. The burden of his choices seemed to hang in the air.

"Not regret," Custer finally said, his voice filled with thoughtful reflection. "Perhaps a sense of disillusionment. You see, war offers unequivocal clarity. There is a defined enemy and a tangible battlefield where the outcomes are clearly visible: life or death. Yet, politics resembles war without the deafening gunfire, an entirely different kind of torment. The wounds it leaves may stay hidden, but they cut into the fabric of a person's soul."

He shifted his position in his seat, seeking the comfort of its familiar embrace, absentmindedly brushing away imaginary dust from his sleeve as if trying to shake off the burden of his thoughts. Although this gesture seemed trivial, it revealed a sense of resignation and an unquenchable longing for something greater.

"At first, I held a vision," he continued, his voice growing more confident as if flashes of ambition ignited in his mind. "A path to lead this extraordinary nation away from the shadows of war and toward a future filled with reconstruction, healing, and strength untainted by cruelty. I truly believed we could rise triumphantly from the ashes. When I shared that vision with the public, I found many who supported it."

When Ethan looked up from his notebook, he asked, "You really believed you could change the system?"

Custer paused before replying. He said, "I wanted to believe it. The system needed repair. Corruption and greed plagued the government, requiring a new approach."

Ethan watched as Custer skillfully crafted his story. Over time, each moment he shared was refined into a tale approaching legendary status. An intriguing thought began to take hold in Ethan's mind: a curiosity about how public perception can distort the truth of heroism, often exposing a gap between myth and real-life experiences.

Ethan understood how important this transition was for Custer and was eager to learn more. "What was most surprising to you about the world of politics?" he asked, showing genuine curiosity.

"The intricacy of it all," Custer responded after a moment's reflection, his brow furrowing slightly. "On the battlefield, the objective is always clear-cut; you know what you are fighting for. But in the realm of politics, it isn't just about winning votes or gaining a prestigious position. You also need to be aware of your constituents' fears, motivations, and feelings as you meet their changing expectations and stay true to your values. It's like navigating a dangerous situation; one mistake can have serious consequences, possibly changing the course of your career or even your legacy."

"However, there is a paradox to recognize: The public wants a champion who represents their hopes and symbolizes victory. Yet, in politics, compromise often plays a key role. To be effective, you need to listen carefully, discern different viewpoints, and sometimes yield on issues, not out of weakness, but to pursue a greater good that benefits everyone involved."

Custer's insights truly resonated, highlighting the demands of civic duty on leaders.

Custer kept speaking with renewed energy. "When I started this journey to serve the public, I imagined a bright and hopeful future. Although the road has been tough and full of obstacles, each setback has taught me valuable lessons. More importantly, it has reinforced my conviction that pursuing greatness inevitably comes with challenges. Every challenge we face is an opportunity to grow and move toward a better future."

The conversations between Custer and Ethan revealed leadership struggles and the lasting impact individuals can have on history and others' lives. Custer's story highlighted the main themes of ambition, sacrifice, and legacy, illustrating a core part of humanity's quest for meaning and purpose amid life's chaos.

Custer let out a short, ironic laugh, pointing out the absurdity of his situation. "It's like trying to lead a cavalry charge armed only with a grin and a well-crafted speech. The challenging task ahead might seem daunting and undeniably intimidating. Yet, at the same time, it could be thrilling, and I compared the experience to standing before a wild stallion, an untamed spirit ready to be caught through sheer resolve and determination."

The campaign had officially begun, opening a new front that would test Custer's strength and resolve in unexpected ways. Ethan looked forward to learning more about the campaign strategies and objectives.

Outside, the wind moved the dry grass, producing a hauntingly beautiful sound that blended with the distant calls of wildlife. Nearby, a young colt whinnied, its call full of innocence and eager excitement.

Custer stood, walked over to a bookcase, and picked up a colorful piece of paper. He handed Ethan a carefully folded campaign leaflet, marking a key moment in their interaction. This eye-catching flyer was decorated with bright red, white, and blue, prominently displaying the words "Custer for the Union!" in bold, attention-grabbing letters that stirred patriotism among viewers.

"He was a decent man, Rutherford Hayes, and a decent candidate," Custer remarked, settling comfortably into his seat with an air of familiarity. "He stood firm on his principles no matter what. However, I must admit that he lacked the spark that ignites others' passion. Just one look at him, and you'd think he was more suited for shining the marble surfaces of a bank than facing the deafening noise of combat amidst the chaos of a battlefield."

Ethan let out a soft chuckle, a spark of amusement flashing in his eye. "And what about you, General? You look as if you've just stepped out of one of those grand buildings, dressed to attract the attention and admiration of everyone around you."

"Absolutely," Custer replied, an enthusiastic sparkle lighting his eyes as a playful grin spread across his face. "People sought something far beyond the limits of normal policies and political decorum; they craved a story, a richly woven narrative that went beyond mere survival and routine governance. They longed to see the individual who faced death bravely and emerged victorious, a warrior not only confronting his own past but also representing the struggles and hopes of others. Hayes had strong backing from Grant's influential group, which could be seen as a reliable ally in that political landscape. Still, I arrived full of energy, accompanied by a group of loyal veterans who had endured similar trials and a nation weary of poor responses and weak leadership. Remember, I also had Samuel J. Tilden, a skilled politician, as vice president. His name added influence to our ticket."

Ethan leaned in closer, clearly curious as he looked for the complete story. "How did you prepare for the debates?" he asked, genuinely interested in uncovering Custer's strategies.

Custer offered a slight grin, with a touch of mischief in his expression. "I must admit, I prepared with a touch of sarcasm. The questions asked during the debates were often disappointingly dull and predictable, while the crowds remained consistently restless and easily distracted. However, within that indifference, I took the opportunity to emphasize my humanity. I was determined to present myself as more than just another name on a ballot but as a real, breathing person, shaped forever by scars, both physical and emotional. I wanted them to remember the struggles I faced in my life's journey and that I had overcome them all with resilience. Hayes, in comparison, was hardly more than a footnote in the unfolding story of that era."

After a deliberate pause, he took the opportunity to light the pipe he held firmly in his hand. Custer continued, "Libbie played a vital role in shaping our speeches. Her steadfastness was unwavering; she stressed that we should fill each word with dignity and clarity so our message would resonate with listeners. Every speech we delivered ended with a heartfelt appeal for unity and healing among our citizens. Our goals went beyond simply winning; we aimed to foster a healing process for a nation that had become painfully divided."

"But," Ethan interjected, unable to hide his surprise, "even with all your hard work and effort, you still lost the popular vote."

Custer's eyes gleamed with determination and conviction as he replied, "Ah, but I managed to win the Electoral College. That result sent my opponents into utter disarray. They dismissed it as invalid, calling the victory an empty triumph. Yet, when I was sworn in, standing before those assembled, I held my head high, wearing my reliable old cavalry boots beneath the crisp, tailored coat made especially for that momentous day. It was a subtle yet meaningful gesture shared only with Libbie, who smiled in recognition of its profound symbolism."

"Hayes never fully embraced my role in the presidency. In fact, many in the political world shared that feeling. I heard those whispers echo through the halls of power in Washington," Custer admitted, his gaze drifting as if reminiscing. "Yet, I would prefer that uncertainty over a path that leads to being forgotten any day. There's an inherent risk in stepping into the spotlight, but I refused to hide in the shadows. History has its own way of choosing favorites, Mr. Thorne," he said, reflecting on our conversation. "I never claimed I deserved my position; instead, I said I was ready to face it with all its challenges head-on."

Ethan carefully transcribed every word from Custer's lips, the pencil nearly worn down to a nub. This moment, filled with significance and gravity, would stay with him forever as the larger-than-life figure leaned in closer, showing his legendary reputation and a genuinely human side, revealing the man behind the myth with an open heart.

Custer rose from his chair and said, "Ethan, I won't be able to join you for our luncheon today, as I have a business matter to attend to. However, Harold will take excellent care of you, and I will rejoin you shortly." Harold entered the room carrying a tray from the kitchen. Custer grabbed a sandwich and left the library. Ethan jumped at the chance to continue editing his notes, trying to capture the plot and Custer's motivations.

When he returned to the library early in the afternoon, Custer's eyes, which were usually bright and full of life, seemed to carry a new heaviness. A strange tension filled his gaze, signaling that a storm was brewing both outside, where dark clouds gathered on the horizon, and inside him, as if he were battling turbulent emotions. The usually lively horses, sensitive to the changing atmosphere, moved to a corner of the paddock, distancing themselves from the approaching storm.

"It was Inauguration Day, March fifth," he began, the steadiness of his tone disguising the layers of memory woven into his words. "The bitter cold was remarkable that day. I remember Libbie's breath forming delicate clouds in the icy air as we entered the carriage and headed toward the Capitol Building. The throngs of eager spectators lining the streets to witness the occasion surrounded us with lively excitement. After we arrived, the crowd erupted into a chorus of cheers and passionate chants, their voices ringing against the grand marble columns that proudly stood as symbols of our democracy. At that moment, a realization struck me: it wasn't me they were celebrating; instead, they were honoring the myth, the monumental figure I was being shaped to embody, rather than the flawed, real person on the brink of a magnificent journey."

Custer fell silent. His hands, steady during battle, trembled slightly on the armrest. "I could practically feel the anticipation electrifying the air around me, a rare combination of hope and fervent expectation. When I stepped onto the grand platform, I sensed the gaze of an entire nation focusing on me, with their hopes resting on my shoulders, a nation yearning for change, eager for someone like me to guide them through the turbulent waters of our historical challenges."

He briefly closed his eyes, letting himself feel the urgency of that defining moment. "The act of speaking was both exhilarating and terrifying," he acknowledged, his voice trembling slightly. "Every word I uttered carried the hopes, dreams, and aspirations of countless people. My goal was to inspire them, to ignite a collective spirit that could rise above our differences and work toward a brighter future."

After a brief silence for both men to collect their thoughts, Ethan asked, "After taking the Oath of Office, describe your encounter with President Grant."

Custer reached for his pipe, lit it, and said, "Libbie and I were driven to the Executive Mansion after the swearing-in ceremonies. Upon arrival, we were greeted by President Grant and Julia, who welcomed us as they were leaving. Grant and I stood close and stared into each other's eyes. Then, quite unexpectedly, he saluted me. For many years, I had always saluted him first, but now this change was quite significant. I was now his commander, and I will never forget that moment."

Ethan listened carefully, intrigued by the vivid recounting of Custer's memories and the emotions they evoked. "Did you feel, at that moment, that you had fully embraced the role?" he asked, delving into Custer's experience.

Custer responded with a gentle smile, his expression thoughtful as he reflected on that pivotal day. "Yes, in many ways. Yet, I couldn't overlook the influence of the remarkable individuals who preceded me. I wasn't simply representing my journey; I was standing on the shoulders of giants, the legacy they had crafted through their struggles and victories as the foundational groundwork upon which I intended to build my own mission."

His words moved Ethan. He paused writing and looked at Custer's face. "Sir, that is quite profound." A serious tone crept into his voice. "It must have been incredibly heavy to carry the weight of history and everything that comes with it."

"Indeed," replied Custer, his tone becoming earnest and reflective. "However, it is also a great honor to serve in such a capacity, to be part of something greater than oneself. What true value remains in our leadership if we do not constantly strive for progress and unity among our people?"

After a brief pause, Custer confidently explained, "I was well aware that the obstacles ahead would be incredibly demanding and challenging. Certain individuals, both inside and outside my circle, doubted my abilities, seeing me as a young figure in a crucial role, lacking the required experience and wisdom. Yet, I stayed committed to my mission to prove them wrong and showcase my abilities. I aimed to embody our nation's spirit: strong, resilient, and fully ready to face upcoming challenges."

As the conversation progressed, Custer's insights into leadership during challenging times illuminated the complex nature of the role. He remembered his successes and failures, realizing that both were crucial for his growth. Every decision Custer made in the cabinet room had ripple effects that went beyond immediate issues; they shaped the very fabric of a nation trying to define its identity after a devastating conflict that left scars on the nation's soul.

Custer shared inspiring stories about colleagues who initially doubted him, showing how their skepticism ultimately fueled his determination to succeed. He openly discussed how each harsh criticism he faced energized his commitment to become a more effective and compassionate leader. "The responsibilities of the presidency can often lead to feelings of isolation and overwhelming emotions," he acknowledged thoughtfully. "However, it is also a tremendous privilege, a unique chance that allows one to unite the people and amplify the voices of those who often feel overlooked and marginalized. I aimed to create a government that included every citizen, not just favored the few in power. I wanted a nation that genuinely reflected equality and justice, the core principles it was built on."

Ethan quickly recorded the statements and realized that this man had ridden into battle at the head of a thousand men and had led the entire nation, but on this day, Custer was a leader to only one person.

Custer continued, "Do you know I was the youngest elected president in history? I was only thirty-seven when I took office. They whispered behind my back, derisively calling me 'The Boy President.'" Custer's brows lifted slightly in amusement, a small smile spreading on his face. "Oh, I was fully aware of that."

Ethan's pencil slipped off the page, and he felt a sudden shock wash over him. "You knew?"

Custer returned a knowing smile, his expression a mix of playfulness and comprehension. "Of course. In Washington, knowledge is power. It flows through the corridors like an endless stream of gossip, and staying connected with your scouts and allies is crucial. You must stay informed about the nation's current events. I learned these lessons early on, and there was still much more to learn."

As the interview went on, Ethan's view began to change, and he saw that the meeting wasn't just a chance to hear a man talk about his life; instead, it was a key moment where a leader shared his growing understanding of what it truly means to take responsibility and accept sacrifice. With each insight Custer offered, he became more than just a military figure; he appeared as a strategist with a vision beyond the usual, a forward thinker capable of imagining a better future, and ultimately someone with depth who was unafraid to admit and accept his flaws.

The term "The Boy President" took on new significance for Ethan, symbolizing more than just a nickname or a historical label; it became a powerful emblem of the strength found in vulnerability. For Custer, it served as a heartfelt reminder of the unwavering determination and resilience needed to face and conquer the many challenges that life naturally presents.

# Chapter 9: The Custer Presidency

The air in the library smelled of smoldering wood, aged paper, and the faint, lingering smoke from Custer's pipe. The fire had died down to embers, but the room still felt warm, not just because of the hearth but also due to the heaviness of the conversation.

As Custer sat in his chair, his demeanor looked serious and focused; every movement showed purpose as he stared at the softly flickering embers, their warm glow contrasted with the rising emotion in the room.

Ethan carefully asked, "Do you regret choosing to become president?" His voice was filled with curiosity.

Custer turned toward him, a thoughtful expression on his face. "I only truly understood the impact it had on those closest to me when I was no longer in the office and could see things clearly. The role didn't change who I am, Thorne; it simply revealed the real me, exposing my true character to the world. Like in the war, with each battle I fought, I shed layers of pretension that had hidden my true self, showing the person I was meant to be all along."

Ethan nodded, jotted down an essential phrase in his notes, and felt an intense, lasting respect for Custer. The complexities of his character were now more apparent than ever.

"And who is that person?" he asked, driven by his desire to investigate, examine, and dig further. He aimed to uncover the key traits that defined Custer and reveal the true qualities of his nature.

Custer replied slowly, his furrowed brow and intense gaze emphasizing each word he spoke. "A man who continuously pushes forward, undeterred by the obstacles that lie in his path, even when the road gets extraordinarily tough and fraught with uncertainty."

Ethan had learned to give Custer a few moments of quiet reflection before asking tough questions or switching topics. He found this usually resulted in more detailed answers, which was his goal. Eventually, Ethan said, "Your transition from general to candidate to president was complete. How would you describe your time in office?"

After a moment, Custer replied, "I faced the difficult challenge of leading. Half of Congress saw me as a decorated hero who had gained battlefield fame but lacked the true wisdom and experience for effective leadership. The other half saw me as just a figurehead, willing to follow their agenda without personal conviction or passion. Despite the doubt surrounding me, I had ambitions and goals focused on reconstruction, healing, and societal progress. I imagined a nation ready to rise from the broken remnants of war, emerging united and stronger than before."

Eager for more insights, Ethan inquired, "What was the first significant decision you made as a leader?"

Without hesitation, his voice full of authority, Custer responded, "The withdrawal of troops from the South. I firmly believed that building trust was essential for genuine healing, a process that could only happen by stepping back and granting the Southern states autonomy. I assessed that by withdrawing our soldiers, we would give them a chance to regain independence and begin healing from the scars left by the war. The backlash from that decision was quick and severe, with a barrage of criticism from all sides. Detractors condemned me, calling my actions reckless and naive. Nevertheless, Libbie's unwavering faith in me and my vision gave me the encouragement and support to persevere and stay true to my convictions."

As Custer spoke, he briefly rose from his seat. "Time and again, I found myself labeled as impulsive, mockingly dubbed the 'Boy President.' Yet, I privately took pride in that name, using it as a shield against the relentless tide of doubt that often beset me. In the unpredictable world of politics, being underestimated by others gave me a strategic advantage. These characteristics allowed me the freedom to maneuver and outwit my opponents, showing them there was more beneath the surface than they could ever fully see."

Outside, the sun slowly sank behind a thick, looming cloud, casting a shadow over the room that highlighted the seriousness of their conversation. Ethan leaned back in his chair, feeling a sense of humility wash over him, and was moved by this poignant revelation. He also felt a quiet pride in himself and a sense of satisfaction from the progress of the interview. In his view, Custer had become something even greater, a symbol of resilience and a steadfast spirit unshaken by life's relentless challenges.

Ethan pressed on, recalling quotes from Custer's inaugural speech and their significance. "You once commented during an important address, 'The battlefield has given me discipline, clarity, and purpose. These are the tools I use in leadership, not the secret arrangements of those seeking power.' Reflecting on those powerful words, how foresighted do you think they were?"

Custer returned to his chair, slowly soaking in the warmth and comfort of the fire as he pondered his response. At that moment, a brief softness appeared on his face, not from happy memories but from the complex mix of remembrance and reflection.

"I shared those thoughts when I hadn't fully grasped how quickly the doors of power can close once the thunder of cannons falls silent. Major challenges emerged during my transition from military leadership to guiding our nation. Sometimes, navigating the established political system that had been the norm proved to be a tough and demanding task," he replied, his tone full of reflection. "In the heat of battle, orders are clear. You either push forward with determination or withdraw with tactical caution. There's no room for doubt or quiet compromises." He shook his head gently in a sign of resignation. "Politics is filled with far more hidden traps and snares than anything I ever faced on the battlefield."

Custer's gaze shifted toward the portrait of Libbie hanging on the wall, perhaps seeking inspiration or comfort in her likeness. "Still, I meant every word I said back then. I believed that discipline and clarity would speed up progress. For a while, those principles did lead to success. But the secret deals I warned about never completely disappeared. They stayed, greeting me with false smiles while they plotted and schemed to win their votes out of my sight." Speaking softly as if sharing a secret, he said, "Idealistic? Maybe. But I had seen what war could do. I wanted to believe peace could accomplish more."

A flicker of amusement crossed his eyes, and a subtle smile played on his lips. "Even so, I would willingly pay to see the reactions on their faces when they finally realize that the 'Boy General' still can lead effectively and decisively."

A shadow crossed Custer's face as he spoke again, his voice growing lower and more serious. "During that time, the Ku Klux Klan lurked in hiding, patiently waiting for the right moment to commit violence and intimidation against marginalized communities. I sent courageous agents, people willing to infiltrate their ranks, gather intelligence, and shed light on their secret operations. I dedicated all my resources to disrupting their networks, aiming to cut off the connections they relied on to conspire in secret. But for every leader we managed to eliminate, another, more powerful and vicious figure would inevitably rise in their place, like a relentless hydra fueled by resentment and rage, continuing a cycle of adversity."

Intrigued by the conversation's growing seriousness, Ethan felt compelled to ask more questions. "In the middle of all this chaos, did your supporters stay loyal? How did your public reputation hold up during such challenging times?"

Custer relaxed comfortably in his chair, a slight crease forming on his forehead as he thoughtfully remembered the varied reactions of those around him. "Popularity changes like the waves," he remarked, his tone reflective. "At first, many saw my efforts to promote peace in a positive light. I was considered a war hero who had stood up for our country during turbulent times. But when I took unexpected actions back then, I faced strong backlash from many sides. People found it difficult to reconcile the traditional image of a military figure, which usually meant strength and conflict, with the practical work of nation-building and reconciliation."

A brief silence filled the room, creating an emotional atmosphere as Custer and Ethan shared a moment of rapport. They both recognized the heavy burden of leadership on Custer's shoulders and the complexities of his role.

Ethan asked with sincere curiosity, "Did you expect the resistance you faced?" His investigative nature was precise in his expression.

A gentle sigh from Custer highlighted the gravity of his memories. "I expected some opposition, of course.

Still, I believed that once the effects of the war started to fade, a shared desire for healing and reconciliation would develop among the people. I greatly underestimated how complicated and unpredictable human emotions can be. Fear, identity, and nostalgia can cloud even the clearest judgment and sabotage the best intentions. I wanted my calls for empathy and cooperation to break down these barriers. However, I found that people often cling to familiar stories and narratives, even when those stories can be harmful to their progress."

Ethan absorbed the seriousness of Custer's thoughts, fully aware of the complexity and depth of the situations described. "What course did you take when faced with those difficulties?" he asked.

Custer's tone became more determined as he outlined his strategy. "I stayed firmly focused on my purpose. My main goal was to create a workable path to unity and insight among divided groups. I listened carefully to the stories of those willing to engage in dialogue, who could look past their fears and misconceptions. I looked for any sign of progress, no matter how small, as these moments motivated me to keep going. It was crucial to surround myself with like-minded individuals who shared a vision of a more inclusive and harmonious future, where collaboration could thrive."

As they talked, the heavy rain outside mirrored the somber mood of their discussion on healing the nation's emotional wounds.

Ethan tentatively asked, respecting Custer's insights, "Given the tensions of that period, do you believe that the ideals of unity you aimed to promote have stood the test of time?"

Custer considered the question carefully, his face serious as he reflected on the implications of his answer. "In many ways, yes," he responded after a moment of thought. "Hope still thrives in our community, supported by individuals and groups who work tirelessly for knowledge and cooperation. But it is also true that the shadows of our divisive history remain stubborn and troubling. It takes care, courage, and a strong commitment from all of us to build a shared sense of purpose beyond past disagreements."

Their conversation flowed smoothly. The rain had turned to sleet, blurring the edges of the outside world. Both men felt a growing bond as they connected through their stories. By sharing thoughts and insights, they not only had a heartfelt talk about a past era but also sparked a strong commitment to addressing and healing the divisions that still existed, work that remains essential and urgent today.

Custer gave a sardonic grin, his lips curling slightly to show a touch of self-awareness and recognition of the ironies of perception. "Upon further thought, the reactions to my ideals largely depend on who you ask. In Richmond, I received admiration; people enthusiastically raised their glasses to my name, celebrating my role as a loyal supporter of their beliefs." The warmth of their cheers lingered within him, strengthening his sense of purpose during turbulent times. "However, if you went north to Boston, you would have found a different response. There, my effigy was burned, turning me into a symbol of contempt, a target for their anxieties." The stark contrast between the two cities highlighted the era's factional divides and the complexities of his public image.

While the wind howled outside, swirling through the trees and sending chills across the landscape, the orchard trees stood tall and stark against the dull, overcast sky. Their branches were bare, resembling skeletal hands reaching for the indifferent heavens.

Ethan's brow furrowed with a reflective sadness that shone in his eyes. He thought about how time might gradually erase the complexities that defined the General, leaving only hints of his legacy. He couldn't help but wonder which remnants of Custer's life and choices would survive the relentless march of centuries to come.

Sensing the impact of Ethan's reflective thoughts, Custer softened his tone, becoming more contemplative. "You see, Reconstruction was not just about regions or politics." He tilted his head slightly, his demeanor turning more serious as the gravity of the topic settled in. "It was connected to heritage and memory, and memory can be the harshest battleground of all. In this place, wounds persist, and triumphs blend with defeats, shaping the stories we leave behind and the legacies we carry far into the future." His words carried the emotional depth of personal experience.

A heavy atmosphere surrounded them as the two men sat quietly, each lost in their own thoughts. Meanwhile, the autumn wind howled outside, chilling everything to its core and setting a stark natural backdrop for their serious conversation.

Custer's expression softened further, and a thoughtful smile appeared as he absentmindedly touched his lapel in a respectful salute to her memory, a gesture full of admiration and unwavering devotion to the woman who had profoundly influenced his life.

"She was the heart of the Executive Mansion, radiating grace, wisdom, and influence that shaped the very essence of governance within its walls," he stated, his voice thick with emotion, layers of affection woven into his words. "Libbie filled the rooms with elegance and, in return, provided the nation with its moral compass." His words lingered, filled with sentiment.

Sitting at a distance, Ethan looked up from his notes, briefly captivated by Custer's sincere words. "Her campaign for suffrage...could you please describe her contributions? What aspects of the project originated from her?"

"Every bit of it," Custer answered decisively, his conviction palpable. "From the moment I accepted the nomination, she stressed that she would not be a silent partner, hidden away like some ornamental piece. No, she possessed a strong voice and utilized it relentlessly." He recalled her fervent ardor and tireless efforts with admiration and respect. "She campaigned tirelessly, wrote passionate letters, and energized the public. With fierce clarity, she consistently reminded this nation that its promises would be meaningless if they silenced the voices of half its population. His reverence for her unwavering spirit grew stronger as he spoke, revealing their powerful connection.

"Did she have to deal with criticism?" Ethan asked, his anger fueled by the hardships and challenges Libbie likely faced in her tireless efforts to secure justice and equality for women.

"Absolutely," Custer replied, his voice sincere and honest. "She faced opposition and hostility from both men and women, which made her task even harder. Yet, despite all the challenges, she stayed strong and determined; nothing could break her resolve. She once told me, 'I have used your reputation in battle to push our cause. Now, you will work to uphold mine and make sure our efforts are recognized.' And I did my best, putting all my energy into that promise." The meaning of her words struck a chord in him, confirming the strong bond they shared, forged through passionate love and shared beliefs.

A bittersweet smile crossed Custer's face as he remembered her resilience. "She was instrumental in bringing the women's suffrage issue to Congress. When the 19th Amendment finally passed in 1920 after years of struggle and tireless advocacy, my dear Libbie had been gone from this life for two years. I often wondered how she would have celebrated if she had seen her cause succeed. She would have taken immense pride in casting her first vote."

Ethan paused in his writing, taking a moment to absorb the significance of Custer's thoughts. "Do you think she altered history?"

Custer quickly responded, his eyes shining brightly with pride and conviction. "I am wholeheartedly certain she did," he declared with unyielding confidence. "Her influence and impact reverberated through the very foundations of our society, shaping its evolution far more significantly than any charge I ever commanded on the battlefield. I reflect on the battles fought, recognizing that they were not merely contained to the physical confrontations on battlefields but also encompassed the life-changing struggles within the minds and hearts of a nation striving to evolve."

A silence surrounded them, honoring Libbie's enduring legacy. Outside, a gentle breeze moved a lone shutter, the soft sound serving as a subtle reminder of the world beyond their quiet talk. Inside the library, Libbie's portrait seemed to watch over them, radiating her quiet strength and lasting influence.

Custer softly commented, his voice filled with fondness and longing. "She was the last spark of hope even in the darkest moments of every failure, a beacon of resilience and inspiration that illuminated the path forward." Each statement he uttered was a heartfelt tribute, a lasting reflection of her essence in his life, and a gentle reminder that the fight for justice was a journey they undertook together. He reached for his beloved pipe resting on the ashtray, but as he lifted it, it slipped from his fingers and rolled closer to Ethan. Ethan, who had finally learned to maintain his composure in such moments, met this minor accident with a sense of calm. He now accepted that Custer refused to accept help when he believed he could fix his mistake.

Ethan carefully turned to a fresh, blank page in his well-used notebook, mentally preparing to continue this rich and meaningful conversation.

A glow of admiration spread across Ethan's face. "Her extraordinary courage in confronting such formidable challenges is truly inspiring. In what ways did her activism shape your own military career and leadership style?"

Custer smiled, a playful glimmer shining in his eyes. "Libbie's activism had a profound effect on my worldview. It heightened my awareness of the complex connections between civil rights, women's suffrage, and genuine leadership. In fact, many of my military campaigns were often guided by the same core principles she championed: equality, freedom, and justice. Ultimately, her beliefs inspired me and shaped my approach to service as well."

"I can clearly see the thread that connects her advocacy with your position," Ethan said, eagerly jotting down more notes. "It's fascinating to see how personal relationships and experiences can shape and guide larger societal movements."

"Undoubtedly," Custer affirmed, his voice growing more serious. "History is rarely made in isolation. The cooperation and encouragement we give each other, both in our private lives and in the public arena, are essential for meaningful progress and societal advancement. Libbie's influence on my life clearly demonstrates this powerful truth."

Ethan paused to consider the value of strong relationships, both personal and professional. "Do you believe future generations will keep spreading Libbie's message of equality and justice?"

Custer looked directly at Ethan. "Yes, I firmly believe so. The ongoing fight for equality is a long journey. Libbie's voice, along with those of many others from our past, will inspire people committed to justice and fairness. Her legacy will guide them through their personal struggles and efforts."

As the wind calmed into a gentle breeze, both men felt a renewed commitment to their discussion. Custer leaned forward, emphasizing the urgency of his statement. "We must honor those who fought openly for change and those unsung heroes like Libbie who worked tirelessly behind the scenes. Their relentless efforts deserve our heartfelt acknowledgment and respect."

A wave of inspiration swept over Ethan, causing him to set his notebook aside briefly. He wanted to fully determine the importance and seriousness of the conversation that had started between them. "You've given me a lot to think about, General. The impact we have on the world is a result of our willingness to support each other and recognize the shared history that unites us," he said, his voice reflecting both gratitude and thoughtfulness.

Custer nodded in response, his gaze fixed intently on Ethan, showing he was engaged in their conversation. "We need to acknowledge the sacrifices made by those who came before us and share the important lessons we've learned from our experiences as we reflect on our past," he emphasized, highlighting the importance of collective memory.

Light poured through the large, sunlit library window, filling the space with a warm, welcoming glow that felt almost magical. Outside, the remnants of the earlier rain shimmered on the pathways, sparkling as if celebrating the renewed hope from their thoughtful discussion. The light added a spiritual feel to the room. Both men understood they were part of a powerful story that would echo through the ages.

"Although my cabinet was filled with those in the highest positions of power, I must admit, it never truly felt like it was mine," Custer began, his voice calm but tinged with nostalgia. "What I inherited was far from a unified plan; instead, it was a complex mix of factions, ambitions, and egos, each eager to follow their own path. My choices often involved compromises to satisfy different regions or maintain fragile alliances, sacrificing the pursuit of the highest quality or competence in governance for political expediency." His expression grew somber as he recalled his many struggles during that turbulent time.

Ethan leaned in closer, captivated by the small details of Custer's journey. "Did you really have a chance to pick your own members?" he asked.

Custer nodded in agreement, though reluctantly. "A few key instances," he replied. "However, I must confess that party brokers, individuals eager to consolidate their power, essentially dictated the cabinet names. These brokers supported my nomination with the unspoken recognition that they would be allowed to insert their choices among my advisers, effectively manipulating the political landscape for their interests."

Ethan keenly observed the flicker of annoyance that revealed Custer's usually calm exterior. "And they didn't always see eye-to-eye with you?" he asked, fully aware of the complex dynamics unfolding before him.

Custer let out a brief, humorless laugh, with a trace of irony. "Not at all. In fact, they often disagreed more strongly with each other than with me. The Secretary of War often clashed with the Secretary of the Interior, and the Treasury regularly opposed my Southern policies. It was a constant barrage of requests for political favors, endless memos detailing conflicting demands, and subtle threats hidden in diplomatic language. Every day felt like navigating a maze of bureaucracy, with documents passed around colleagues more concerned with appearances than real accomplishments."

Ethan raised an eyebrow, intrigued by the chaotic world of governance Custer described. "Were there any parts of that work that brought you satisfaction?" he asked, fully expecting a response filled with annoyance.

Custer's tone was briefly jovial. "I took great pleasure in having my loyal scout, Bloody Knife, move into the Executive Mansion after I took office," Custer recalled, a warm smile crossing his face as he reminisced about those days. "I can only imagine the gossip that must have spread among the social elite. People may have wondered, 'How can an Indian reside in the Executive Mansion?' Their discomfort was obvious."

"However, before their speculation could last too long, Bloody Knife made his position clear. Disliking the confinements and restrictions of indoor life, he set up a traditional teepee on the east lawn, creating quite a scene. Politicians in Washington hurried to make sure no picture of the house showed his tepee, scrambling to preserve an image that aligned with their narratives. I found that quite amusing," he noted, pausing as fond memories lit up his eyes.

“I also remember when Judge Bacon, Libbie's father, first visited us at the Executive Mansion. We hosted a social gathering and invited him to join us. He appeared to enjoy himself, but I wasn't sure if he fully approved of me marrying his daughter, even after I had become president. We always had family members visiting. In fact, they still come to visit me here.”

"As for everything else, I faced many obstacles and frustrations during that time," Custer continued, the influence of his past evident in his voice and expression. "I wasn't a seasoned politician; instead, I was a military leader suddenly thrown into a tough environment filled with court members and political figures, each secretly pushing their own interests rather than genuinely caring about the needs and well-being of the public."

Ethan tilted his head slightly, trying to compare Custer's well-known history with his carefully crafted public image. "But you had the people's support; didn't that give you some degree of power?" he asked, curiosity clear in his voice as he leaned forward in his chair.

"Yes, among the public," Custer admitted with a sense of acknowledgment in his voice. "Popularity can rally support and generate momentum, but it cannot enforce laws or change where needed. In the military, orders are meant to be followed without question; in Washington, though, things are quite different. They will stall, delay, and complicate the simplest matters there."

Ethan carefully took notes, the deliberate scratch of his pencil breaking the silence. Sunlight streamed through the curtains, casting long shadows as the hours passed.

As Custer recounted his challenges, Ethan's usually calm and measured voice now carried a striking intensity, reflecting his engagement with the topic. "Your economic team resigned in protest because you refused to seek advice or heed warnings about inflation and unemployment. What do you say to that?" he asked, his eyes sharp and steady, as Custer's expression tightened in response to the direct question.

Custer didn't flinch in response. His face showed no sign of discomfort, maintaining a calm demeanor that conveyed a lot. The magnitude of Ethan's question hung in the air, filled with meaning and implications that resonated throughout the room. He shifted slightly in his cushioned chair, the leather softly creaking as he settled into a more reflective posture. Bringing his hands together below his chin, he looked at Ethan with a sharp gaze, shaped by years of leadership experience, challenges, and hardships that had defined his career.

"I remember the day they left," he began, his voice low and resonant, filling the sudden silence in the room with an air of command. He chose his words carefully and deliberately, each one sounding confident and assured, as if shaped by years of thought and experience. "They didn't storm out armed; instead, they walked out with nothing but press releases and serious faces, leaving an atmosphere heavy with their self-righteous anger." A slight smile appeared on his face as he spoke, a flicker of amusement in his expression. "They criticized me for being reckless and told me not to trust my instincts instead of listening to their sound advice." He exhaled slowly, almost dismissing the criticism without letting it bother him.

"They were not entirely wrong."

Suddenly, he leaned forward, pressing his elbows firmly against the polished surface of the desk, showing a strong sense of purpose and determination. His voice, steady and commanding, reverberated through the quiet room. "Tell me, which general ever asks his lieutenants whether to climb a hill? When action is necessary, you don't consider the wind; you move through it without hesitation or doubt. You don't stop checking reports when the cavalry charges ahead at full speed and the battle is near. I made the decision."

His gaze now sharpened and intense, directly fixed on Ethan as if daring him to question further. "I implemented major tax cuts, strictly regulated rail speculators, and avoided draining the Treasury for their preferred ideas of endless stimulus, which would only cause more problems. And yes, I recognized that inflation was a serious concern. Many people faced tough financial hardships, cut back on spending, and were anxious about what the future might hold. However, the public often feels stressed when the elite emphasize abstract economic theories over practical solutions, prioritizing theory instead of the real-world struggles faced by a nation's spirit and its people."

Ethan wrote quickly, capturing Custer's words along with the conviction, passion, and resolve behind them. Custer was straightforward, his confidence shining through every aspect of his demeanor. However, Custer raised a hand, signaling for silence, and his gaze became challenging, as if daring anyone to disagree. "Note this, Mr. Thorne: I never guaranteed comfort. I offered stewardship, which sometimes means making tough decisions and carrying the burden of responsibility."

A thoughtful silence filled the room as Custer's words lingered in the air. Recognizing their significance, Ethan understood the essence of Custer's struggles and successes in leading a divided administration through tough times.

"Leadership," Ethan said softly, contemplating its significance and implications. "How did you balance upholding your principles with making compromises to progress in a challenging environment?"

Custer's tone softened briefly, becoming more reflective and sincere. "The reality is that true leadership is more than just holding power or giving orders. It also involves dropping pretenses and showing our humanity." He leaned back in his chair, immersing himself in the moment.

Ethan sensed the impact of Custer's words. After a deliberate pause, he asked, "Was there a specific moment when you faced this conflict directly, when the tension between your principles and the need for compromise was especially intense?"

Custer leaned back and seemed to sift through memories. "There were many instances," he answered thoughtfully, "but one event stands out vividly in my mind. It centered on a crucial military funding bill that I saw as vital to national security. However, another faction within my cabinet strongly pushed for social programs inextricably linked to that bill. They threatened to withdraw their support for military funding unless I backed their initiatives, which left me in a dilemma. It was a clear case of prioritizing politics over principles, and I faced enormous pressure to give in to their demands."

Ethan listened carefully; his pencil seemed forgotten as he absorbed Custer's story. "I had to ask myself: Should a leader compromise safety and security to please those pursuing personal gain or political advantage? Ultimately, I supported the military funding bill, clearly stating the nation's urgent need for strength during tough times. But the consequences of that decision were significant, splintering my party and creating a divide that took a long time to repair and reconcile."

"The aftermath must have been complicated," Ethan remarked.

"Certainly," Custer replied, his face becoming serious as he reflected on the significance of his experiences. "Dealing with the consequences required a careful approach to rebuilding trust, not just within my own team but also with various groups in the public eye. I had to reaffirm my strong commitment to security while working to repair relationships with many stakeholders. I made it a point to show that I genuinely valued their input and concerns, even when I clearly couldn't meet all of their demands."

"When you look back, how do you think your presidency will be evaluated?" Ethan asked, his curiosity clear as he leaned in eagerly to hear Custer's thoughts and reflections on his time in office.

Custer straightened up, embodying the determined and resolute leader once again. "My administration was not just a collection of policies or measures I implemented during my time, nor can it be properly judged by how liked or popular I was at any point. It hinges on the key decisions made during tough times, the persistent effort to pursue a clear vision, and the steadfast dedication to principles I valued, even when following them was arduous. If future generations remember me for anything, I hope it will be because I led with purpose and intention rather than simply conforming to societal expectations or popular opinion."

As Custer spoke, Ethan learned a powerful lesson that goes beyond just one man's leadership journey. He understood much more than Custer's personal story of leadership. Ethan discovered important lessons about the heavy responsibility that comes with power, the key decisions that influence history, and the ongoing need to maintain integrity through the toughest leadership challenges.

Custer slowly lifted his head, a subtle yet genuine smile spreading across his face. "It is essential to remember, Mr. Thorne, that during times of conflict, a true leader remains steady in their resolve. The most important lessons often come after turmoil and strife. These lessons carry the weight of time and guide those who follow."

At that exact moment, Harold quietly entered the room. The soft clatter of china caught their attention. He carried a carefully arranged tray of steaming cups of fragrant tea, presenting it with subtle professionalism that enhanced the warm, inviting atmosphere. After gently placing the tray on the wooden table in front of them, he gave a silent nod of acknowledgment before stepping back and leaving, allowing the two men to continue their conversation.

The late afternoon sun peeked through the clouds, casting a warm, golden glow over the library's wooden shelves. Custer found himself lost in thought in that peaceful space, filled with the rich aroma of old books and polished wood. His hands rested heavily in his lap, embodying a haunting memory and foreshadowing what lay ahead.

"One of our country's greatest leaders was Ulysses Grant, but I never saw him as a rival," Custer began softly but steadily, "and I never hoped for his downfall." This statement lingered in the air, filled with tacit emotion, demonstrating that our respect for others can sometimes outweigh even the fiercest ambitions and rivalries.

"Are you referring to his later life?" Ethan asked, eagerness clear in his voice as he tried to learn more about this unfolding story.

Custer nodded slightly; the creases on his face intensified, reflecting a significant memory he was about to share, one he had kept in mind for years. "After the scandals from his presidency, he nearly went bankrupt," he explained with a serious tone. "His investments failed, and his advisors' betrayals left him with little, except for his pride, which was a heavy burden," Custer spoke sincerely, with his words carrying regret and empathy. He quickly looked away, hesitant to fully accept the emotional burden of his recent admission. "It was unfair," Custer finally admitted, his voice dropping to almost a whisper, marking a striking change from his usual image as a strong, confident leader. "Regardless of our differences, he played a key role in preserving the Union." The impact of his words lingered in the air, heightening the historical insight and emphasizing the immense responsibilities Grant faced.

Ethan asked, clearly curious, "Did you arrange for assistance to be provided to him?"

"I initially proposed the idea of giving former presidents a lifetime salary, with backing from a small group of colleagues in Congress," Custer confirmed, his voice steady as he regained his composure. "We drafted a bill to ensure that former presidents received a lifelong pension, an effort aimed at preserving the dignity of the office, if not for the individual himself." His resolute tone showed his commitment to his duties and principles.

"You also added an important provision," Ethan remarked, his engagement with the details of our political efforts evident in his expression and speech.

Custer nodded thoughtfully, his expression showing he understood the importance of that moment in their legislative history. "I did not propose the provision granting lifetime salaries to all elected officials in Congress; that decision was unrelated to the bill I championed for former presidents," he clarified. "That was the bargain Washington made in exchange for supporting Grant." A brief flash of disappointment crossed his face, highlighting the compromises often involved in the complex world of political decision-making.

Ethan furrowed his brow as he kept writing. "Did you ever regret signing it?" His question examined Custer's views on justice, responsibility, and the ethical aspects of political deals.

He leaned back in his chair, causing it to creak under his weight as he contemplated the question and sensed its seriousness. "I regretted the need for the motion," Custer said thoughtfully, "but I do not regret the act itself." His voice was filled with certainty, a clear stance from reflection. "In the end, Grant faced his last days with dignity, and that was what truly mattered." The long breath he took showed a man grappling with complex choices but ultimately finding comfort in the legacy those choices left behind, a reminder that sometimes dignity in life can overshadow the harsh judgments of history.

A reflective silence filled the room. Ethan, recognizing the importance of the moment, understood the essence of Custer's experiences, including his many challenges, accomplishments, and the complexities of leadership.

Ethan believed this conversation was more than just a simple talk; it was a rare opportunity for Custer to reflect on the choices he had made in his life. It allowed him to reconcile his accomplishments with the regrets that still haunted him. "General, what do you believe your legacy will be?" he asked, fully aware of how important and potentially transformative the question was for both of them.

Custer paused briefly, taking a moment to consider his response carefully. "People's perceptions of you and the stories surrounding your life's work often shape your legacy. I implemented policies to promote progress, unity, and causes I believed were vital for the greater good. However, many of my decisions during critical moments of my career have been subject to significant criticism and scrutiny. Ultimately, how I am remembered may depend on the stories told by those who saw me as a soldier growing into a leader with visions that went beyond my own goals and aimed at the prosperity of my nation as a whole."

"We often find ourselves in our youth trying to outshine each other," Custer said softly, his tone filled with thoughtful sadness. "At the end of our journey, we hope to be remembered for our light, not our shadows." This touching remark captured a human longing for recognition that goes beyond mere rivalry and ambition.

As twilight neared, their talk for the day wrapped up. They stood, shook hands, and said farewell.

After Ethan was taken to the railroad station, he and the other regular travelers boarded the train. They settled comfortably into their worn seats, used to the familiar rhythm of their journeys. The steady, rhythmic sound of the train wheels against the tracks created a calming backdrop that helped keep his thoughts flowing smoothly. He glanced beyond his reflection in the window, briefly ignoring the handwritten notes in his notebook, and instead thought about the man behind the many stories. To Ethan, Custer had become more than just a former general and president. His identity remained that of a sharp strategist who, even in retirement, approached each interview with the precision and skill of a battlefield tactician.

Each visit to Laurel allowed Ethan to learn more about this extraordinary figure, strengthening his emotional connection to Custer's story. As the country admired his heroic military actions, inspiring speeches, and legendary tales, Ethan focused on the individual's true essence, uncovering the intricate layers of personality and doubt that shaped his legacy from a personal perspective.

# Chapter 10: The Early 1880s

The next morning, October's chill had settled over the estate, frost blanketing the ground. As Ethan approached the mansion, he noticed the trees standing bare against the ominous sky, their branches creaking in the brisk autumn wind. The landscape seemed to be entering hibernation, preparing itself for the long, cold months ahead.

When Ethan entered the library, he cast a worried glance at Custer. The exhaustion on Custer's face was more apparent than ever; his shoulders sagged, and his posture was slouched. The normally lively and energetic storyteller now appeared visibly troubled. He looked tired, and his usual enthusiasm was gone.

After exchanging their usual morning greetings, Custer spoke softly, "My last year in office felt like a slow retreat, not from a fight, but from my sense of importance. New voices emerged from the shadows, demanding attention and passionately advocating for change. While the country reflected on and appreciated past accomplishments, it grew impatient and restless with how slowly progress seemed to happen." He paused, allowing the heftiness and depth of his words to fill the room, as if inviting Ethan to grasp the implications.

He rubbed his forehead thoughtfully, as if trying to soothe the flood of memories, moments blending both cherished times and burdensome regrets. "They wanted new ideas and tangible progress for our rapidly changing society. However, I stuck to old methods like cavalry tactics and traditional approaches that didn't connect with the younger generation."

Ethan remained silent, sensing an untold meaning behind the comparison. It highlighted the unavoidable cycle of change and the difficulty of embracing new growth and ideas.

"I aimed to make a statement," Custer continued; his voice was stoic, and his usual fire was absent. "I vetoed a tariff change, believing it was crucial for our economic stability. Yet it was reversed without hesitation, as if my words were meaningless before the tide of progress. I suggested establishing a national railroad inspection bureau, a proposal I thought necessary to ensure safety and efficiency in our transportation systems. Still, it was dismantled almost immediately, before it could take hold. By the end of my term, even my party had turned me into a relic, using my presence as a symbol of the past rather than a guiding light toward the future."

Custer's eyes drifted away, lost in a daydream of memories. "There were indeed enjoyable times," he mused, his voice turning thoughtful. "My beloved wife, Libbie, had a remarkable talent for welcoming international officials with a charm and elegance that was simply extraordinary. I fondly recall one garden gathering when we hosted the famous Mark Twain; his eyes sparkled with mischief and joy as he turned to me, a wry smile on his face, and remarked that I looked like a man still in constant competition with a horse."

Custer's grin was fleeting, unable to conceal the exhaustion in his eyes. "I'll always have a yearning for the sound of hooves pounding the ground and the thrill of the hunt."

For a brief moment, the room fell silent as both men appeared lost in thought: Custer, grappling with the diminishing significance of his role in a rapidly changing world, and Ethan, contemplating the stories that would inevitably outlive both of them.

Custer firmly insisted that his choice not to run again was entirely his own, holding onto that belief like a sailor in a storm. Yet, beneath this confident exterior, Ethan noticed a vestige of doubt, implying that Custer's decision was more complex, as he was torn between his aspirations and constant pressures.

Custer acknowledged, "I gave them one term," his voice calm yet revealing fortitude. "I allowed them one term to show that a warrior could also lead effectively. I never intended to die in office." His words reflected firm conviction, subtly underscored with implied longing, as if his declaration concealed a truth he hesitated to reveal.

Ethan asked, "Your term ended when you were 41. Would you describe your transition from president to elder statesman?"

"My first realization was how quickly the feeling of power can vanish. Your influence suddenly becomes minimal, and the crowds no longer seem to offer their praise. Frankly, I remembered staring into Grant's eyes before he saluted me on the steps of the Executive Mansion. He knew. He knew I would become disillusioned with how Washington works, but he couldn't warn me. It was something I had to learn on my own. I gained a greater appreciation for the man when I stepped out of the mansion for the last time."

With a look of contemplation, Custer leaned back in his chair. In his silence, he seemed absorbed in his memories. When he spoke again, the weariness had lifted from his voice, replaced with a renewed energy. "When we built this estate," Custer said, "Libbie embraced the land as if it were her birthplace. To her, it became a sanctuary, a refuge from the outside world. She took extreme pride in naming each new colt born on this ranch, pouring the same care and passion into each new day; she supervised their training with meticulous attention. I admired her spirit and her unwavering enthusiasm for life. As for me, I found comfort in riding every day, losing myself in the vast fields for hours, letting the rhythmic sound of hooves hitting the ground guide my thoughts."

"What about the horses?" Ethan interjected, capturing Custer's reflection on his riding adventures and curious about the man's enthusiastic involvement.

Custer's expression changed, and genuine pride lit up his face. "Our Thoroughbreds still rank among the best in the region," he said excitedly. "We've been on the cusp of victory at the Kentucky Derby, but it has eluded us. One day, we will bring home the coveted trophy. Be that as it may, you must realize that the race is just the visible part of the journey. Libbie and I endeavored to build something grander than ourselves, and we focused on creating an enduring legacy."

Custer's passionate words resonated with Ethan. Here stood a man who had faced relentless public scrutiny and overcome numerous professional obstacles while enjoying the victories of his cherished equestrian pursuits. The sincerity of his character was evident, a trait that blended smoothly with the wistfulness that colored their ongoing discussion.

"Do you believe this legacy will stand the test of time?" Ethan asked with genuine curiosity, showing interest beyond the current discussion. "Will the tales and triumphs you passionately cherish endure and persist long after the races are over and the dust settles?"

Custer pondered the significance of the question, its importance lingering in the air. "Legacy," he reflected thoughtfully, "is an intriguing phenomenon. It flourishes and thrives through the passion and enthusiasm of those who remember and share the story. I hope our journey will inspire and motivate those who come after us. Our paths may seem unclear and indistinct now, but they are the foundation for what lies ahead."

Custer's firm belief touched Ethan. He recognized the wisdom in the heartfelt messages Custer had shared.

Custer continued, "Regarding my legacy, did you realize I was a candidate for inclusion in a large granite monument being planned in the renowned Black Hills of South Dakota? The talented sculptor Gutzon Borglum, already known for his designs, was diligently at work on an impressive statue to honor Confederate military leaders near Atlanta. During that time, he met with me here and took the opportunity to share his grand vision for his upcoming project in the majestic Black Hills. He shared his plans to include my likeness in a back corner of the monument, specifically positioned between the esteemed figures of Jefferson and Lincoln. Concerned about the potential perception of my inclusion, I proposed that he consider a different face. I boldly advised him to dedicate an entire mountain specifically for me, where people could celebrate my contributions and sacrifices in their own right." Custer let out a gentle, resonant chuckle, one that reverberated with a mix of pride and amusement. "However, I am honored by having a state park named for me just south of the proposed sculpture," he added almost as an afterthought, his tone mixing recognition and irony.

Ethan realized he needed to guide Custer toward a more relevant discussion about personal matters. "I understand," he responded. "Legacy is ever-evolving; it demands care, attention, and a commitment to remembrance. The powerful tales passed down through generations of families provide a fortifying strength." Sitting together in the soft, warm glow of the library, filled with the lingering memories of

Custer's past, both men understood how closely their legacies would one day intertwine. They were connected through the separate paths that brought them here and through these historic conversations: the General sharing the details of his esteemed life and Ethan documenting and publishing his story.

Custer's journey, shaped by his experiences as a soldier and a leader, combined with Ethan's role as an attentive listener and dedicated storyteller, created a unique and meaningful partnership that intertwined past experiences with the promise of future stories. As they shared treasured moments that defined their lives, they planted seeds of insight and reflection that would grow over time. In that close exchange of ideals, something significant surfaced: the realization that the past unquestionably influences the future and that every story, no matter how nostalgic, continues to shape what lies ahead.

As Custer pointed toward the orchard, sunlight streamed through the branches, creating intricate patterns and shadows that danced across the library's wooden interior. "I also tend to the trees," he remarked with pride. "It's a key part of my mental and physical health regimen."

Ethan remarked, "It certainly appears to work for you." He asked, "What about the current state of affairs in your estate?"

Custer replied warmly, "We often have guests." "Historians eager to explore and analyze the old tales of our past, veterans seeking comfort through shared memories, and, sometimes, curious school groups excited to meet a legend. Also, there's Bloody Knife, who currently manages the stables with his son, an expert in horse breeding who works hard to ensure that the lineage of Custer Horses continues through fine Thoroughbreds. Our horse breeding, selling, and shipping business is thriving. As more automobiles appear, we continue to adapt and improve our methods. Thoroughbred racing has recently seen a big comeback, and we've taken advantage of that opportunity."

A crackling fire punctuated Custer's words as he spoke with passion and conviction. Outside, the wind picked up, playfully shaking the last bright autumn leaves from the branches above, letting them spiral down like whispered secrets carried on the cool breeze. At that moment, Ethan began to appreciate the man Custer had truly become over the years. Custer had grown into an important figure, connected to the land he called home, embodying great stature and significance.

The fire in the hearth burned low, casting a warm glow that flickered around the room. Custer, seated nearby, looked distant, lost in thought.

Ethan took a steadying breath to center himself amid swirling thoughts. He addressed Custer calmly and carefully, "General, I'd like to shift the focus of our discussion and concentrate on your interactions with Indians. There's a topic that seems to have loomed in the shadows of your life: the Washita. It has often been called simply a massacre, a term that carries many connotations and emotions."

Custer clenched his jaw tightly, feeling the familiar strain beneath the coarse stubble on his chin. His captivating blue eyes, which usually sparkled with a restless spirit, turned cold and intensely focused, as if cutting through the room. "That's how they would describe it," he said, his voice low and rough, bearing the full burden of emotion that has been suppressed for too long. "But I refuse to do so. It was the Battle of the Washita River. Let's start from there." His determination shone through him, a clear force, as his words reflected the conviction of someone who had long ago reconciled his views with history, cementing his perspective with unwavering resolve.

Leaning forward, he rested his arms on the polished mahogany desk, which creaked under his urgency and purpose. The fire's flickering light danced across the room, casting shadows on Custer's face, highlighting signs of age, and revealing a fierce vitality that defied his years. "It was November 1868. The early winter cold had just begun to settle in, making the expansive plains brittle and barren, stripped of warmth and color. We had been pursuing the Cheyenne and Southern Arapaho tribes relentlessly for months, enduring harsh, unforgiving terrain. General Sheridan had given clear orders, telling us to hold back until the snow fell, believing the weather would give us the tactical advantage we needed. The tribes, in their desperation, were conducting brutal raids, attacking settlers often, devastating wagon trains, and setting fire to isolated homesteads on the fringes of their territory. Their dire situation drove them to savage, unyielding attacks, fueled by a strong will to survive.

This conflict was far from the heroic spectacle of war seen in parades or legendary stories; instead, it was a primal struggle over land that barely supported either side, a raw, violent contest testing the limits of endurance and resolve."

Custer paused in his recounting, his gaze drifting away from Ethan, perhaps wandering through the lonely expanses of his past, where memory mingled with pain. "When we reached their camp, we did so under the cover of night and silence. A biting wind pierced through our uniforms, yet we pressed ahead with steely determination, each soldier merely a shadow against the stark backdrop of the night sky. I dismounted and moved closer, feeling the sharp, thin air fill my lungs, a bitter reminder of the brutal conditions. In the darkness, I noticed faint wisps of smoke rising from their lodges, a quiet hint of warmth inside that sharply contrasted with the bitter chill surrounding us. I decided to split my regiment into four strategic groups, each commanded by trusted officers, all prepared to launch a coordinated strike from different angles, a carefully planned attack timed to coincide with the first light of dawn."

He took a breath, clearly immersed in the memory that unfolded within him; it was as if he were reliving that fateful night. "When the notes of 'Garry Owen' filled the air," he whispered almost to himself, his voice carrying a sense of longing. "I felt my blood ignite with adrenaline. That sound represented action and purpose; it served as a clarion call announcing that battle was near, stirring something primal within every soldier present, invoking courage that compelled us forward into the unknown."

Custer's confidence resonated strongly through the air as he vividly recounted the chaotic moment of the attack. "We engaged shortly after dawn, when the sun was just beginning to cast its first light over the landscape. The initial volley erupted like thunder, shattering the peaceful morning with a sudden burst of rifle fire that echoed ominously in the cold air. Muzzle flashes lit up the somber dawn. The air was filled with the shouts of soldiers and horses, blending into a chaotic symphony of noise across the vast open ground. Within minutes, a flood of sabers and gunfire swept through the valley, breaking their previously organized defense. Then reinforcements from the south arrived: Kiowa and Comanche warriors, drawn by the sounds of battle, rushed in like a fierce tide, determined to push back against our steady force. My well-trained troops, no strangers to battle, quickly regrouped under the immense stress, their spirits lifted by a fierce resolve to face this new threat with everything they had. Though we held our risky position on that battlefield, the ground beneath us was forever marked by the toll of our fierce fight, stained with the remnants of our struggle."

Leaning back in his chair, the old wood creaked in protest as he sighed, clearly weary from the burden of his memories. "We recorded the deaths of one hundred and three warriors that day. Additionally, fifty-three women and children were captured, their faces etched with fear and grief, haunting reminders of the cost of conflict. However, I will concede that in the confusion of those early moments, noncombatants perished. In warfare, disarray inevitably prevails, and it's nearly impossible to separate the chaos of battle from the desperate struggles of individuals trying to defend their lives and those of their loved ones. It is a relentless force that shows no mercy. However, we do not equate the events at the Battle of the Washita River with those at Sand Creek. Colonel Chivington's actions in 1864 were a calculated slaughter of innocent noncombatants, carried out under the pretense of peace. Our actions stemmed from the harsh realities of war: devastating, yes, but involving direct clashes with a hostile enemy determined to fight us. That is a crucial difference, a distinction that is meaningful in the pages of history."

Ethan listened quietly, allowing Custer's words to settle heavily in the space between them. The only sound was the steady movement of his pencil as he carefully tried to capture not just the words but also the raw passion and emotion behind them. Custer's intense gaze fixed on Ethan, almost daring him to respond. Still, Ethan chose not to meet the look, letting the silence linger, thick with the fervor and fire of Custer's account.

"I do not wish to justify war," Custer finally said, his tone softer now, with a touch of self-reflection. "Yet even within the turmoil, I grasp its very essence. You conquer the frontier with weapons, not with kindness or compassion. That day, we sent a message that resonated far beyond our bullets, a harsh and unyielding lesson in the savage realities of westward expansion, a crucial part of the relentless machine of progress."

Harold entered the room, breaking the heavy, somber mood that had filled the conversation. Carefully, he placed a wooden tray on the sturdy oak table, which stood out against the muted surroundings. It was a comforting yet straightforward gesture: freshly baked biscuits, jam, and a pot of steaming tea that rose in delicate wisps, like ghostly whispers swirling into the air. He paused briefly, bowed his head slightly, and then stepped back from the room, leaving a lingering sense of warmth in the chill of the autumn day.

They ate silently, taking a moment to relax before continuing their discussion.

Ethan flipped back a page to review his notes, creating a quiet atmosphere for Custer's thoughts to resonate. Finally, he lifted his head, his expression a mix of neutrality and thoughtfulness. "General," he asked, choosing his words carefully, "what are your views about the Dawes Act? How do you see this legislation shaping the future interactions between our culture and the Indian tribes?"

Custer considered the question carefully, his eyes narrowing as he thought about the broad consequences of such important legislation. "The Dawes Act," he started calmly, giving himself time to analyze its effects, "is of great significance in our national history. At first glance, it seems aimed at civilizing the Indians by integrating them into American society and splitting tribal lands into individual plots. In essence, the act sought to promote agriculture and a farming lifestyle, encouraging Native peoples to adopt practices that fit with mainstream American society."

He paused briefly, his facial expressions revealing the challenges and complexities of the situation. "Yet, the truth is much more complicated than it might initially seem. This law was designed to reduce tribal control and, in doing so, weaken the cultural identities that have been central to these communities for generations. It aimed to shift from communal living to emphasizing personal ownership over shared living, which ignores the core of Indian culture, rooted in mutual support. We divided the reservations into plots of land for farming, and in most cases, we gave the land to white settlers." After a pause, Custer continued, "A closer look at history shows that policies like this have often led to the decline and erosion of Indian cultures and societies, proving that such laws can have devastating and far-reaching effects on the very fabric of their communities."

Custer's gaze grew more intense, emphasizing the gravity of the message he was about to deliver and its importance. "Moreover, how the Federal Government has managed those lands has often been shocking and disturbing. The Federal Government frequently broke promises to assist different tribes, resulting in increased poverty among many indigenous peoples. Even if their intentions were noble at first, the outcomes mostly favored the interests and needs of settlers and investors, further intensifying cycles of exploitation that marginalized Indian communities."

Ethan listened carefully to every word from Custer's lips, thoughtfully considering them within the broader context of history and the ramifications for future relations. "It's evident," Custer continued, his voice steady yet forceful, "that a fragile power dynamic exists, one that has consistently favored a specific vision of advancement at the unfortunate expense of Indians' rights and sovereignty. The Dawes Act stood out as a pivotal moment in this ongoing conflict, illuminating a larger story of displacement and loss reverberating through time."

The impact of that statement lingered in the air as Ethan carefully thought about the harsh truth revealed by Custer's insights. Their conversation looked at the past and explored the current situation and prospects regarding relations with the Indians. There was a clear perception that understanding history and the vital lessons it offers is crucial to shaping future policies in meaningful ways.

Ethan asked after a long, meaningful pause, "What do you see as the way to heal these rifts?"

Custer furrowed his brow, his expression becoming more serious as he reflected. "We must confront uncomfortable facts directly. Recognizing historical injustices is the crucial first step toward genuine healing. A path grounded in mutual respect rather than dominance or control is essential. Progress involves starting honest conversations, fostering greater recognition, and rebuilding relationships based on trust and respect, even when the difficult journey tests our resolve."

This depiction of historical events, thoughtfully placed within a larger context of responsibility and awareness, stirred something within Ethan. Their conversation went beyond simply recounting past events; it examined the moral complexities and their far-reaching effects on society.

Ethan tilted his head, lost in thought over a lingering question. "But didn't Indians receive citizenship in 1924?" he asked, genuinely seeking clarification.

Custer grew irritated at the attempt to oversimplify a complex issue. "Yes. But at what cost?" he shot back, his tone becoming more intense and forceful. "Land taken without consent, spiritual ties severed entirely, identities shattered in the process. If you grant a man freedom while simultaneously erasing the very essence of his past, can you genuinely call him free? Freedom without acknowledgment of history and tradition is a hollow promise."

Custer's voice had grown sharper, and Ethan quickly jotted down notes, trying to catch the emotion in his words.

Ethan looked up from his notes, his expression serious and focused. "General, what about Wounded Knee? December 29, 1890?" "What does that date mean in the larger context of our discussion?" His question hung in the air, a mournful silence that only occurs when discussing such grave topics.

The mood shifted dramatically, and Custer's eyes seemed to darken as memories flooded back, bringing a sense of sorrow. "Wounded Knee is a tragic chapter in American history that is woven into the fabric of this nation. It's more than just a date marked on a calendar; it symbolizes overwhelming loss, intense confusion, and a heartbreaking failure to bridge significant cultural gaps. It is a devastating failure for everyone involved, serving as a poignant reminder of the consequences of neglect and indifference. The command was given to confiscate all the firearms that the Indians carried. A small group of men was in the crowd of Indians, taking their guns, when a shot rang out. Soldiers standing guard around the perimeter hesitated at first, but many Indians drew knives and attacked from all sides. The men opened fire. Yes, women and children were in the line of fire, and many were killed. It was a day of severe sadness."

Ethan listened intently, sensing Custer's powerful, tumultuous emotions about that crucial historical moment. "What do you think could have been done differently?" he asked, seeking a different perspective.

Custer paused, leaned back in his chair, and shared his thoughts. "Conversation. Awareness. First and foremost, the firearms should have been confiscated long before they arrived at Wounded Knee. There was a reluctance to truly appreciate the complexities and nuances of the diverse cultures involved. In a broader sense, instead of seeing Indians as mere obstacles to progress, they could have been seen as valuable partners in building a shared future." Custer reflected, "The narratives of our lives could have been intertwined, fostering unity rather than being violently torn apart by miscalculation and conflict."

Custer's somber, raw honesty-laced words reflected on several peaceful outcomes that could have resulted from a different approach. He stated firmly, "What we witnessed at Wounded Knee was not merely a tragic incident; it was a stain, but not one I'll denounce." His words spread through the room like a fog, thickening the air with unwritten truths and hidden regrets. A lump formed in Ethan's throat, a poignant reminder of the discomfort he always felt when confronting such a painful subject.

Ethan stayed silent, the severity of the comment hanging in the air as he waited for Custer to explain. After a moment, Custer fingered his temple, as if trying to brush away memories that haunted him, before continuing to speak.

"I wasn't there," Custer said. "But I read every report. I had the opportunity to talk with the men who were there. The Seventh Cavalry had orders. They were afraid. And they might have been too proud. But they followed the command." His words were deliberate, showing more than just obedience; they revealed a truth about the bonds forged in the fire of battle, capturing the essence of duty, unwavering bravery, and the heavy burden they carried.

Ethan interjected, his voice rising slightly in agitation. "They fired into a crowd. Women and children." His words carried a mix of anguish and defiance, a heartfelt plea for Custer to face the harsh truth of that tragic day, when innocent lives were lost in the chaos of battle.

Custer didn't flinch at the accusation. "Yes. Yes, they did. And many regret it still," he admitted, his tone firm but touched with sorrow. "But in the Army, discipline is paramount. We are taught to follow orders, to obey commands with unwavering loyalty and dedication to duty."

Custer looked into the fire. "That day was a total disaster. Everything that could go wrong did. But I can't call my old regiment murderers."

After a pause, he continued, "When I was in command, I poured my heart into training those men, shaping them into soldiers I believed in and trusted with my life." As he spoke about his men, a range of emotions flickered across his face: pride in their bravery, sorrow for their sacrifices, and an awareness of the thin line between fulfilling duty and maintaining moral integrity.

A heavy silence filled the air between them. The gentle ticking of the clock in the background reminded them of how much time was passing as they faced a somber moment.

"What if you had still been in command?" Ethan asked finally, his voice steady despite the air's tension.

With the bitterness of experience etched on his face, Custer grinned piteously. "If I had been in command, there would've been a charge instead of confusion, a standoff, not a slaughter. Or maybe I'd be another name on the marble. It's difficult to lead men through dust and shadows." His gaze drifted out the window, fixating on something far beyond the horizon, perhaps lost in reverie or regret.

"But I can tell you this," he continued, his voice carrying somber authority. "Wounded Knee was chaos. And when chaos wears a uniform, it stains everything." The depth of his words resonated in the air. It reflected soldiers' moral struggles, highlighting the conflict between their duty to the nation and their own humanity.

In stark contrast to his earlier lively movements, Ethan's pencil now moved slowly across the pages of his notebook. Each stroke felt heavy, burdened with the sheer gravity of history and the complexity of truth. There was no excitement in his task, only the heavy burden of telling a story filled with contradictions and pain.

Custer's voice dropped low, almost to a whisper, as he shared a core truth that took years for warriors to comprehend. "You want to write the truth? Write that a soldier carries two burdens: his orders and what he sees when he closes his eyes. Write that, and maybe you'll grasp why I still ride the fields each morning in my dreams." His words hung in the air, inviting a closer look into a soldier's mind and the ghosts of the past that can never truly be laid to rest.

Ethan hurriedly wrote, his heart pounding as he absorbed the force of Custer's passionate speech.

"They were souls with stories, families, and dreams brutally extinguished." Custer's voice carried the gravity of remembrance. "If we allow history to repeat itself without reflecting on its lessons, we miss the valuable chance to learn from the past. We must preserve those narratives and draw on their inherent wisdom."

As Custer finished his remarks, a hush fell over the room. The fire in the hearth flickered gently, providing a comforting warmth that contrasted with the cold, harsh reality of the history uncovered. Outside, the wind whispered through the trees, a soft reminder that time moves endlessly forward, carrying a reflection of everything that had transpired.

Grateful for the honest exchange, Ethan was eager to learn more about the situation. "What do you foresee for the future of these stories and the connections they create?" he asked, curious about how history might influence what lies ahead.

Custer's expression softened as he considered Ethan's question, a flicker of hope shining through his serious face. "Healing and transformation hold endless possibilities. This process begins with a commitment to recognize the past, affirm our shared humanity, and carefully build meaningful bonds based on trust and respect. By listening instead of imposing, we create a future that respects our different histories and aims for a more inclusive and fairer world."

Ethan felt a renewed sense of purpose flowing through him. He had a strong desire to uncover the hidden details buried by layers of history and to give voice to the silenced stories of those marginalized and overlooked. Custer's words resonated within him, urging him to reflect on past stories and to actively work toward creating a more just and compassionate future.

The conversation shifted as they discussed Custer's leadership, Ethan's ethical views, and the enduring impact of the Wounded Knee tragedy. Ethan and Custer saw the importance of protecting this complex, emotional story. Driven by a common goal, they set out on a journey to face the past honestly, forging a path guided by healing and insight.

Outside, the first snow of the season blanketed the orchard. As Custer stoked the fire, he said, "You will write what you believe is true." After a brief pause, he added, "And that is how it should be."

Harold entered the room, still holding the door open, disturbing the poignant atmosphere. "You're needed at the front door," he announced urgently, breaking the moment. Custer nodded in acknowledgment, excused himself, and grabbed his cane, hesitant to end the conversation.

Left alone in the quiet library, Ethan let the silence envelop him like a heavy, comforting blanket that muffled any outside noise. Driven by an inexplicable urge, he moved across the room to the window near Custer's desk. Outside, the orchard stretched out before him in a barren state, its branches stripped bare. Ethan felt a wave of surprise flood over him. From this new vantage point, the neatly arranged rows of trees resembled a ghostly cavalry formation, four rows wide, extending to the horizon with an eerie yet captivating symmetry. The sight was striking, creating a strange blend of order and stillness that appeared to freeze the air around him. In the back of his mind, he could almost hear the faint sound of the traditional tune "Garry Owen," a melody that seemed to resonate in the quiet. The scene held Ethan frozen for a moment, his breath catching in his throat as he felt a connection to something much larger than himself.

He felt an urgency to preserve this vision and returned to his chair to record the striking tableau in writing. This spectral regiment seemed forever standing at attention on the parade ground.

# Chapter 11: Visiting the Plains

After a brief pause, Custer entered the room. Ethan was still hurrying to document the scenic view through the window. When he reached a stopping point, he leaned slightly forward, fixing his gaze on Custer's. "After your presidency, did you have the opportunity to return to the plains?"

"We did, twice," Custer said, his voice escalating with nostalgia as he began to share his experiences. "The first was in 1885, when Libbie became an unstoppable force in the growing suffrage movement. She was often invited to speak at functions." Custer had a slight smile as he recalled the trip.

"Those were years when the raw wounds of war began to heal, slowly replaced by a quiet yet firm desire for societal change. I hoped to show Libbie the frontier again, not as soldiers on duty but as relaxed guests and active participants in a nation in transition. We traveled in private railroad cars, which were not just a luxury but a thoughtful choice, as their silence provided us with peace. At that point in our lives, we had grown tired of craving public attention and praise, now preferring to watch the world unfold outside our window, safely protected by the smooth, clear glass that separated us from the busy world beyond."

Custer shifted slightly in his chair as if bracing himself to explore a well of memories. He paused briefly to recall the joy of those moments, a smile slowly forming on his face. "Our first destination was Chicago, a city that had transformed dramatically. It had been built from the remnants of nearby plains and wetlands and had evolved into a bustling hub filled with the lively energy of commerce and innovation. Libbie, usually composed and thoughtful, was genuinely captivated by the sight of our first skyscraper, a symbol of progress that stirred a sense of wonder. The Home Insurance Building had just been completed, and it was a breathtaking structure, an awe-inspiring creation of stone and steel that seemed to reach confidently toward the sky. In her characteristic style, she humorously compared it to a grain silo dressed in a necktie, a remark that showcased her wit. I told her that human ingenuity often starts in shapes that don't look appealing initially; finding their beauty and elegance takes time and patience."

“We wandered through the sprawling rail yards, the largest in the country, and the noisy mix of steam engines and clanking metal, along with the massive scale of activity, was truly impressive. I turned to her and said, 'If victory can be measured by movement, then Chicago has already won.' This was a new kind of struggle, a different battle centered around logistics and industry. I began admiring the innovative refrigerated cars that travel across the landscape. The war experiences had taught me to value the importance of logistics, and here, in this dynamic city, I could see a nation being built without a single bullet being fired."

Captivated and fully engrossed in the story, Ethan furiously wrote in his notebook, frowning slightly as he concentrated on capturing every detail. "Had Libbie been invited to speak there?" he asked curiously.

Custer nodded slowly, a slight pride showing in his expression. "Yes, at the Chicago Woman's Club. It was an intimate gathering of refined women and a few serious political figures, mostly men, who had attended out of duty to listen. Libbie seized the opportunity to speak on enfranchisement issues, emphasizing the moral obligation of representation, and delivered her message clearly and with firm resolve. I vividly remember one man in particular, his face flushed and arrogant, trying to interrupt her with a misguided remark about women's roles and their alleged unsuitability for voting."

"Patience characterized Libbie's demeanor as she waited for him to finish, her gaze steady and unwavering. Then, in her calm and measured tone, she asked a thought-provoking question: had he ever voted on a tax he hadn't personally paid? That question left him speechless, I assure you. Soon, the room began to rumble with murmurs of agreement and gentle applause, demonstrating the power of her words and their impact on those present."

"And what transpired after Chicago?" Ethan inquired, eager and genuinely interested in unraveling the next chapter of this tale.

"We continued our train ride to Minneapolis," Custer responded, a subtle smile forming as he recalled the events. "We were scheduled to attend the American Woman Suffrage Association convention, an important gathering dedicated to the fight for women's right to vote. Henry B. Blackwell was set to deliver his speech. Lord, help us all," he chuckled, reflecting on the familiarity of the situation. "He had developed a habit of rambling on in a way that turned his voice into a steady drone, capable of filling the hall but ironically tiring the audience with boredom. By then, Libbie had listened to his speeches many times. Although he was undoubtedly a good man with noble goals and intentions, someone who takes thirty minutes to say what could be said in five should probably not be in the spotlight at the forefront of such an important movement."

Ethan chuckled, enjoying the humor of imagining how annoyed Libbie and others must have been during the long speeches. "Was Libbie given a chance to speak?"

"They did give her an opportunity," Custer confirmed, his voice warm with fondness as he remembered. "Mr. Blackwell introduced her, but his lengthy introduction was just as unnecessary as always. However, when she finally took the stand, the atmosphere in the room changed dramatically as she captured everyone's attention. Her voice wasn't harsh or overbearing; it was clear and steady, effortlessly reaching every corner of the hall. The captivating quality of her delivery lay in the beauty of her carefully chosen words, which flowed smoothly from her lips, and in her undeniable presence. She didn't try to persuade anyone with flowery language or emotional appeals. Instead, she stated her position confidently and with authority. Like a general taking control of a battlefield, she laid out the undeniable logic for women's suffrage in a straightforward yet powerful way."

Custer's gaze briefly drifted toward the library door as he reminisced about the experience. "However, the real reason for our journey was connected to an invitation we had received, which heightened our anticipation. Full of his usual enthusiastic energy, Teddy Roosevelt had just established his ranches in the Badlands of present-day North Dakota. He wrote to me in his lively, exuberant handwriting, inviting us to join him for a hunting trip in that wild and scenic landscape. He mentioned the promise of 'fresh air and great company,' a phrase that has stayed with me ever since I first read it."

"Ethan, let me take you on a journey through the Badlands. Once you leave the plains in western North Dakota, you enter an area radiating wild, untamed energy. The air is fresh and crisp, and the land displays nature's power, with striking buttes and spires rising like ancient landmarks beneath a vast, open sky. You face one gully after another, making it almost impossible to cross with wagons. The hillsides, worn away over centuries of erosion, show layers of different rock types, creating a colorful mosaic. While the buttes are barren of vegetation, life flourishes in the draws and valleys, where patches of green offer a haven. The Little Missouri River winds through the center, its waters carving a path through the landscape, shining like a silver ribbon in the sun. The elements test the resilience of bison, elk, and wild horses, while prairie dog mounds dot some of the flatlands. Every detail, from petrified wood to the serene grandeur of a lone butte, speaks of a resilient spirit and a beauty worth preserving."

Leaning in slightly closer, Custer's eyes sparkled with excitement, a faint smile playing on his lips as he recollected the treasured invitation. "The Marquis de Morès, a French aristocrat known for his association with Teddy Roosevelt and his unconventional lifestyle, had also invited us. He and his wife, Medora, owned a chateau near the town named after her in the beautiful Badlands. Despite his French aristocracy seeming like an odd match for the rugged terrain of the Americas, they were wonderfully down-to-earth folks and gracious hosts. I had met Medora's parents, Louis von Hoffman and Athenais, in New York City several years earlier. He was one of the founding members of the Knickerbocker Club, a gentlemen's club for the upper class to socialize, and that's also where I first met Teddy."

He continued, "Medora's parents built a beautiful brick home near the chateau for their visits. The Marquis offered to let us stay there during our trip." He continued, "As fate would have it, Libbie and Medora quickly connected over their shared love of horseback riding, and a natural bond formed between these two intelligent, spirited women."

Custer carried on with a sense of wistfulness washing over him, his demeanor subtly shifting as he examined the memories swirling in his mind. "As Libbie and Medora strolled gracefully along the banks of the river, engrossed in their lively conversation about everything from the latest fashions to the ideas shaping their lives, I found myself in the company of Teddy and the Marquis, engaging in adventurous hunting excursions in the rugged landscapes along the Little Missouri River. Our main targets during these outings were the elusive pheasants, which would suddenly launch themselves skyward out of the tall grasses, creating a flurry of excitement."

"On a particularly memorable day, we spent our time searching for elk, but despite our efforts, they remained out of sight. Still, the excitement of the hunt lifted our spirits and made us hopeful. The elk turned out to be elusive."

"I had a chance to speak alone with Teddy one night, and we discussed his departure from politics. He felt he needed to step back, regroup, and take care of his health. You see, he suffered from severe asthma. His decision to fight it with exercise seems to have worked for him. I encouraged him to return to politics when he felt ready, but I knew not to push too hard. I explained that the Battle of the Little Bighorn helped propel me to the presidency, and he needed to find his own battle."

Custer chuckled, "Roosevelt, with his characteristic vigor and enthusiasm, regaled us with tales that sometimes made me question their authenticity. He had a remarkable quality that resonated with me. He possessed an unwavering belief in the stories he shared, and his storytelling ability was such that he could convince anyone of their veracity."

“Teddy had strong convictions and passionately defended them. Conversely, the Marquis felt entitled and arrogant, quick to anger. Their ranches were nearby, and their fiery personalities often led to disputes, but they mostly stayed friendly. After a short pause, Custer chuckled and added, “The time I spent with them was extremely stimulating and entertaining. The hunting was exhilarating, and the conversations were spirited.”

Ethan shifted forward in his seat, fascinated by the glimpse of personal interactions amid the rugged, demanding landscape. "How did Libbie engage with such a wide variety of characters?” he asked; curiosity was clear in the sharp expression on his face.

Custer's features brightened as he began recounting their experiences with fondness. "Libbie thrived in various settings, showcasing her adaptability and strength. Whether navigating the complexities of high society or immersing herself in the wilderness, she commanded respect through her sharp intellect and vibrant presence. She never shied away from confronting challenges head-on or participating in meaningful discussions about issues that resonated with her. In the person of Medora, she discovered a friendship that transcended cultural and national boundaries, creating a rare and special bond. They exchanged dreams, shared ideas, and cast visions for a future where women’s voices could finally be recognized.”

As Custer's tone softened, filled with a sense of wistfulness, he continued, "One unforgettable evening at the elegant chateau, Libbie and Medora took it upon themselves to host a gathering that drew a mix of local acquaintances and notable dignitaries. The conversation naturally turned toward the changing roles of women in society, sparking a captivating dinner dialogue filled with laughter and personal stories. You could almost feel the electric energy in the room as Libbie spoke passionately about the importance of women's representation in all areas of life. Her heartfelt words inspired the women there and left a lasting impression on the men who listened closely. That night, I saw firsthand how her persuasive speeches and firm beliefs resounded with everyone present, igniting sparks of motivation and reflection."

Custer relaxed, a satisfied smile lighting up his face as he thought about his experiences. He knew his engaging storytelling was creating a legacy to inspire future historians. Their stories set the stage for more exploration of how two remarkable lives were intertwined against the backdrop of a changing America.

"Libbie seemed genuinely happy," Custer observed, his voice filled with warmth and contentment that showed his admiration for her. "She appeared more cheerful than I had seen in quite some time, radiating a contagious energy. Even with the widespread European influence around us, the appeal of the West offered a uniquely refreshing sense of freedom and a landscape full of endless opportunities. Together, she and Medora envisioned a future that included improvements in women's voting rights and a better quality of life on the frontier, aiming to bring civilization to the wild expanse. Medora dreamed of building thriving theaters and schools to create a cultural haven within the vast, untamed wilderness. Meanwhile, Libbie, always the practical and strategic thinker, considered the fundamentals of democracy, such as voting stations where women could voice their opinions in this new frontier."

The flickering shadows from the fire, representing the passing of time, beautifully highlight Custer's detailed story.

After Custer finished his story, he fell into a quiet, reflective silence. He thought about the personal tales he had just shared and memories of better times. Ethan used this pause in the conversation to continue writing his notes and jot down his thoughts and observations.

After their lunch, Ethan asked, "Did you attend the statehood celebration in the Dakotas?"

Custer's hearty laughter erupted, filling the room with warmth and energy and evoking a sense of nostalgia. As he settled back into the plush leather chair, a flicker of memory lit up his eyes. "Yes, I did," he confirmed, his voice full of certainty. "In 1889, Bismarck was the capital of the Dakota Territory. Later that year, the territory was split and officially became the states of North Dakota and South Dakota. That spring, I received a letter from Arthur Mellette, the territory's governor, inviting me to take part in their July 4th parade in Bismarck, which I eagerly accepted. It was quite a grand celebration, and even Sitting Bull had appeared."

"President Harrison had encouraged the territory to pursue statehood, leading to an extraordinary Constitutional Convention. It was a truly spectacular event, brimming with enthusiasm; brass bands filled the air with music, cannon volleys echoed in the distance, cavalry troops performed impressive displays, and stirring speeches lifted everyone's spirits. The excited crowds cheered both Libbie and me as we delivered our speeches. Having a former president present and speak before any celebration is always memorable. Still, when I began telling stories about our three years stationed at the nearby Fort Abraham Lincoln, the audience erupted into thunderous applause. By then, I suppose I had become seen as a living symbol of the frontier, embodying the wild lands gradually woven into the fabric of the Union."

Custer continued, energized by the memories from the exchange. "A few days later, on July 8th, Henry B. Blackwell held the convention's attention for hours with his talk on women's suffrage, introducing Libbie to loud applause from the audience. While I'd like to think that most of the cheers genuinely celebrated her, I can't ignore the possibility that some attendees also appreciated the break from his oratory as well."

Custer chuckled softly, a wry grin spreading as he admired Libbie's boldness. He added, with a gentle smile and his gaze drifting momentarily as if he were imagining his beloved wife among the cheering crowd, "However, I sense her thoughts resided more with the cause at hand rather than solely on the festivity itself."

He paused for a moment, a playful glint in his eyes. "Nonetheless, true to my entrepreneurial spirit, I envisioned more than just a series of festivities. I saw a significant business opportunity on the horizon. We traveled by rail, and I arranged transportation for several of my finest Thoroughbreds, known for their extraordinary speed and endurance. These magnificent horses caught the interest of the HT Ranch, which was determined to expand its livestock and diversify its breeding programs. While in Bismarck, I made valuable connections with A. C. Huidekoper and Sidney Tarbell and successfully sold several horses. They were excited about building a modern stable and eager to combine the strength of Percherons with the agility of Thoroughbreds. They wanted speed. After a brief round of the expected horse-trading conversation, they took ownership of four beautiful breeding mares, $2,000 each. A fortune then."

"That's quite impressive," Ethan remarked, nodding with respect and newfound realization, fully recognizing Custer's sharp business sense amid the festive atmosphere.

Ethan leaned in closer, a thoughtful expression forming on his face. "Did the two of you have other opportunities to address the crowds during the trip?" he asked, his voice full of respect and admiration for the remarkable couple he was beginning to discern more acutely. Custer burst into a hearty laugh that boomed through the room, filling the space with infectious warmth and disbelief. Shifting slightly in his well-worn chair, he leaned back, a playful sparkle lighting up his eyes, clearly savoring the memory before he began. "Oh, Libbie most certainly did, and that's an understatement," he replied, his enthusiasm obvious. He kept going, clearly enjoying the story and its impact on those around him. "Without needing any cues, Libbie transformed every train stop into an unexpected stage for suffrage activism. Picture it: dusty train depots bustling with activity, onlookers filled with curiosity, and sometimes bewildered stationmasters trying to make sense of the unfolding scene. As soon as it was fully stopped, she would leap off the train, confidently claiming her platform wherever she pleased. She always made herself heard loud and clear, whether at the imposing courthouse steps, lively market areas vibrating with chatter, or quiet schoolyards after classes. Her voice rose above the usual small-town murmur, demanding attention and sparking intrigue."

Ethan's expression shifted as he reflected on the societal norms that required women to remain silent and follow traditional roles. He recognized the importance of social conventions, and such bold actions were clearly brave and unusual for a woman of her status. "Was that customary for that period?" he asked, his words carefully chosen to highlight the significance of the conversation and the historical context they discussed.

Custer chuckled softly and grinned as he reveled in Libbie's courage advocating for women's suffrage. "Radically unconventional," he asserted with confidence, the significance of history underpinning his statement. "A woman in her position was traditionally expected to embody decorum, to please those around her with nothing more than her presence, and to maintain silence, contributing only a pleasant smile when appropriate. However, Libbie," he paused deliberately, allowing his words to make an impression, "defied those expectations at every opportunity. She rarely remained seated, and any smile she offered was preceded by a bold declaration, made only after she had clearly articulated her point. Rather than passively requesting attention, she seized it with both hands. She didn't look for a soapbox; she transformed herself into one by boldly sharing her truth, leaving a permanent mark with her passionate rhetoric. She truly earned not just the silence but also the respect and admiration that permeated those amazed audiences."

As he gazed at the portrait hanging gracefully above the fireplace, Custer's eyes shone with admiration and remembrance. The woman in the frame, even in the stillness of the paint, radiated undeniable strength and resolve; her gaze was direct, intelligent, and captivating. "Libbie contributed so much more to the movement than simply delivering powerful speeches," he continued softly, his voice filled with reverence. "She infused it with dignity. Her courageous actions showed that the fight for equal rights was not based on hysteria or rudeness but on rational discussion, unwavering bravery, and innate grace. Her authentic nature amplified her voice and uplifted the entire cause, inspiring many others to join the fight."

Enthralled by Custer's stories, Ethan leaned forward. "You mentioned Fort Abraham Lincoln. Could you describe your experience of living at the fort during your years there?" he asked.

"It was a captivating blend of military life and the shifting aspects of American culture," Custer elaborated, his eyes lighting up as he reminisced about those times. "The fort served as a gateway to the West, and we were right at its center. Soldiers trained hard, families thrived in that unique environment, and the camaraderie among officers created a community full of shared goals and hopes. It was quite different from Army posts back in the States. It was one of the largest and most significant forts in the northern plains. It had initially been an infantry post, but in 1873, when we arrived, it was quickly expanded to include the Seventh Cavalry."

"It was also a place of tension, a frontier where inevitable change was always on the horizon and shaping our daily lives. Our main objective was to ensure the progress of the Northern Pacific Railroad, protecting the surveyors and construction crews. Additionally, because of our location, we played a central role in the growing conflict with the Indians, who were upset about treaty violations and settlers moving into the area."

He paused briefly, allowing his words to settle as memories flooded back. "Libbie played a crucial role in that environment. As the commanding officer's wife, it was her duty to set the social tone of the post. We had a large house, and she enjoyed hosting many events for officers, their wives, and visiting dignitaries. Essentially, she acted as 'First Lady of the Post,' unknowingly preparing herself for her future role during my presidency."

"With respect for my command position, Libbie held back on her enthusiasm for promoting the idea of women's suffrage, revealing it only when she believed she was with like-minded people."

"And how did the military community react?" Ethan asked, genuinely curious about the mix of acceptance and resistance that often comes with waves of change.

Custer chuckled softly, tenderly recalling the memory with a touch of disbelief. "Reactions were indeed mixed. Some wholeheartedly embraced her message, likely driven by her unwavering conviction and passionate delivery. Others, however, viewed her efforts with skepticism or even outright disapproval. A woman speaking openly on public issues was considered, at best, unconventional and, at worst, a threat to the social order. Yet, often, her determination inspired and motivated those around her to reconsider their views and challenge their preconceptions."

The golden afternoon light streamed through the study window. Ethan, his interest burning bright and his respect clear. "Did you have a chance to return to Fort Abraham Lincoln after the statehood celebrations?" he asked softly, almost reverently, as if he were handling delicate memories that deserved the utmost care.

"Indeed, we did," Custer replied, his voice tinged with reverence. "After weeks filled with celebrations, parades, and inspiring speeches that seemed to ripple through the community, heading back home felt natural and necessary. Fort Abraham Lincoln was more than just a military post for us; it had become a refuge where we found a sense of normalcy amid the chaos of our ongoing efforts in a rapidly changing world. Here, we could reflect on our goals, gather our thoughts, and consider the broader impact of our actions on the community and the nation."

Custer's voice, rich with experience, continued to evoke powerful imagery. "What remained of Fort Abraham Lincoln was strikingly different in 1889. I observed that relentless winds and bitter winters had dramatically changed it, reducing it to a mere shadow of its former glory. The skeletal remains of the fort cast an eerie outline against the expansive prairie sky, while the foundations, overtaken by weeds, left only the weathered traces of painted wood behind. It had become a somber relic, a poignant symbol of the relentless passage of time and the impermanence of human effort." A slight tremor passed through his hand as he gestured, illustrating the haunting scene with his evocative words.

"Libbie, bless her heart, went straight to where she remembered our officers' quarters. She ran her fingers over a worn stone, possibly part of the foundation that once was the lively center of military life, and softly said, 'Goodness, George. It's much smaller than I recall.' I wrapped my arm around her, trying to comfort her, and assured her that it felt smaller because we had both changed so much; we grew older and experienced many things, while Fort Abraham Lincoln remained a steadfast guardian of our youthful, grander memories."

Custer leaned back in his chair, making his face pensive, as if briefly lost in a well of memories. "It was a mix of nostalgia and grief. Seeing the remains of a place where vibrant life once flourished was extremely moving. I could hear children's laughter, the busy energy of military life, and the camaraderie that once filled the fort with warmth and purpose. It seemed as if the very buildings and land had absorbed our experiences, struggles, and joys over the years, only to stand now in silent testimony as remnants of a bygone era."

Ethan's pencil stopped, a physical sign of the heavy thoughts now filling his mind, capturing the meaning behind Custer's reflections. The General's insightful comments drew him further into the complex web of history, blending personal stories with the larger societal changes that have shaped the world we live in today. "What do you believe that deserted fort signifies today?" he asked softly, his voice almost reverent, hoping to gain more insight from the experienced officer whose stories seemed to bridge the past and present.

“The fort will certainly remain in history. It is situated on the west bank of the Missouri River, south of Mandan. Despite the removal or decay of the buildings, the stunning plains landscape persists. In 1907, Teddy Roosevelt signed a deed transferring ownership of the fort’s land to North Dakota, and it became the state's first state park: Fort Abraham Lincoln State Park. I trust they will be excellent stewards of the park and ensure future visitors can enjoy the rolling hills and the bluffs overlooking the Missouri River.”

Their conversation was engaging and filled with detailed insights, enhancing their observation of a time marked by both progress and hardship. Custer’s vivid memories painted a picture of two lives connected through hopes and struggles tied to their shared dreams. Ethan absorbed every detail, recognizing that the story was more than just a recounting of history; it was a tale of resilience, bravery, and the often-turbulent journey toward justice that defined their era.

Harold carried a tray of hot coffee and set it on the table. Meanwhile, the shadows grew longer in the study, creeping across the furniture like the passage of time itself.

"Thank you for sharing your experiences, General,” Ethan replied sincerely, his tone reflecting a newfound determination and quiet respect. "They will live well beyond my notes, affecting not just this moment but possibly many others in the future.”

As Custer's words faded into the room, Ethan felt the heavy weight of history settle over them like a shroud of time, wrapping both men in its significance and respect. The General's memories painted a vivid picture of a past filled with bold dreams of expanding voting rights, hopeful aspirations for social progress, and steadfast perseverance in the face of challenges, embodying the spirit of a lively and thriving community.

"We continued our journey west through the Dakota and Montana Territories to the breathtaking wilderness of Yellowstone National Park, a place renowned for its incredible beauty and wonder. We boarded one of the Yellowstone Observation Coaches at the rail terminus at Cinnabar, each pulled by an impressive six-horse team. Our destination was the Grand National Hotel, located near Mammoth Hot Springs. The building was a grand structure, four stories high and over 400 feet long, quite an unexpected sight amid the rustic surroundings. Guests were treated to a level of luxury equal to that of the finest cosmopolitan hotels. Libbie and I found this a bit humorous, as we knew how shocking the wilderness would be for many guests as they explored the park in the following days. Most guests traveled the 'Grand Loop' in a stagecoach, an uncomfortable journey because the roads were rocky and muddy, unlike the paved paths we have today. However, the views would have made their discomfort worthwhile."

"The 1st Cavalry was stationed at the park, patrolling and protecting its natural resources. Its commander, Captain Frazier Boutelle, greeted us upon our arrival.

He had arranged for us to spend a day relaxing at the hotel, after which the cavalry would serve as our personal guides through the park, and we would travel with a small unit of soldiers for the rest of the week. It was a wonderful experience to ride with the cavalry again. The views were breathtaking. The vastness of the landscape surpassed anything I had seen before, filling me with awe and grandeur. Geysers erupted spectacularly, sending plumes of steam and water high into the sky like nature's artillery display. The canyons were painted in rich reds and oranges that felt surreal, as if the earth had come alive. The waterfalls thundered with untamed force, creating a sight that moved me intensely. I told Libbie that despite the chaos of war, nothing had ever filled me with such awe and wonder."

"On most nights, our destination was one of the conveniently located hotels around the park. However, we had requested one night of camping with the soldiers to relive how our lives had once been. It was an unforgettable night, sleeping under a sky full of bright stars while hearing the gentle roar of a nearby waterfall, which reminded us of the vast universe above."

"Libbie kept a diligent diary during our journey, filling its pages with thoughtful reflections and descriptions of the spectacular magnificence of the park."

Custer paused, as if recalling the sights and sounds he described. "Much has been written about Yellowstone over the past decades, but words cannot do it justice. It is a place you have to see and experience yourself."

"After such an eventful trip there, how was your journey back east?" Ethan asked, his pencil poised and ready to capture every word of the response.

"Our return route was not as direct because we took a side trip through Lexington, Kentucky," Custer said, a familiar glimmer lighting up his eye as memories flooded back. "I kept, and still keep, in touch with several esteemed horse breeders from my time stationed in Elizabethtown, maintaining connections that have proven invaluable. While there, I focused on two exceptionally bred Thoroughbreds, descended from the illustrious Eclipse lineage, acclaimed for their speed and remarkable character. Unable to resist the allure of such magnificent creatures, I acquired four in total. One, a stunning animal in appearance, never raced, seemingly lacking the competitive spirit that defines champions. The other two proved to be good, dependable horses, commendable in their own right, but they did not show any exceptional potential. The fourth, ah..." His words trailed off with an air of mystery, a knowing smile spreading across his face.

"So, the horses aren't just a business but a vision for the future?" asked Ethan, emphasizing Custer's focus on horseflesh.

"I want Custer Horses to be remembered long after I am gone. Like the Eclipse breed, I hope to create a distinguished line of Thoroughbreds, and I believe we are close," Custer explained, conveying his unwavering confidence.

"Returning to the side trip, did you have any memorable encounters with any notable individuals?" Ethan skillfully redirected the discussion to its primary focus and sought further clarity.

"Yes, we did," Custer affirmed confidently. "We met Laura Clay, who was the president of the Kentucky Woman Suffrage Association. She and her sister, Mary Barr Clay, were key figures in the Southern suffrage movement, fighting to secure women's voting rights amid fierce opposition. Libbie and Laura strolled under the ancient, sprawling oaks, engaging in thoughtful conversations as they carefully planned their speeches and strategies to promote their cause. Their voices formed a soft hum filled with genuine determination and passionate dedication. Laura radiated passionate, righteous anger that energized every point she made. Meanwhile, Libbie consistently showed strength and steady confidence, staying calm and composed despite the external pressures they faced. Together, they created a remarkable partnership, two unique forces working in harmony toward a shared, meaningful goal, blending their talents and inspiration for the greater good of society."

"Did she ever doubt that women's suffrage would happen in her lifetime?" asked Ethan.

Custer exclaimed, visibly shaking, "She always believed it would happen and almost lived long enough to see it. In every town we traveled through, at each busy station we passed, and in every simple hall where Libbie stepped up to deliver her speeches with steady determination and clear thinking, I was constantly reminded that the fight for justice was very much alive and ongoing. She had stood at the forefront of this movement, not wielding a sword to conquer foes, but armed with eloquent words that can shape a hopeful and inclusive future."

His gaze returned to the flickering flames of the fire, enwrapped in a moment of reflection as he considered the importance of those memories. "That journey, Ethan... It helped us reconnect with our true selves, awakening a sense of purpose beyond the faded headlines and distant memories of history. We emerged not only as symbols of a nation eager to showcase its legends but also as individuals shaped by war and the complexities of Washington's political system. It was a journey rooted in reflection yet filled with enormous promise for the future."

Custer then focused on Ethan, with a sincere, almost fatherly intensity lighting his face. "We must never underestimate the ability of history to inform our current lives and influence our future. Our lives are woven into a larger tapestry, and it's crucial to determine the patterns set by those who came before us. Each generation faces unique struggles and tough challenges that seem impossible to overcome. Nevertheless, the timeless ideals of perseverance, courage, and the importance of teamwork remain constant through the ages. Our past should never be a burden; with wisdom and kindness, it can become a powerful source of strength. By actively studying history and listening closely to the voices of those who came before us, we extend our knowledge and build greater empathy. This engagement helps us make thoughtful and meaningful decisions in the future and honors the sacrifices and struggles that have laid the foundation for where we stand now."

As Ethan started taking notes with renewed excitement and energy, he realized that the depth of the conversation was changing his view of historical events and the common human condition that connects us all.

"Thank you, General," he said, sincerely appreciative. "I value your insights and reflections."

Ethan had planned to mention Libbie's passing, but it was getting late, and Custer had shared many thoughts that needed careful consideration. The topic could be saved for another time, allowing focus on the hopeful opportunities still to come.

As their conversation naturally concluded, Custer's demeanor softened from its previous intensity and focus, revealing a gentle warmth. "It's my honor, Ethan. Grasping our history helps us to shape our identity and face the future with purpose. We must respect those who came before us, as their sacrifices paved the way we walk today," he said, his reverence clear in his voice.

Ethan noted that Custer's vivid memories highlighted how the strong bond between a place and its memories can turn any location into a sacred space of remembrance, regardless of its significance. What time does not erase, it redefines. Additionally, Ethan observed that our minds reshape the people who once filled our lives, their memories becoming the foundation of our inner world.

# Chapter 12: The Rising Storm

The next morning arrived quickly. Ethan was taken to the library, and he and Custer remained quiet after exchanging greetings. This brief silence was broken when Ethan turned a page in his notebook, a subtle yet deliberate gesture indicating he was ready to begin the day's session.

"General, I'd like to move on to more recent events. Let's start by discussing your views on the Spanish-American War. After witnessing it firsthand, what can you tell me about that turbulent period?"

Custer let out a soft exhale. "In 1898, it was undoubtedly a conflict driven by newspaper sensationalism," he stated, his voice showing a mix of contempt for the hyperbole of that era and a reluctant acceptance of its inevitability. "This conflict was born from lurid news that captivated the public's imagination and was further fueled by widespread public anger."

Ethan poised his pencil over the paper, ready to write but paused in anticipation.

Custer shifted in his seat, the firelight casting a serious glow on his weathered face, each wrinkle telling of his life's battles, both on and off the battlefield. "The war indeed started with the catastrophic explosion of the USS Maine. Was it an accident or espionage? That tragic event, which took the lives of 268 Americans in Havana Harbor, sparked a frenzy across the nation, leading to the rallying cry, 'Remember the Maine!' I strongly believe that the widespread use of yellow journalism fueled the intense public outrage and demand for action."

Sensing the bitterness in Custer's words, Ethan was eager to explore the topic further and gain a better assessment of his perspective. "Do you truly believe the newspapers were instrumental in creating such overwhelming excitement among the people?" he asked, his eyebrows raised as he aimed to uncover the nuances of his answer.

Custer slowly lifted his head, his expression becoming focused as he organized his thoughts to answer Ethan's question. "Without a doubt," he replied, his conviction clear and steady. "They fueled the flames of war with their reckless and sensational headlines, carefully igniting passions and effectively handing Congress the matches that started the fire. The Hearsts and Pulitzers of that era were more than just publishers; they held immense influence, shaping public perception and directing the country toward war like skilled puppeteers pulling at delicate strings."

His gaze grew reflective, and as he stirred the lukewarm tea in front of him, the liquid swirling harmoniously with his thoughts, he continued, "War is, in truth, a striking contradiction, frequently fought under the veneer of noble principles that are, in fact, cloaked in half-truths and self-serving agendas. We claimed to send our brave soldiers to 'liberate' Cuba, but beneath that surface lay an unquenchable thirst to expand our land and plant the American flag more substantially higher on foreign soil. During that four-month conflict, we gained control of Cuba, Puerto Rico, the Philippines, Guam, and the Hawaiian Islands."

"What would you have changed?" Ethan asked eagerly and firmly, wanting to learn more about Custer's diverse experiences, wisdom, and lessons from his long career. He understood that the insights shared might reveal the complexities of that war and the true nature of conflict.

Custer responded immediately, his single statement embodying a philosophy shaped by years of victories and regrets. "Restraint," he said plainly, his voice steady and determined. "Patience. And for heaven's sake, we need far fewer parades that celebrate our wins, which only serve to hide the terrible toll that came before and after them. I had carefully read the casualty reports, taking in the grim details of our losses. I saw the harsh truth of disease spreading through our ranks, claiming lives at a pace more ruthless than the Spanish bullets ever could. Did you know that diseases killed nearly as many of Roosevelt's Rough Riders as the Spanish gunfire did? War isn't a show. We sent young men overseas to 'liberate' people we had no real understanding of. We covered conquest with the American flag and called it freedom."

Reflecting his inner conflict, he gently shook his head, his silver hair shimmering in the flickering flames. "However, in the chaos of that war, a significant revelation arose: America experienced a radical transformation, redefining its identity and path. We are a young nation compared to Spain, England, and Portugal. The conflict went beyond defending the Union or expanding the frontier; it became a battle for image and reputation. We became a world power then. In the grand arena of international relations, where the stakes are high and complex, perception often outweighs the harsh realities of bloodshed and combat."

When silence settled once more in the room, Custer's demeanor shifted, and his voice softened noticeably, shedding its sharp critique and showing greater awareness. "I harbor no resentment toward the soldiers," he said gently, his tone full of empathy and acknowledgment. "They did as they were told, following orders without question. But what I believe is crucial to recognize is the true cost of a war sparked by words and documents, which is sorrowfully paid in coffins, not in the headlines that often glorify it. I will say, however, that Teddy proved to be the best leader of the whole bunch. I spoke with William McKinley just before Christmas in 1899, when he was seeking a new vice president following the death of Garret Hobart. I suggested Teddy, and I guess the Republicans remembered my rise to the Executive Mansion and jumped at the chance to have him as vice president under McKinley in 1901."

The air was filled with the rich aroma of aged leather and burning wood, wrapping the room in a warm embrace that sharply contrasted with the cold outside. Ethan leaned back in his cozy, well-padded armchair, feeling the soft leather gently creak beneath him as he moved. He watched the fireplace, where the flames had dimmed to embers, casting a gentle amber glow that flickered around the room.

Shifting the subject, motivated by his natural curiosity and an innate desire to uncover as many details and perspectives as possible, Ethan asked, "I've come across a range of opinions about the statue erected in your honor in 1910 in Monroe, Michigan. It's larger-than-life, and its detailed design featuring you on an elegant horse is quite impressive. However, what are your thoughts on this monument? What elements do you find most striking or meaningful?"

Custer let out a quiet laugh, conveying amusement and weary reflection on his legacy. "Ah, yes, the monument," he replied, slightly shaking his head, a subtle yet knowing smile dancing across his lips. "The George Armstrong Custer Equestrian Monument was unveiled in a ceremony filled with much pomp and circumstance in early June 1910, marked by elaborate speeches and a sense of solemnity. I suppose it was a grand occasion, filled with drawn-out speeches that seemed to stretch forever, accompanied by those uncomfortably rigid uniforms designed for show rather than comfort. The atmosphere must have been filled with pride and reverence." He shifted in his seat, showing clear signs of restlessness, as if eager to escape the impact of the memories.

Custer said, "Did you know there was an earlier design for the monument? The first scale model, on display at the Monroe County Historical Museum, showed me on a horse with both front legs raised, and

I immediately objected to this portrayal. Although it's not an official rule, it is generally understood that if the rider was killed in battle, the horse's two front legs are raised."

His eyes flickered briefly toward the dancing flames of the nearby fire before settling back on Ethan, revealing a complex mixture of feelings that shifted like the shadows in the room. "Frankly, I've never truly known how to regard it. I often feel trapped in bronze, ensnared by the rigid confines others impose on me. However, people crave symbols, Ethan. They need something concrete to hold onto and solidify their memories as time's fleeting nature begins to obscure their recollections. They search for a constant, a touchstone amid the ever-evolving narrative of history itself."

He let out a long, thoughtful sigh, as if carrying his burdens and the influence of countless victories and defeats. "Facing one's own monument, an embellished portrayal of one's identity shaped by others' perceptions, evokes a mix of introspection and discomfort, revealing the complexities of how history memorializes individuals. It can be unsettling to see strangers venerating a statue instead of embracing the complexities and nuances of the man it depicts. The harsh reality we must face is that a bronze likeness will likely endure long after one has departed from this world, and its story will be shared and reshaped long after one's voice has faded away."

Ethan wrote passionately for a long time, with the only sound in the quiet room being the movement of his pencil. Each word he inscribed on the page felt like a form of liberation and an acceptance of a new responsibility.

“After that, the Great War began in 1914,” Ethan suggested, his tone gentle and almost reverent as he shifted his focus back to the imposing figure sitting across from him, fully aware of the historical importance carried in their conversation. "What are your thoughts on the conflict?”

Custer didn't answer right away. The silence stretched on, broken only by the occasional pop of the fire. His typically intense gaze fell to his hands, rough and strong from years of hard work and leadership, his fingers interlaced on his lap. A life defined by command, battle, and critical decisions seemed almost carved into their stillness, telling stories of bravery and consequence. He took a slow breath, calming his mind.

"Ghastly,” he finally muttered, the word slipping from his lips in a low sigh, filled with discontent. It wasn’t just a description; it was a harsh condemnation. He saw it as a conflict that lacked the influence of a bold leader on his men. No spirit. There was no room for daring or innovative tactics, only mindless slaughter. He shook his head, expressing extreme disappointment with the war’s unimaginative approach. "Where was the quick thrust, the flanking maneuver, the decisive charge? All that was lost..."

Ethan keenly watched the noticeable change in Custer's attitude, feeling the impression of his apparent discontent. It was like a thick cloud had covered Custer, shifting his behavior and manner.

With genuine curiosity and a desire to figure out the underlying factors, Ethan carefully asked, "Can you elaborate on that further? What might have caused this significant shift in battle tactics?" His tone showed eagerness to gain insights into this strategic change and determine its rationale.

Custer observed that "The nature of war has changed," his tone steady yet subtly melancholic, reflecting both his personal experiences and the evolving nature of conflict throughout history. "In my era, people approached confrontations with strategic daring, eager to engage in battle openly and with resolve. The skillful execution of battle tactics and formations instilled a sense of honor, weaving bravery into the fabric of combat. However, the Great War marked a drastic shift toward mechanization, relying on technologies that strip away the inherent humanity from the battlefield and diminish the true essence of conflict."

He paused briefly, his gaze drifting as if he were recalling distant memories, and seemed lost in thought before continuing. "Strategies that once represented bravery and nobility on the battlefield have now been overshadowed by the harsh realities of trench warfare and the devastating effects of industrial-scale destruction. In this new era, soldiers are often reduced to mere statistics on an ever-growing casualty list, made anonymous and overlooked by a society eager to move on. Instead of courage shining through the chaos of prolonged combat, we now face an unfathomable dread. On this clouded battlefield, suffering is measured not by valor or personal stories but through cold, impersonal data."

Ethan wrote passionately in his notebook, driven by the urgency and depth of Custer's remarks. "What do you think has been society's reaction to this change? How has public perception evolved in the wake of such widespread destruction and loss?" he asked, captivated by their conversation.

Custer paused to reflect on how society reacts to conflict, his expression thoughtful. "Public perception has unfortunately become more disconnected," he said, the seriousness of his words showing his concern. "The initial shock of war often fades into numbness, causing the horrors and realities of combat to blur into distant memories, preventing a full recognition of the destruction that has taken place."

"Do you think this disconnection reduces the respect owed to those who serve?" Ethan asked, carefully connecting Custer's poignant thoughts to current societal issues and their effects on veterans today.

"Undoubtedly," Custer responded, his look intense and filled with steady conviction. "Such detachment greatly undermines the very essence of honoring the sacrifices made by those in the field. When we categorize their experiences as just numbers, we strip away their humanity, failing to adequately acknowledge the deep and lasting impact that war inflicts on the spirits of those who fight. It represents a heavy price that cannot simply be measured by the victories achieved or the lands acquired; those figures are devoid of the true cost paid in emotional suffering and loss."

The room fell silent once more, filled with a solemn stillness that weighed heavily on Ethan as he absorbed Custer's powerful words.

The door opened with a soft creak, and Harold came in carrying a tray of tea, ham, biscuits, and cheese. He left the two men to their conversation.

After a brief break for food and drink, Ethan said, "General, I appreciate you sharing your views. Your perspectives clarify the complexities of warfare, its different strategies, its far-reaching effects, and most importantly, the human experiences intertwined with great loss connected to it."

Custer looked at him steadily, showing a slight sign of appreciation in his tough features as he understood the significance of their discussion. "Thank you for engaging with these reflections, Ethan. Conversations like this are vital for keeping memories alive and ensuring we respect the invaluable lessons learned through the trials of history, as they shape not just our knowledge of conflict but our very humanity."

Custer took a breath as if trying to clear the troubling thought of sacrificing more lives in futile battles lingering in his mind. "Trench warfare epitomized a grievous misstep, a savage descent into barbarism that modern civilization should have surpassed ages ago. Men embedded in the soil like abandoned roots, covered in the heavy mud of decay and ruin, resigned to the dark grip of their coming doom. Every update from Europe filled me with a sense of foreboding, Ethan. Young and impressionable soldiers were stuck in mud that reached their knees, gassed like vermin in their confined pits, and then absurdly sent over the top into relentless hailstorms of gunfire, not for honor or courage, but to gain a few pointless feet of land. They called this gruesome practice strategic warfare; I view it instead as an open form of mass suicide. The practice isn't warfare as we once understood it; it's a heartless display of destruction." He let the final words slip from his lips with a biting disdain that lingered heavily in the room's silence.

His gaze, which earlier seemed to drift into the depths of some internal struggle, now held a distant, almost haunted look. "In my era, a charge had real significance, Ethan. It represented bravery, refined skill, and admirable leadership. You could face your enemy directly, breathe in the sharp scent of gunpowder, listen to hooves pounding, and feel the rush of battle coursing through you. There was a raw, primal bond between soldiers. In France, though, soldiers died without ever seeing the face of the man who killed them; they were faced only with faceless, impersonal death, dealt by hidden rifles and choking fumes. An empty, haunted existence defined their days, a cruel facade of honor where no true honor existed." He exhaled a pained sigh. "It was a hollow void, lacking purpose or comfort, a hint of what life should have been."

Ethan, who had been leaning forward eagerly with his pencil poised above his notebook, quickly jotted down a few key points while keeping his gaze fixed on the old general. He noticed every slight shift in Custer's expression and the faintest tremor in his voice with great interest. "What are your views of the tanks used in battle?" he asked, sensing a change in the atmosphere, a spark of renewed energy lighting up Custer's once-distant eyes.

A slow, mysterious smile spread across the old general's face, lively and knowing, not soft or comforting, but more like a predator waiting for its next unsuspecting prey. "Ah, the tanks." He leaned closer, a new energy bubbling inside him.

His voice grew stronger, shedding the fatigue that had recently weighed on him like a heavy cloak. "In that horrific conflict, the truth was that they were undeniably too slow to change the course of events effectively. The enemy's artillery treated them as easy targets because of their small numbers and clumsy, mud-covered operations. Yet, I saw the potential lying dormant within those armored giants, Ethan. I could clearly see their promise. If only they had moved with the agility and ferocity of cavalry: quick, agile, and fierce. Imagine if those iron giants could move with the grace and speed of a Thoroughbred at full gallop; we could have sliced through those treacherous trenches as easily as a sickle cuts through ripe wheat. There would have been no need to crawl in the mud, just a pure, relentless charge."

He shifted slightly in his seat, his demeanor changing, as if he were about to deliver an unplanned speech to an unseen assembly of soldiers ready for battle. His hand cut through the air deliberately, emphasizing and punctuating his points for greater impact. "What I see, what fills my thoughts day and night, is a style of mobile warfare that redefines our approach to engagement. This approach is characterized by continuous, fluid movement across the battlefield. Flanking tactics can disorient the enemy's front line and ultimately transform the strategy and deployment of entire forces. The atmosphere is electrified, charged with speed and thunderous momentum. Think of long lines of armored vehicles, like powerful beasts, crashing through enemy lines, scattering their ranks like startled birds taking flight, taking ground rapidly, not step by step but by the mile with unstoppable force. Such swift and fierce assaults would significantly weaken the enemy's morale and spirit, striking fear into their hearts."

Custer added, "The horse's role in warfare is dying, but so is the soul of war."

Ethan looked up. "The soul of war?"

Custer nodded. "War was never clean, but it was human. A man faced another man. He led from the front. He shared the danger. Now? Commanders now sit far behind the lines. Men die by hundreds, thousands... Victory is measured in miles gained, not lives spared."

Custer paused, then passionately declared, "The cavalry, Ethan, will return in a new form: on tracks, exhibiting superior speed and agility."

Ethan, eager to capture every word, wrote fervently, his pencil moving smoothly across the thick, textured paper of his notepad as he aimed to contain the flood of ideas and the electrifying energy radiating from the general. Custer's bold vision stood in sharp contrast to the stagnant, blood-soaked fields that had defined the Great War, serving as a captivating rallying cry for change.

"Speed and adaptability, Thorne, are the keys to unlocking this monumental potential," Custer continued, his voice adopting a captivating rhythm, full of conviction. "Each tank will operate as a standalone unit, working collaboratively with others, like a well-organized squadron, and with the agility to execute individual tactics, quickly adjusting and flanking in response to the ever-changing battlefield dynamics. They must be armed with lighter, rapid-fire weapons designed for suppressive fire and formidable machine guns ready to destroy anything that dares to block their path. These vehicles should be engineered to rearm and refuel on the battlefield, allowing them to stay in action rather than retreat to a distant base. They should not move slowly; they must dash forward with unstoppable momentum. They should operate like hounds unleashed on a fox, relentless and driven, pursuing their prey tirelessly."

The room fell silent for a brief but powerful moment, with only the soft crackle of the fire and the lively exchange of ideas flowing freely between them. The world seemed to sense the potential impact of this critical perspective on the course of warfare, carrying hopeful anticipation of great possibilities.

He suddenly shifted his focus from the mesmerizing dance of the flames, locking eyes with Ethan, a challenging spark igniting in his gaze and taking on an almost rebellious intensity. "Tanks in combat... I think of them like armored cavalry. And mark my words, Thorne, one day someone will wield this concept to achieve victory before their adversary can respond adequately. They'll advance further into the front lines, and the enemy command structure will implode completely from the pressure."

"Have you discussed this concept with anyone?" Ethan's voice strained as he tried to keep up with the flow of ideas from Custer's vibrant imagination.

Custer's mouth contorted into a narrow smile, a grimace indicating both recognition and a trace of frustration. "My words are meant for anyone willing to hear them and truly understand their importance. Also, many others either cannot or willfully refuse to face the reality I present." He sneered, dismissively waving his hand as if to ignore their opinions, saying that most of the top brass in Washington think he is just dreaming. "They believe I am clinging passionately to a past that has already slipped away, relentlessly chasing the ghost of a legendary battle that now only exists as a memory. They see a tank as just a large, slow-moving tractor, failing to grasp its vital role in modern warfare. Yet, I assure them, this expedition isn't about what's behind us or longing for past glories. It represents growth from everything I've faced, the lessons learned from battles fought, the ambitions kept close, and the constantly changing landscape of conflict that demands we adapt and innovate. This operation represents the logical progression in the field of mobile warfare."

He pointed outside, beyond the heavy, plush velvet curtains that hung gracefully over the window. "Those horses you see out there? They symbolize my legacy; indeed, they do. But soon, cold, unfeeling machines will replace the noble living beings I have cherished. The overwhelming, thunderous roar of engines will drown out the beloved sound of their hooves, each delicate step reflecting history and connection. It will be louder, faster, and ultimately uncontrollable, drowning out the essence of what we've known."

Ethan paused, his pencil hanging in the air, wrestling with a fleeting personal thought that fluttered through his mind like a restless bird. "Do you long to ride with them, General? With the proud, armored cavalry you envision?"

For a brief moment, Custer's shoulders drooped slightly, and the lively spark in his eyes faded, a shadow of reflection crossing his face. He spoke softly, regret lingering in the room like heavy fog. "Every day. Every single day."

A heavy silence enveloped the two men. The crackling fire disrupted the stillness, with embers flickering and dancing, and a single spark shooting into the air like a desperate glimmer of hope trying to break free.

The fire had dwindled to just embers now, its orange-red glow casting shadows that moved slowly across the library's walls. Outside, a gentle yet steady breeze pressed against the glass, producing a soft, mournful whistle that reflected the melancholic mood inside the room.

Ethan said, "I'd like to delay our discussion about the Nineteenth Amendment in 1920 until later. Before we get to that, can you tell me about the dedication ceremony for the Lincoln Memorial in Washington? What was it like to be there when it was officially unveiled?"

"I vividly recall that momentous occasion when I attended the dedication of the Lincoln Memorial in 1922. It was a cool spring morning filled with dignitaries and a sense of reverence." He began speaking calmly and respectfully, recalling a treasured memory that left a lasting impression on him. "The air was brisk, but the sun promised warmth and renewal as it started to rise. I stood there among notable figures, including President Taft and other distinguished individuals, surrounded by a sea of dark suits and serious faces, as a large, silent crowd gathered. We stood in awe together, looking up at the magnificent seated giant."

Custer's eyes, filled with reverence, gazed beyond the room, as if he were transported back to that moment when he saw the grandeur of the marble statue symbolizing strength and resilience. "In that moment, I felt something within me awaken, not a trace of fear or doubt, but a sincere realization that resonated through my very being. Lincoln wasn't a general; he didn't lead cavalry charges or command troops in battle. No, he fought with words and determination, embodying the very essence of the nation. He remained committed to fighting for the country. In my opinion, Lincoln sought unity and healing. What happened afterward... was the opposite."

After a long pause, a slight tremor shook his hand as he gestured, serving as a subtle reminder of the military discipline and steadfast dedication that had defined his life and shaped his identity. "I proudly saluted him one last time," Custer added.

As they talked, the conversation flowed smoothly, allowing both men to explore their thoughts about duty, honor, and history's lasting influence. The surroundings felt tense, filled with memories of those who came before: victories, struggles, and legacies that lingered like a thick fog. At that moment, the library transcended just being a place filled with books and artifacts; it became a sanctuary for memories, a space where the histories of those who fought, resisted, and dreamed blended with the hopes and aspirations of the living.

Custer continued speaking, his tone more thoughtful and sincere. "During that commemoration, I gained the perception that the heart of our nation goes beyond just victories or defeats; it's in our shared courage to face the moral challenges that shape who we are. Giving voice to everyone, especially those pushed aside and ignored, is a huge challenge. Navigating this conscience is a delicate and complex fight that requires moral fortitude, wisdom, and empathy."

Ethan recognized the subtle nuances in Custer's eloquent words. Each phrase carried significance, highlighting the complexity of historical stories and implying they demand careful consideration.

"What aspects of Lincoln's character and leadership did you find most admirable?" Ethan asked softly and cautiously.

Custer slowly nodded, a quiet sign of his intentions. "He stood out clearly from most men I have known. His character and leadership had a profound impact on those around him, as shown by his ability to inspire loyalty and bravery even in tough times. I earned my stars under his command, Mr. Thorne, a great honor that recognized my achievements and showed his belief in my potential. He had a remarkable talent for seeing good qualities in a young, impulsive officer, qualities that many others missed or failed to see."

He continued, "Few could handle the burden he bore without faltering under the pressure of leadership and expectation. That statue, his likeness, was so skillfully crafted that his eyes were depicted with perfect detail. That is what initially drew my attention and held it strongly. They radiate kindness while revealing compassion and an awareness of the human condition. Beyond that, they exhibit indomitable drive and an unyielding resolve to face challenges directly. It feels as though they observe everything with sharp awareness, taking in the world around them while quietly contemplating the complexities of life and leadership."

A heavy silence surrounded them, as if the entire library had come to a standstill, quietly honoring the significance of history in the air.

Then, almost hesitantly, Ethan turned a page in his notebook, the soft yet distinct sound signaling the gentle end of a reflective moment that seemed to last forever. As the noise faded, he looked up, his face turning contemplative, his mind racing with ideas. Ethan then suggested discussing the Indian Citizenship Act of 1924.

Custer silently absorbed the fading warmth of the fireplace, feeling the fire's heat gently caress his face, like a comforting hug. After a moment, he finally moved, breaking the silence. He said unexpectedly softly, "When I was informed that President Coolidge enacted the Indian Citizenship Act, I stood in this room, at this very spot, and tipped my hat to the empty space around me." A brief smile touched his lips, mixed with a trace of bittersweet pride, recognition, and respect. "Maybe for the departed souls, maybe for the bygone years."

Ethan suddenly stopped his meticulous note-taking. His pencil hovered uncertainly, close to slipping from his fingers. "You supported it? What happened to your animosity toward them?" he asked, a suggestion of surprise in his voice, his brow furrowing slightly in disbelief at the unexpected revelation. Even in his later years, the standard view of George Armstrong Custer was rarely associated with progressive ideas or reforms that acknowledged the complexities of human rights.

Custer turned fully to face Ethan, the flickering firelight illuminating the subtle expressions on his face; his eyes revealed a complex mix of exhaustion and firm resolve. "After the Indian Wars, they were no longer enemies. Much like the Civil War, we needed to work together for the good of our nation. Yes, I favored that legislation," he affirmed, his tone growing more confident as he spoke, emphasizing the importance of his action. "It was certainly overdue. It gave Indians what they should have received long ago: the dignity of full citizenship. It was not granted as a favor to those who comply with us. It wasn't handed to them as a condition for land or peace. It is an inherent, undeniable right that belongs to them, just like any other person born in this land." His unwavering gaze remained fixed on Ethan's, determined to show the strength of his conviction.

With a purposeful gesture, he pointed Ethan toward a polished mahogany sideboard, where a scattering of books and a half-filled decanter contrasted with several faded sepia photographs. One image showed Bloody Knife, his Arikara scout, who had become a lifelong friend. "I fought against the Lakota and the Cheyenne," he continued, his voice softening and carrying a certain seriousness as a shadow crossed his features. "I led my men into battle against them, yes. But I knew many of them personally. I sat with them by their firesides. I shared meals with them. I witnessed their remarkable bravery in the face of great challenges. And I experienced their sorrow firsthand, the resonating kind that empties a man inside, leaving only dust where once happiness had thrived."

He paused intentionally, allowing the seriousness of his words to fill the room with a somber mood that called for reflection. The silence persisted, broken only by the soft crackle of the fire, disturbing the calm.

"Time after time, I wondered why we couldn't embrace our shared humanity," he whispered, his voice filled with frustration and longing. "We often overlook that behind every adversary is a story, a life. History is more than just military victories and the praise of conquest. It's also about the bonds we form and the knowledge we seek, or, as is often the case, the lies we spread."

"We took their land," he said. "We crushed their spirit. Then we presumed to validate their existence with a piece of paper that says, 'You belong.'"

Ethan did not write. The words were too substantial for mere pencil and paper. They were etched in his mind and lived in the silence.

## Chapter 13: Libbie

Ethan gently tapped the well-worn pencil against the rugged edge of his leather-bound notebook, the soft sound blending with the comforting crackle of the nearby fire that kept the space warm. He softly tried to bring Custer back into the conversation. The General had been stretching his legs, strolling around the room. As was his custom, he stopped before Libbie's portrait, his eyes gazing up at her. It was stately and magnificent, enclosed in an ornate, gilded frame and hung prominently above the grand fireplace's mantle. The lively sparkle in her eyes contrasted strangely with the room's silence. Her likeness projected a serene power, inspiring reverence, admiration, and respect.

As Custer sat down, he looked at Ethan, signaling he was prepared to proceed.

Ethan nodded and calmly asked, “I'm interested in learning about life before West Point. Would you tell me about your and Libbie's formative years?"

"In a humble village named New Rumley in Ohio, my journey unfolded,” Custer recounted.

Ethan recognized that Custer would instinctively talk about himself first. Custer naturally tended to draw attention to himself, always ready to steer conversations in his favor.

"It was less a village and more a stark testament to endurance, a place shaped by the breath of winter's wind and the unyielding resistance of granite-hard soil," Custer said. "It was hardly a cluster of homes at all. It was a wider, muddier spot on a dirt road, where thin smoke constantly curled from stone chimneys, fading into an indifferent sky. Mornings there didn't wait for the sun or for the roosters to stir; they appeared in the harsh predawn dark, filled with the raw, metallic smell of iron tools biting into earth still stiff with frost, with the scent of damp soil and wood smoke clinging to everything. My father's boots, heavy and steady, echoed across the thin plank floors before the first sign of daylight, each heavy step a firm decree: the work would find you, always, like the relentless pull of the tide, whether your spirit welcomed it or not." Custer paused and shifted in his chair.

A smile slowly appeared on Custer's face. "When I was young, I struggled to pronounce my middle name. I tried repeatedly, but I couldn't say, 'Armstrong.' The best I could do was 'Autie,' which became my family nickname. As an adult, only Libbie called me that name."

His smile faded into a stern look. "My father worked as a farmer and a smith, and we weren't poor," he said firmly, tapping his cane against the stone hearth, the sound resonating through the quiet study. "Not destitute, not ragged and starving like the truly wretched. We had a roof and barely enough food to fill our stomachs. But we were nobody. A family among dozens, unremarkable, forgotten before we were even noticed. There were too many hungry mouths and chores that demanded immediate attention in that kind of life. As a boy, I asked 'why?' about the sun, the dirt, and authority more often than I worked with a hoe or chopped a log." He paused, a flicker of that old, youthful frustration at his inability to find answers crossing his face.

"My mother," he recalled, "was a whisper of quiet strength and unshakable resolve, a constant presence whose quiet prayers at the kitchen door seemed to hold the ramshackle house together through sheer will." He conjured vivid glimpses for Ethan: the rough, weathered texture of his father's hand resting unusually gently on his shoulder; the terse, almost pained words, "Go if you must," a reluctant blessing on the day he decided to leave. And then, the stark image of the muddy, well-worn boots George deliberately left behind on the porch, a symbolic shedding of his past as he boarded the clattering train to Michigan, the steam whooshing a final, definitive sigh of farewell.

Ethan struggled to connect the years and experiences to imagine what Custer was like at sixteen. He imagined a lean, hungry boy, pockets empty but a mind burning with ambitions and dreams, possessing a razor-sharp vision. He was driven by a passion he wielded like a honed blade, carving out his destiny and reshaping his future. This was a youth who, through the hard work of New Rumley's demanding soil and strict routine, had grasped a vital, strong truth: simply existing wasn't enough. The first big obstacle was getting noticed and rising above the anonymity of "nobody." And the second, even more formidable challenge? It was a steady, unwavering refusal to look back, to ignore the dust and shadows he left behind, and to always charge forward into whatever was next.

"I found myself in Monroe," Custer began, the name slipping from his lips like a gentle sigh, a whisper that seemed to hover. He settled back into the comfort of his plush armchair, taking a breath, and the sound faded softly into the cozy atmosphere. "I chose to live with my half-sister, Lydia, and had better educational prospects in Monroe than I ever would in Ohio. Lydia's husband, David Reed, owned and operated a drayage business."

Ethan's furrowed brow and slight tilt of his head signaled he was not familiar with the term.

Custer continued, "A drayage company specializes in the shipment of goods. Under David's kind tutelage, I learned valuable lessons in logistics."

"After graduating from McNeely Normal School, I earned a teaching certificate and briefly worked as a grammar school instructor in Ohio. However, teaching did not interest me. I was determined to pursue a military career and secure an appointment to West Point. As a sixteen-year-old Democrat, I wrote to our congressman, John A. Bingham, who was a Republican, expressing my desire to attend the U.S. Military Academy at West Point and asking for a congressional nomination. Bingham replied that someone else had already received an appointment. I responded immediately, including a list of my physical and educational qualifications, and asked him to recommend me for any other vacancies. I believed my determination and persistence would impress him. My strategy worked, and he nominated me for the next available cadetship."

Ethan's pencil tip broke from the pressure of taking notes so quickly. He quickly grabbed a replacement from his satchel and kept going. "What about Libbie? How would you characterize her early years?" asked Ethan.

"Both privilege and tragedy shaped Libbie's childhood. She lost her mother and siblings before turning thirteen. Her father, Judge Daniel S. Bacon, promised his dying wife he would care for their only surviving child. He was a caring, protective father who gave Libbie a refined, high-quality education. She excelled in school and graduated as valedictorian from the Young Ladies' Seminary and Collegiate Institute. She had a rare and desirable mix of sharp intellect, confidence, and witty charm."

"Judge Bacon's home," Custer continued, a subtle smile dancing on his lips as he recalled fond memories, "was a symbol of respectability and community standing. It had a white picket fence, painted so often that it gleamed like polished bone under the sun. The garden was meticulously maintained. Each rosebush was pruned to perfection, blooming vibrantly as if presented to the world. The windows were so spotless that one could see the shine of their reflections before knocking on the stately oak door, which stood guard like the threshold to timeless memories."

Ethan meticulously documented every detail, capturing not only Judge Bacon's physical presence, a man of discipline and precision, but also the spirit of an era, highlighting the importance of community, respectability, and the intricate web of lives woven into the story of history.

"I never believed he thought I was adequate," Custer shared, with a playful smile flickering across his worn face, emphasizing the lines that showed his physical and emotional struggles. "He called me a reckless country boy, full of spirit but lacking common sense, a free soul trapped in an unyielding world."

His smile broadened slightly. "He insisted that I had mud running in my veins, a wildness that would tarnish his daughter's flawless reputation, an asset he held dear. He made it clear to Libbie that marrying me would be a risky decision."

Custer's eyes involuntarily drifted toward Libbie's portrait, as if the sight alone summoned a flood of cherished memories that blended with the present. "Yet she remained steadfast, never wavering in her determination," he said, respect clear in his tone as he recalled her loyalty. "Not a single time did she falter, not in the face of criticism or doubt. She would stand on that porch, her hair neatly arranged in a manner befitting a lady of Monroe, her hands gently clasped in front of her, embodying decorum. Yet she held my letters so tightly, clutching them as if they were lifelines. I swear, sometimes the ink would seep through the delicate paper and stain her white gloves, leaving faint blue marks on the crisp fabric, evidence of her emotional investment. Her quiet defiance was more powerful than any spoken vow, a silent proclamation of her feelings."

Ethan appreciated Custer's depiction of Libbie as Monroe's steady strength, a woman of unwavering loyalty and quiet resilience, and a beacon of steadfastness amid the storms of judgment.

"I would come back from West Point during those years," Custer reminisced, his tone softening as he let the memories wash over him, each tinged with a bittersweet feeling. "Wearing my finest uniform, every button gleamed with a nearly overwhelming pride. I polished my boots until they reflected like mirrors, catching the light and reflecting my hopes. My saber belt was tied so tightly that I had trouble breathing, all to present myself as a suitable suitor, a man worthy of her affection. I stood stiffly before her father, a man who judged a man's worth by a ledger of actions and financial achievements, linking ideas of honor and bravery to what could be counted and measured. It wasn't until I had stars on my epaulets that her father's opinion of my prospects shifted in my favor, ever so slightly."

A hollow laugh escaped him, more a sigh than humor, heavy with nostalgia that seemed to linger like the scent of a forgotten cologne. "But Libbie," he said, tenderness returning to his voice, "she judged me by an entirely different standard. She saw the boy beneath the shiny surface. She could see a young man gazing out at the distant orchard, not just as fruit trees enclosed in a space, but as a vast horizon, waiting for a thousand galloping horses. She understood the dreamer inside me, the one willing to abandon a life of comfort for the fleeting but brilliant moment of victory on the open field, even if that journey ended quickly and carried uncertain risks."

As their conversation went on, Harold quietly brought in the noon meal.

After eating, a silence lingered, broken only by the soft sounds of Ethan's pencil gliding across the smooth page. Ethan said, "I appreciate your rise from humble beginnings to launching your career in the military. Libbie's dedication to you and her support are evident. You mentioned your letters, but I'd like to learn about her letters."

"Her letters..." Custer murmured, a spark lighting up his eyes with fond memories and emotion.

Custer paused to reflect, his demeanor thoughtful and introspective as the memories surfaced. "Those letters were invaluable treasures, imbued with a sense of intimacy that transcended distance. I kept them hidden beneath my cot, a sacred collection I often revisited by the dim light of a flickering candle. Each carefully penned word resonated with her insight and the connection between our souls, strengthening a bond society often tried to break or weaken."

"She wrote every week, rain or snow, battle or peace. Always the same salutation: 'My Dearest Autie.' Each letter was a lifeline, a link bridging our separate lives, allowing me to share my dreams and unspoken fears while she offered steadfast support and unshakable faith, fueling my resolve," Custer said. His story continued, revealing how their lives were intertwined in complex ways. It was a testament to love and strength that thrived despite society's pressures and rules.

Ethan wrote, "Every letter Libbie composed served as a lifeline, not just for 'Autie' but also as a way for their shared hopes to survive and flourish despite the relentless challenges of a rapidly changing world."

"In the aftermath of each battle, her letters arrived like rays of sunshine and love, illuminating the darkest moments with their unwavering support, offering solace and strength amid the chaos of conflict," Custer reminisced, his voice filled with gentle affection and admiration. "She would send me letters rich with hope and love. Each word shone like a guiding light in the encroaching darkness of conflict. They lifted my spirits during the toughest days, those dark moments when defeat felt temptingly close, and the influence of my duties seemed overwhelmingly burdensome."

"Those letters, marked with her unmistakable and unique script, were more than just notes; they represented a sincere reaffirmation of our shared mission and commitment, acting as lifelines that connected our hearts across the distances. She reminded me of our joys, that familial comfort of home, and the hopeful future we dared to dream of—a life beyond the wars and turmoil surrounding us. She kept writing letters to me even when we were together. Writing was her way of expressing her fears, hopes, dreams, and love."

Ethan's pencil moved smoothly, capturing the scope and breadth of Custer's heartfelt disclosures. The core of their partnership shone brighter amid the shallow judgments and misconceptions often directed at them. Libbie's quiet strength wove seamlessly through the fabric of history, creating a story filled with love and honor—one that deserves recognition and validation. Uncharacteristically sharing personal details, Ethan said, "I write letters to my fiancée when I can, but moving forward, I intend to put a greater effort into communicating with her. Your description of the letters between you and your wife is inspirational."

Custer responded with a knowing nod. "Ethan, you understand the true value of words better than most people do. It would serve you well to remember that consistent communication with the person you love, along with kindness and respect, is an investment in your relationship's long-term health. An investment that continues to grow, like interest earned in a bank, is worth far more and yields more rewards than any money could. That is something Libbie's father could never grasp about our marriage."

After a brief pause, absorbing the depth of Custer's words, Ethan then said, "Now that I have the stories of your beginnings, describe how your partnership matured and flourished."

With a knowing smile that conveyed affection and wisdom, Custer leaned back once more, reflecting on a time marked by hardship. "Through the struggles of separation, societal expectations, and personal sacrifices, our bond grew stronger and thrived. Libbie understood my restless desire for broader horizons and shared my lofty dreams. While I was away pursuing my path, she immersed herself in the town's activities, diligently maintaining her family's respected reputation and nurturing her ambitions. The locals usually viewed her with respect and skepticism; she was the daughter of a respected judge, and I stood as a challenge to the status quo. Yet, Libbie faced this tension boldly and openly."

Even as his pencil moved across the page, Ethan's mind wandered to his fiancée living in upstate New York and their struggles with being apart. In a short time, he was able to rise above his emotions and regain his focus.

Custer's tone changed noticeably as he described the heavy responsibilities and personal sacrifices required for leadership. "There were moments when doubt slipped in quietly," he reflected, letting his emotions show in his words. "I wondered if I was truly doing enough, if my successes justified the high costs they imposed on others. Yet, Libbie's unwavering faith in me kept me steady amid the uncertainty. Like the eternal flame of our love, she was the light that never dimmed, a constant beacon in the darkness. I was never truly alone on this journey; her spirit walked with me, offering lasting support. They called me fearless, but I was afraid," Custer said. "Above all, I feared failing her more so than I feared any enemy."

As he continued, Custer's voice shifted, revealing layers of longing mixed with steadfast pride. "Whenever I returned from the field, it felt like an intense reunion of spirits that had traveled more than just physical distances. The desire to be together became our shared goal, driven by intense hope and resolve. We built a relationship that thrived within society's constraints, constantly challenging the boundaries that tried to divide us, thereby redefining the very story of our love."

Ethan nodded enthusiastically, captivated by the story of resilience and enduring love unfolding before him. "And when did your commitment truly take shape?" he pressed, eager to learn more.

"The moment I asked for her hand," Custer declared confidently, his eyes shining with the memory of that crucial moment. "I remember gathering every bit of courage, as if preparing for a formidable encounter. The visit was tense as I stood before Judge Bacon, his narrowed gaze skewering me. I spoke sincerely, revealing my true feelings and risking rejection. His reaction, as expected, was filled with disbelief and judgment, his skepticism clear."

A shadow crossed Custer's face as he confessed, "In that moment of doubt, it was Libbie's unwavering love that steadied me. Her loyalty, a beacon defying her father's stern disapproval, became my anchor through the storm. She illuminated my goals, fueling a resolve to win her hand and finally earn the respect that had often seemed just out of reach. Her father ultimately conceded that his daughter's wishes and strong determination were more powerful than his reservations or objections, and he had no choice but to approve."

Ethan grasped the depth of that emotion, thinking it over as he understood the core of their struggle. "And during those instances," he murmured, "both of you were not only challenging societal norms but also carving your unique path, one marked by commitment, resilience, and a refusal to be confined by the expectations of others."

"Undeniably," Custer replied, his face showing a mix of pride and sentimentality that revealed the depth of his connection to the past. "Our adventure, in many ways, was a series of confrontations. Genuine love often grows from hardship, balancing expectations, and facing resistance that tests the very fabric of our beings. Throughout it all, Libbie never wavered in her faith in me; each challenge we faced only strengthened our bond, intensifying the connection that tied our souls together."

While they talked, the grand library radiated a peaceful atmosphere, filled with a sense of calm that resonated with the energy of their heartfelt conversation. Each detail Custer shared became a victory over the long-standing struggles of their past, emphasizing the powerful and lasting impact of love, closely tied to intention and shared dreams.

He shifted his position in the cozy armchair, exuding controlled energy despite the exhaustion in his eyes. His elbows rested on his knees as he sat thoughtfully, while his cane's shiny, polished surface lay across his legs like a quiet, heavy reminder of the past, more meaningful now than any rusty sword could ever be.

Nearby, Ethan held his pencil ready, listening closely to every word. The fire crackled softly in the hearth, emitting a gentle, honeyed light that seemed to ease the General, and his words flowed freely.

"From Monroe's grand porch, where our paths first crossed in a dance of fate, she journeyed with me to Fort Abraham Lincoln's windswept plains, through the glittering ballrooms of the Executive Mansion, and beyond into the uncharted territories of our shared destiny." Custer began, his voice slightly hoarse from the hours of talking, yet full of a personal touch, warm and familiar.

He absentmindedly touched the cold pipe, a familiar gesture that reflected his thoughtful nature. He took several slow sips from his now-cooled tea and continued. "They dismissed her as naive, just a society girl thought to be unfit for the rugged demands of the frontier. They called her a cavalry bride, implying she was only a delicate counterpart to my strong will, a fragile bloom struggling to survive in a harsh, unforgiving environment. Yet Libbie, my beloved Libbie, never faltered, even when the whispers grew louder, the criticism became relentless, or when outright slander aimed to tarnish her name and reputation. Her gaze stayed steady and true, as unwavering as my aim, steadfast in the midst of the tempest."

Ethan's pencil moved smoothly across the paper, effortlessly capturing the essence of her spirit: Libbie, the quiet yet resilient heart amid the ongoing chaos. Ethan hesitated, considering how to phrase his next question. He didn't want to seem disrespectful to Custer or Libbie's memory, but it had to be asked. "I need to ask you about the rumors I've heard regarding another woman. What can you tell me about Monahsetah?"

"Ah, yes, the tale of Monahsetah continues." Custer's voice grew sharper and more determined. His jaw clenched tightly as he spoke, revealing his intense emotions. "After the Battle of the Washita River, she had been a translator for us for several weeks. That is the extent of my knowledge of her. Much later, some people proposed that her child was my son. Yet, this was simply a false tale spun from bits of campfire stories and white men's thirst for scandal. People sought to create sensational news for cheap newspapers, driven by a desire to seek retribution and sow discord."

He struck his cane with resolve, the impact resonating strongly against the cold stone of the hearth. "However, the claim that I had a son with her is nothing but a fallacy, a mere reflection created from the falsehoods perpetuated by a society far too eager to pursue revenge over the more complex facts obscured by broken agreements and shattered promises." He let out a sigh that spoke volumes of the frustration and pain this rumor had caused.

Outside, the cold air wrapped its icy arms around the estate, while the bare branches of the trees rhythmically scraped against the wooden fence. The sound of the branches outside mingled with the faint scratching of Ethan's pencil on paper. The unique medley served as a reminder of the sharp contrast between speculation and the hidden truths known only to Custer and Libbie, a divide that seemed to grow wider with each passing moment.

"Libbie saw the truth despite the chaos," Custer continued, his tone softening as the earlier intensity of his emotions began to fade. His eyes looked thoughtfully at the portrait that gently hovered above the mantel, where Libbie's calm, wise face was framed in ornate gold, capturing her likeness and spirit. "She absorbed all the chatter, every cruel insult carelessly hurled from the officers' wives, and every sharp, whispered remark exchanged in dimly lit corners of their social gatherings, standing firm against the relentless storm of judgment and hardship. She read every letter and article that tried to tarnish my name and reputation. Through all the seasons of uncertainty and fear, her gaze remained fixed on mine without flinching; her trust stayed strong, reflecting a faith that no adversity could dislodge."

Filled with admiration and respect, Ethan captured her loyalty on the page, firmly underlining his note with deliberate strokes and writing "Loyal. Unfaltering. Fearless."

"Beyond your marriage, how do you believe she will be remembered by history?" asked Ethan.

A long, weary sigh, laden with countless memories, fell from Custer's lips. "She didn't disappear when I received my various honors," he began, his voice, though tired, warm with the sound of her name. "Libbie never wore a general's sash, nor did she lead soldiers from atop a noble horse. Instead, she excelled at inspiring audiences far more than any drum ever carried in battle, more powerfully than any bugle announcing dawn each day." He shifted slightly in his seat, the leather creaking softly beneath him as he leaned forward, almost conspiratorial, as if about to reveal a long-held secret. Even in the dim, gentle light of the library, his eyes sparkled with youthful excitement. "While they painted me as a hero or a villain, depending on the storyteller's bias, she worked tirelessly behind the scenes, penning letters that shaped our private world. Hundreds of them. Strong, clear letters that flew like homing pigeons to senators and governors, reaching women whose names weren't carved into stone or etched into history, yet who had steadfastly supported this nation through its many challenges while men were caught in muddy battles and preoccupied with drawing pointless borders on maps."

Ethan wrote, "Libbie, the general of suffrage."

Custer continued speaking, gazing around the peaceful, wood-paneled room as if he could feel the presence of the determined women who had fought for their rights. "She welcomed them right here, Ethan." With a steady and resonant tone, Custer stated, "Their discussions took place in this room and the neighboring parlor, where significant decisions and debates were held. Outside, spring blossoms adorned the twisted branches of the apple trees, their delicate petals scattering in the breeze and spreading sweet, fragrant scents through the warm air. Inside, ideas clashed with the intensity of a coming storm. The rooms buzzed with conversations, laughter, and chatter, with delicate teacups and shining silver spoons."

He chuckled softly, feeling a mix of pride and nostalgia wash over him. "Some men, feeling secure in their detachment, cautiously peered through the parlor door, oblivious to the gravity of the forged alliances. They'd sneak hesitant glances into the room, seeing only bonnets and lace, hearing the gentle chime of teacups clinking together, all while thinking the real threats, those genuine struggles of the time, lay far from their cozy drawing rooms."

"Fools," he repeated softly, a warm hint of affection coloring his tone as he remembered their naivety. "Unseen by many, she carefully sketched maps on napkins, cultivated complex relationships over tea and pie, and built alliances with whispered promises, all helping to advance the noble cause steadily."

Custer leaned back again in his chair, his rugged face illuminated by the nearby fire. "By the time women finally received the vote," he continued, his voice soft and filled with a sense of historical righteousness, "my dear Libbie had already passed away. She helped pave the way for that pivotal moment in history. I know some people credit the ultimate victory to the energized younger generation. During the start of the Roaring Twenties, bold and daring women, sporting stylish bobbed hair, eagerly flocked to the voting booths, leaving a lasting mark on the democratic process. Yes, they did arrive riding a wave of popular sentiment. However, this glorious achievement was only possible because of the strong foundations and strategic paths Libbie's long, unrecognized efforts had built long before anyone even thought to wave a flag to celebrate such a feat. She wasn't the only voice: the Clay sisters, Susan B. Anthony, Henry Blackwell, and many others fought to advance women's rights. Still, I sincerely hope the historical record will show the true extent of Libbie's work."

Ethan, thoroughly captivated by Custer's passionate storytelling, observed that history is shaped not only by those who are loud and famous but also by those who work quietly behind the scenes, making a notable impact through persuasion and friendship rather than raw force. Libbie and her peers' legacy was marked by perseverance and unwavering dedication to a cause that ultimately defined their era. It serves as a timeless reminder of the powerful effect that a single devoted person can have on a larger movement and future generations.

Custer's tone grew softer and more contemplative as he penned his thoughts about the passage of time and Libbie's enduring influence on those around her. "Like a river fed by tributaries, her legacy joins the countless women who found the courage to stand firm, express their beliefs, and fight for what they hold dear. The subtle, less dramatic conflicts often go unnoticed in the major events that capture the public's attention. Yet, these quiet struggles shape the world as impactfully as any large confrontation on open fields, leaving an everlasting mark on society's fabric."

Ethan listened carefully, absorbing these heartfelt insights and gradually recognizing the broad and complex nature of true heroism. With each realization about his changing role as a keeper and recorder of these often-overlooked stories, he began to sincerely appreciate the importance of honoring and protecting the stories of those who often fade into the background of history. A renewed sense of purpose grew within him, transforming his duties from simple documentation to a passionate mission to amplify the voices of individuals who significantly impacted the world through their tireless dedication and intense passion.

Custer said, his voice warming with memory, "She never cared about superficial praise or acknowledgment. Her joy came from witnessing others break free from their invisible barriers. It was a relentless joy; she radiated hope to everyone around her, especially for those who most needed light during the darkest times."

In his notes, Ethan carefully wrote in a dimly lit library: "The ballot was her battlefield; she triumphed without using a sword. It was a victory of belief and conviction, not sheer might."

Custer raised his head, locking eyes with Ethan with a fiery intensity. As Custer's gaze remained fixed on him, his voice gradually gained strength and seriousness. He stated, "When you tell my story, Ethan, your piece will depict me as either a hero or a villain. Let my reputation be what it may, but I humbly request you honor my wife's memory with grace. Remind them that every single vote cast by a woman, without exception, carries her spirit in the ink. Her perseverance, quiet yet steadfast will, and enduring essence carried her through numerous challenges."

They maintained their gaze briefly. The silence between them was meaningful, as Custer revealed a rare, vulnerable side. He gave Ethan a glimpse of the fragility he usually hid from the world. In their quiet moment, Ethan instantly understood, and no words were necessary.

As Ethan carefully transcribed Custer's words, a tremor ran through his pencil as his hand shook slightly, a fact he hoped would pass unnoticed. A final inscription quietly appeared on the page: "Suffrage was her mission, graceful but unyielding." The atmosphere was filled with the essence of a woman who fought unconventional battles, achieving victory through steady progress, one letter, one meeting, and one speech at a time.

The appetizing aroma was the first sign of Harold's perfectly timed arrival. He was carrying a tray of freshly brewed coffee and warm cookies from the oven. As they enjoyed their afternoon snack, the silence in the library grew more intense.

As the grandfather clock ticked loudly, each rhythmic sound heightened the solemnity between them. Narrow afternoon rays of sunlight streamed through the tall, framed windows. Dust particles, previously unseen, slowly floated in the light, reflecting brief traces of the lives that had passed through these walls.

Following this quiet pause, Custer looked calm and collected. Ethan knew it was the right moment to ask a more personal question. “Now that we have covered her life, can you talk about Libbie’s death?”

Custer settled into the large armchair, moving slowly, the influence of years showing in his body. As he leaned forward, he gripped his cane tightly, the slight tremors in his aged hands reflecting the hardships he had endured. Time dimmed his gaze, but it stayed fixed on the dying flames in the hearth, flickering faintly against the encroaching ashes. When he finally spoke, his voice was frail and delicate, like aged paper, yet it carried the faint impression of a once-vibrant life filled with dreams and aspirations.

"She fell victim to pneumonia in the spring of '18," he said softly, his words barely above a whisper, trembling in a throat long used to silence. “In retrospect, I’m not sure if it was just pneumonia or one of the early cases of the Spanish Flu. I remember her sitting by that window,” Custer reflected, his gaze drifting from the flickering flames of the fire. Soft light streamed in, illuminating the intimate space with a gentle glow. "Often, Harold would bring her tea, which she barely sipped, the steam rising and evaporating aimlessly into the air. She would observe the orchard budding outside, her eyes fixed on the first hesitant green daring to show through the lifeless branches, and listen to the sparrows arguing in the porch rafters above. Every morning, no matter how high her fever was, she would slightly turn her head and say, ‘Autie, the blossoms will be late this year. I can feel it in the air.’"

Outside, the orchard's branches trembled slightly, as if recalling her gentle spirit or the touch of her hand on the cool glass she gazed through, a barrier dividing her from the lively world beyond.

Custer struggled to speak. "She passed away in her bed upstairs, surrounded by doctors who couldn't save her or ease her suffering. Her body weakened from the fever and pneumonia. Her cough revealed her pain. Her grip on my hand loosened as she took her final breath. I closed my eyes tightly, not in prayer, but in a desperate attempt to escape the pain.”

"It didn’t work.”

Ethan’s pencil hovered over the paper, hesitant and unsure for a moment. There was no honor, no strategy, and no glorious story to tell in this sad account. Instead, it told a tale of anguish, a battle lost before it even began, set in the library's quiet, where history, memory, and emotion intertwined.

"I genuinely thought she would win that fight,” he continued, his voice trembling slightly as his sorrow surfaced, revealing the depths of his despair. "Libbie consistently managed to persevere through overwhelming challenges. Her spirit was much stronger than mine; she was a beacon of resilience. She faced the dusty, harsh, desolate cavalry camps, enduring the constant whispers of yellow fever that haunted every summer and the petty scandals that a general's spouse might endure. But that cough..." He paused, his eyes growing distant, filled with the pain of a memory replayed repeatedly in his mind's theater. "First, it stole her voice, silencing her cherished songs and laughter. Then the world seemed to fade into a muted gray. It was as if time itself paused, holding its breath in mourning."

Ethan wrote with passion, pressing the pencil harder against the paper so the graphite made a deeper mark, etching his emotions into the surface: "The orchard bloomed late, after she was gone." The stark reality was overwhelming, serving as a tangible reminder of the remaining emptiness.

Custer raised his hand to his chest pocket, gently patted it, and said, "I keep her last letter here. She wrote it just before she became ill and asked if I was happy. I find myself unable to answer her question."

Custer didn't dare glance at Libbie's lively portrait, which showed a bright young woman smiling down from the framed canvas, her vibrancy captured forever in that moment. Perhaps he feared that the joy in her painted smile would be too painful to face, a cruel contrast to the void filling his life. "Her final resting place is on the ridge beyond the orchard," he said, his voice growing tired yet noticeably strong, filled with fervent tenderness, as if trying to summon her presence through his words. "I could have chosen Arlington, where she'd rest beside my comrades, among the regiments, flags, and cannons. But she wasn't theirs; she was mine. This land was the only flag she ever needed, weathered by frost or blooming with life, through muddy paths in harsh winters and the bright springs. This land, this orchard, was her true home, where her spirit could flourish forever."

As Ethan took a moment to gather his thoughts, he looked carefully around the library. Over the past few days, he had admired the impressive collections of books, telegrams, maps, and transcripts, while privately longing to explore the history at his fingertips. Now he saw the room differently, beyond its historical grandeur to the countless intimate moments that had also taken place within its walls. It hosted gatherings filled with important discussions, decisions, and personal conversations, and private moments.

A wave of nostalgia washed over them as the fireplace softly crackled, offering cozy warmth. Custer's silence reflected his absorption in memories of love and the pain of grief. However, his stillness revealed a man caught between two strong feelings: the piercing sorrow of losing loved ones and the steadfast, fierce resilience of his spirit.

"How have you managed to move forward in the eight years since she passed?" Ethan asked.

Custer then leaned back, feeling the aftermath of his years not as a burden but as a lively canvas for capturing vivid memories of an exceptional woman. "Libbie was not just my partner; she was a fighter, a quiet yet powerful advocate for justice and equality. Her presence was always with me wherever I traveled, gently urging me to remember the noble ideals we both championed. She stayed resolute, consistently reminding me that our victories were not solely ours to celebrate but also belonged to all who dared to dream and work toward a better future."

"From that day in the spring of '18," Custer began, his voice gentle and reflective, echoing the wisdom of his journey. "I felt her strength, and I knew I had to persevere. I find a sense of peace among the trees when the flowers bloom in vibrant glory. The air is sweet and heavy with the enchanting scent of apples, while bees flit about, joyfully intoxicated by the nectar they gather with such care. I often go back to that familiar ridge, talking to her as if she were there, resting comfortably against the well-loved fence post, just like in those precious, cherished moments in my memory. She would have quietly reminded me not to leave my boots carelessly strewn in the hallway or playfully chided me for the bits of mud I tracked across the shining floor."

"Our partnership lasted and thrived for over fifty years. Even in its early days, we recognized how special our bond was. We cherished the time we shared and promised never to let a single moment go unnoticed. Our marriage lasted more than five decades, a milestone few couples reach, and every challenge and success strengthened our commitment. We were fortunate to grow old together, and I treasure every moment."

"Especially every spring, she speaks to my heart in a silent language, a whisper on the breeze. If I listen closely, her presence will come alive once again."

While he spoke, Ethan finished writing his heartfelt thoughts on the crisp, blank page, capturing Custer's unwavering belief in the enduring power of love and memories. "Peace blooms in the orchard," he wrote, each word carefully chosen to reflect the quiet resilience and emotional significance of the old man's cherished memories.

"I keep her shawl on the chair near the fireplace," said Custer. His eyes were distant, fixed on the empty seat as if she still occupied it. "I pause each day and put my hand upon it."

In the quiet library, a poignant silence hung in the air. Ethan sat peacefully, realizing that some gestures were too personal and meaningful to write down. He gently put down his pencil and closed his notebook.

## Chapter 14: The Final Session

The arrival of winter brought a sharp chill on the morning of the final visit when Ethan came to the estate, signaling the change of seasons and the bittersweet feeling of goodbyes. A familiar companion during his visits, the once-gentle breeze shifted into a steady hum that rustled through the surrounding trees, with the cold biting at the edges and corners of the grand old house.

Ethan arrived following the carefully practiced routine he had used since their sessions began a week earlier. As always, the dependable black sedan glided smoothly up the gravel driveway, the accustomed ritual a steady constant to his growing anticipation. Getting out of the car, Ethan felt a freezing dampness seep through his coat, sharpening the cold and intensifying the sense of finality in the air. His driver, a man of few words but with a knowing look, nodded briefly before driving away.

The estate looked the same as always, its stillness intensifying with winter's approach. It emitted a silence that felt less like seasonal change and more like a final farewell. It was as if the air was holding its breath, aware of the moment's significance and the emotions it carried. The back fields, usually bustling with the sounds and motion of hidden wildlife, stood quiet, covered in a silvery frost that glistened in the early light as the sun's first rays brightened the landscape, patiently waiting for whatever fate might bring.

As Ethan arrived at the grand oak doors, Harold, the faithful butler, greeted him with his customary steady presence. Harold replaced his usual polite greeting with a more serious nod today, a small gesture that sent a strong message. His usually inscrutable eyes showed a glimpse of comprehension intertwined with a touch of emotion and sadness, reflecting the day's significance. The precision in his movements had become slow and deliberate as he guided Ethan into the library, where the air was thick with an unsettling feeling. Without saying a word, Harold tended to the small antique silver tray on the table, which held a steaming pot of rich coffee and warm, freshly baked bread. The pleasant smells offered a fleeting moment of comfort as Harold stepped back, allowing Ethan to prepare for the critical conversations ahead.

Within the quiet sanctuary of the library, a space filled with leather-bound books and histories, General Custer sat in his large, high-backed leather chair. The dark, polished surface of the chair seemed to absorb the little light available, while the flickering fireplace's uneven, warm glow sharply outlined his figure.

Custer raised his head, greeting Ethan with a reserved smile, "Good morning, Mr. Thorne. I trust you are well prepared for our final day together. This should prove to be an interesting day." Ethan returned the greeting, stating that he felt prepared and was looking forward to their discussions. Custer added, "Before we begin, warm yourself with some hot coffee," motioning to the tray.

From his less commanding seat across the low, polished table, Ethan noticed a subtle stiffness in Custer's posture. Ethan understood that the General's body, which might be stiff from the cold coming in from outside, also bore a much heavier burden: the lasting effects of many years and scars from battles fought not just in open fields but also in quiet struggles within his own memories. Each ache, every slight tremor, seemed to testify to a life lived on the edge of legend and loss.

As he sipped his coffee, a familiar heaviness settled in Ethan's chest, a mix of anticipation and solemnity. He carefully, almost ritualistically, rearranged the stack of notes on the dark wooden table before him; the only sound was a faint rustle of paper. He paused briefly, allowing the atmosphere to breathe, expand, and contract until he sensed Custer was ready to proceed.

The General's usually steady hands now trembled almost imperceptibly as he fumbled with his unlit briar pipe. Usually grasped with purpose, the polished wood slipped from his weakening grip, falling softly with a nearly reverent thud onto the plush rug below. It was a small, seemingly insignificant action. Yet, to Ethan, it was a powerful display of raw vulnerability, a crack in the formidable facade of strength and authority the general usually projected.

And yet, Ethan hardly noticed the event as an anomaly anymore. It had gone beyond being a mistake; it had become a quiet, repeated action, a subtle, almost automatic surrender of control that had become a key part of their unusual experience and shared arduous journey. He vividly remembered the rich, commanding tone of Custer's voice from a previous encounter, the authoritative tenor in which he had once told him to "leave it," a simple phrase that etched itself into Ethan's memory.

Ethan cleared his throat, the soft sound amplified in the quiet reverence of the library. "General," he began, his voice steady despite the thrill of excitement coursing through him, "may I inquire about your perspective on prohibition? Do you believe the Eighteenth Amendment has truly fulfilled the promise it set forth?"

Custer's piercing eyes, sharp as any eagle's, lifted from the delicate porcelain cup cradled in his hand. A short, dry laugh escaped him like the rustle of dried leaves. "Promise?" he parroted, the word laced with a lifetime of skepticism. "I've lived long enough to witness every promise made by man curdle into something bitter. Men drink. They have always, and will always. In my day, the roughest men hid whiskey bottles in their saddlebags. No law could pry it from their hands, only their discipline. And if a man lacks that inner fortitude, no amendment enshrined in the Constitution will magically plant it within his belly."

Ethan's pencil moved quickly, the lead scratching the paper. "So, General, would you advocate for its repeal?"

Custer, with a casual flick of his hand, a gesture still carrying a surprising breadth and strength despite the faint tremor that now revealed his age, waved the question away. “Leave such matters to the younger generations,” he stated dismissively. “I have little appetite for debates with zealots and puritans. My horses, you see, do not beg for gin; frankly, they are far better company for that reason.”

Ethan quickly jotted down a note and then asked, "General, in the years since you left office, have you kept in touch with the other men who held the position? The fraternity, so to speak?"

Custer smiled, a gentle, genuine warmth touching his lips, immediately taking him back to a bygone era. "Roosevelt and I were kindred spirits, you see," Custer started, nodding slowly. "Teddy. He had that fire, that endless, almost reckless drive. The same fierce love for the wild, for the challenge of the untamed continent. When he was in the Executive Mansion, we kept in touch regularly over the years, though our paths diverged quite a bit after his time in office."

Custer leaned forward slightly, his eyes sparkling with shared memory. "We always spoke of taking one last great hunting trip out west, to see the country as it once was, a final venture into the mountains of Montana or the Dakotas before the railroads finished their work. It was a promise made and remade over a dozen dinners. Life, however, has a savage way of interfering with such plans."

Custer chuckled, a dry, knowing sound hinting at old battlefield dust. "He invited me on his South American venture, you know, to the Amazon. I told him flatly, 'Teddy, that's a younger man's folly and a fool's errand besides.'" Custer shook his head, the memory still fresh. "He nearly died of a fever down there in that green, humid hell, lost in that jungle for months. That proved my point, I suppose. I was saddened when we lost him, far too soon for a man of such vitality, but I'm glad to say I still hear from his boy, Teddy Junior. A fine young man, carrying on the family name with honor."

Custer's hand rested on the arm of his chair, the gesture laden with the burden of years. "At present," Custer noted, his tone turning somber, "it is only Mr. Taft and I still walking the Earth. Billy Taft, bless his soul. Two entirely different temperaments, he and I, yet we carry the same memory of that burden. A rather exclusive membership, wouldn't you say? Membership gradually dwindles with each passing year. The longest-lived former president was John Adams, the second president of the United States. He achieved a remarkable milestone of living to the age of 90, and I intend to surpass his record and establish a significantly higher benchmark."

A silence filled the room before Custer spoke again, his voice becoming softer with emotion. "The largest gathering of the fraternity I remember was a decade ago, at Libbie's funeral." He swallowed hard, the memory clearly affecting him. "Politics completely fades away in moments like that. All the anger, campaigning, and disputes over tariffs or foreign policy become meaningless when you stand before the earth, covering the most precious part of your life. When Libbie passed, the support was... humbling."

"President Wilson and his wife, Edith, attended, of course, offering the formal, expected condolences of the sitting administration. Privately, he confided a heartfelt personal message that I found touching. He lost his first wife in 1914, and he understood the pain. Billy Taft and his wife, Nellie, were there, their faces etched with sincere sympathy. And Teddy and Edith. I can still see Teddy's face, raw with grief, not only because he had respected Libbie but also because he knew the sorrow of loss. He was a young man when his first wife passed, and I believe her death was a sadness he never truly overcame."

He paused, gathering his thoughts, momentarily lost in the image of those figures assembled beneath the cold winter sky. "To have two former presidents and the current president, men who had commanded the attention of the world and carried the fate of the Republic on their shoulders, stand with you in your grief is a testament to the overwhelming, shared burden of the office. It was a great comfort to know that in the end, we were simply men who had served, standing together against the inevitability of loss. That is a bond that, once forged by the Executive Mansion, never truly breaks."

In that quiet moment of reflection, the bold, flamboyant cavalry officer from history faded away, replaced by an elder statesman who not only outlived his legend but also survived the political turmoil of his time. George Armstrong Custer found his most lasting and meaningful camaraderie not on the sunbaked plains of the battlefield but in the quiet, dignified, and exclusive fraternity of the American presidency.

"Even with the Great War still raging on, several military personnel attended Libbie's funeral. Among them were two generals who had also fought in the Civil War: Aaron Daggett and his wife, Rose, as well as Peter Hains and his wife, Virginia. Pete and I had graduated together from West Point in the Class of 1861. The military presence at my wife's service was a touching and respectful tribute that I will always remember."

Throughout the morning, Custer discussed the large crowd at Libbie's funeral, including the Vice President, Tom and Lois Marshall, Levi and Anna Morton, Charlie Fairbanks, and many others. He shared numerous stories of visitors and conversations, providing impressive detail. He also showed several letters and telegrams from those who couldn't attend, including foreign leaders he had met over the years.

Ethan respectfully kept his distance from Custer regarding Libbie's funeral, giving him plenty of time to reminisce and share memories. After a while, Custer paused and returned the telegrams and handwritten notes to their proper places in the library.

Harold entered the room with a luncheon tray and set the items on the table. As he left, Ethan and the General took the chance to enjoy the meal.

After the meal, Ethan moved on to a different topic. "What is your assessment of the situation in Europe, General? Specifically, what do you think of the rise of Benito Mussolini? It seems some Americans, I've heard, hold him in high regard, believing he's brought order to a land mired in chaos. Others, however, denounce him as a brutal tyrant. How do you interpret these different perspectives?"

Custer suddenly straightened in his chair and leaned forward, shifting from weary relaxation to sharp focus. "Order," he declared, his voice a low, steady rumble, deliberate and somber. "It is a word that sings a siren's song. I spent much of my life chasing it myself, trying to embed it into the souls of men and the very fabric of nations. But order that is born of fear... that's no true order at all. Mussolini," he concluded, his gaze distant, "rides a storm he can't possibly tame. Storms, young man, hold no loyalty; they don't care who claims to control them. I've spoken with Coolidge about Mussolini, and I believe Cal has the situation well in hand. I have nothing more to add."

Ethan scribbled furiously, his heart pounding a wild, desperate rhythm against his ribs. This was a reporter's goldmine, far surpassing his initial hopes. Yet, as he looked up, ready to ask another probing question, a subtle shift in Custer's expression caught his attention. The General had already leaned back into his chair, his earlier fire seemingly fading, replaced by a powerful silence. His gaze had drifted beyond the room's bounds, past the sturdy walls, through the window, and out toward the distant, silhouetted shapes of the barns.

The silence was suddenly and smoothly broken as Custer's voice cut through it. "Give me your assessment, Ethan," he commanded, his words emerging from within his chest with a gravelly, resonant tone that seemed to vibrate through the very timbers of the room. It was a voice rich with undeniable, ingrained authority, yet subtly underscored by a pervasive weariness that belied his usual vigor. "What conclusion have you drawn?" he pressed, his gaze steady.

Ethan paused, eyebrows furrowing in surprise and curiosity, his posture subtly tense. Custer's bluntness was expected; however, the sudden timing of his question briefly distracted Ethan, who had anticipated a more extended back-and-forth. Instead, the question was direct and sincere, a challenge laid bare without any disguise. He met Custer's sharp gaze without flinching, seeing the vast, almost unbreakable well of experience and the hard-earned wisdom carved into the General's weathered face.

"About... you, General?" Ethan asked softly, his tone steady and controlled, seeking clarity in the sudden all-encompassing question.

A sharp, unwavering glint ignited fiercely in Custer's eyes. Custer responded with a sudden, nearly startling burst of spirited energy that filled his words. "You were selected to come here to uncover the full, unvarnished picture. Now that you have removed the veneer and embraced the broader canvas, what is your analysis?"

The gravity of the question pressed down on Ethan, causing him to lean forward in his seat and become more involved in the discussion. This moment signaled a crucial turning point in their knowledge and was a vital conclusion to the lengthy discussions they had shared over the week.

"I believe..." he began, his voice growing stronger and more confident as he carefully chose his words, "that I have gained valuable insights and a greater appreciation for the significance and influence that stories truly hold. Each story, especially those of men like you, carries a heavy, almost unbearable burden: the high cost of becoming legendary, forever subjected to the relentless judgment of history. History, in its unforgiving and steady march forward, has a strange, almost cruel knack for shaping a person, for smoothing out the rough, inconvenient edges of their humanity, and often, for showcasing only the polished, shining myth, leaving behind a carefully refined narrative that may, sadly, overshadow the complex, unembellished truth."

Custer let out a dry, raspy laugh, a sound that seemed to scrape against the quiet of the room, starkly reminiscent of brittle, forgotten leaves skittering across frozen, fallow ground in the increasing chill of late autumn. "Well expressed, Ethan," he acknowledged, the words a gravelly murmur. "In the manner you select your words, you have the makings of a great journalist," he added with a chuckle. "Or a politician." A brief, nearly unnoticed flicker of grim satisfaction appeared on his weathered face, and his lips moved slightly.

He shifted his gaze from Ethan to the grand, oil-painted portrait of Libbie hanging proudly above them. She vigilantly watched their every word and gesture, as if she were a silent, eternal guardian of the intimate memories shared within these walls. Then, Custer's eyes slowly moved to the large window that framed a panoramic, unobstructed view of the sprawling, frost-covered fields. In the distance, but sharply outlined against the muted landscape, a spirited young colt, full of untamed energy and emerging strength, raced carelessly through the pale, fading autumn stubble. The lively scene contrasted sharply with the elderly soldier's quiet presence, showcasing a vivid display of energy and freedom reminiscent of Custer's youth.

"Let's step away for a short break," Custer said softly, his voice gentle. He carefully set his pipe on a small side table. "Enough of these political disputes and talk of conflict. You didn't come all this way to hear an old man repeat the same tired verses. Let me show you what I fill my days with now, what truly occupies the remaining chapters of my life."

Ethan, his notebook held loosely at his side, followed Custer into the crisp October air. The dry leaves crunched softly under their boots as they crossed the yard. When they reached the stables, they found the enormous doors wide open, revealing the vast interior filled with the comforting, earthy aromas of sweet hay, well-worn leather, and the unmistakable scent of horseflesh. Shafts of sunlight slanted into the barn. As Custer stepped inside, the animals stirred in their stalls. Ears twitched, sleek heads lifted, and a collective spark of recognition seemed to ignite in their intelligent eyes.

Moving slowly, Custer entered the stables. In the first stall, a beautiful chestnut colt lifted its head, its dark eyes wide and bright. A blaze of white ran down its nose, and its legs were long and well-formed. It was a creature full of raw potential, brimming with energy just waiting to be unleashed.

“That’s him,” Custer said, and the pride in his voice was warm and genuine. It was a softer, more sincere kind of pride, quite different from Custer’s usual bravado when talking about battle flags and cavalry charges. “This is Prairie Fire. He was foaled in March, and he has the legs and the fire. Maybe,” he added, almost to himself, “he’ll outrun my legacy.”

As they moved along the line of stalls, Custer muttered, “Morning, Duchess.” His fingers softly caressed the velvety neck of a striking chestnut mare. “Easy there, Juno,” he added, his hand resting calmly on the strong flank of a magnificent black stallion, who responded with a gentle snort and a single, rhythmic stomp of his hoof. He addressed each animal as if speaking to an old, trusted friend, his tone free of formalities and full of sincere, genuine affection. The horses, in turn, leaned into his touch, their large, soft eyes showing quiet happiness, nuzzling at the fabric of his sleeves.

“The rest of the horses are in a paddock with the trainers or in the pastures,” Custer said as they walked through the stable. He paused at the very last stall. Within stood a bay stallion marked with a white star on his forehead, his back gently bowed with age, his coat bearing a dusty, muted sheen, and his once-bright eyes clouded with the passage of years. The horse slowly raised its head, its ears swiveling towards the familiar sound of Custer's voice, and nickered a soft greeting.

“This is Dandy Star,” Custer said softly, his hand moving gently over the animal's weathered neck. “He is the great-grandson of Dandy, one of my old warhorses. Star has sired several sure-footed, agile foals; many of them are running in our fields today. I have owned seven generations of this bloodline, starting with Dandy.” His gaze seemed to drift back through the decades, across battlefields etched in memory. “He carried me at Gettysburg, the Washita, and the Little Bighorn.” His voice faltered for a brief, emotional moment, a tremor of feeling breaking through the stoic front. “Strongest creature I ever rode.”

Custer reached for a well-worn grooming brush, its bristles softened by years of use. He began to work, his strokes steady and rhythmic, smoothing the brown coat. The stallion shifted its weight beneath the comforting pressure, its breath seeming to sigh with pure contentment, soothed by the familiar, meditative rhythm. Custer leaned his forehead briefly against the horse’s warm neck, his weathered hand resting gently where the thick mane had thinned with age. “You’ve carried your years,” he whispered, his voice thick with quiet reverence, “with far more grace than I ever managed to carry mine." As he continued grooming the horse with care, he added, "We make a good team, don't we, Star?"

Ethan stood frozen, his hand still. The notebook, a symbol of his purpose, hung aimlessly by his side. He felt overwhelmed by a sense of intrusion, as if he had entered a sacred, private ritual. He thought he had witnessed the primal connection between man and beast that resonated on a level far more fundamental than the grand stories of war and politics.

Custer lingered in the stall, his movements slow and deliberate, humming a tune under his breath, a melody that had once sounded across dusty parade grounds, now softened into a gentle, melancholic lullaby. This once magnificent stallion, utterly at peace, closed his eyes.

When Ethan hesitantly turned to leave, the General did not flinch; he remained in the quiet of the stall, hands working patiently as he brushed the horse with a devotion that seemed as endless as the fading light. The golden glow from the stable doorway cast a warm light over them, a tableau of quiet resilience. Soldier and beast, survivors of vastly different wars, finding solace and companionship in each other’s presence as the long October dusk settled over the land.

A trainer released a few horses from the barn while Ethan waited nearby. Custer put away the brush and had a brief chat with the man. Then he turned to

Ethan, nodded toward the house, and said, "Time to go back."

As they headed back to the house, the sun lowered in the sky, casting long, slanting shadows across the paddocks. In the distance, the young colt, Prairie Fire, suddenly kicked up his heels and bolted, racing the wind for the pure joy of it, a flicker of unbridled life against the fading light.

No sooner had they arrived at the library than Harold set down a tray with two cups of steaming hot tea. They sat quietly, sipped their tea, and warmed themselves by the fire as they usually did. Ethan was keenly aware that this was their last meeting and that he would need to leave soon to catch his train. As he organized his notes, he also reflected on his thoughts: Were there any final questions he needed to ask? Would Custer bring up a new topic that they couldn't explore? How would their farewell unfold?

The moment the tea was finished, Custer began speaking, "I owned a farm just outside of Monroe, Michigan, with my brother, Nevin, which we purchased in '71. I had dreams of raising horses there after I retired from the army. Nevin and his wife, Ann, lived there and managed the farm. When he was 19, he had enlisted in the army, planning to fight side by side with me, just as we used to do with our chores. But when he got to the state camp at Columbus, the army discharged him due to his rheumatism. He fiercely opposed their decision, given the grueling physical work he performed every day on the farm without issue. Furious hardly describes how angry he was, and Nevin was rarely angry. He was a quiet, unpretentious, hardworking, honest man. We made a good team."

Ethan noticed that the phrase 'we made a good team' was the same one Custer had said to his horse, Dandy Star, in the stables. The meaning was clear: you are respected, you are trusted, and you are family.

Custer continued, "Nevin is gone now; he passed in 1915. He lived and worked on that farm until his final day. When I became president, Libbie and I sold our half to him for one dollar. He ran a good business there. Now, it belongs to his son."

"Sometime after the Battle at the Little Bighorn, I bought Dandy from the army and brought him home to Monroe. Even during my presidency, Dandy lived with my brother on that farm. I could have taken him to the grand new stables on the grounds of the Executive Mansion, but he was a warhorse. I knew him, and that environment would never have suited his nature; he would have felt trapped, and I wanted him to thrive. He deserved a better life than that. He survived that last battle and others before it; he earned his respect."

"He spent the rest of his days on that farm. My brother provided him with excellent care, and my father often visited and took a special interest in him. Dandy lived to be 26 and is buried in the old orchard behind the house."

As he spoke, Custer stood up and took down a framed picture from one of the shelves. "Dandy was sure-footed and agile, and my father, Emanuel, often rode him. I believe that was the only time he felt close to his fallen sons because Dandy had been there, too." Custer took a slow breath and then added, "This picture was taken in front of Nevin's house on the farm. My father would have been in his early 70s at the time," handing the frame to Ethan.

While examining the picture of Custer's father atop Dandy, he noticed how the older man carried himself. Ethan commented, "This is an impressive picture. The noble spirit of your horse is well captured. Your father sat that horse tall and proud and seemed to carry himself with the confidence of any commander." He paused and made eye contact with Custer. "He must have been very proud of having a son who became the President of the United States."

Custer got up to stretch his legs and, as usual, walked over to look out the window for a moment. When he returned, his mood had lightened, and he carried a large scrapbook he had taken from the bookshelf. Sitting down, he opened the book filled with black-and-white photographs, some weathered and faded. He invited Ethan to pull his chair closer, and as he pointed to certain pictures, he began to talk. He shared many intimate stories of family gatherings and special occasions. He spoke of memories with his siblings, the 'tomfoolery' of childhood innocence, and the trouble and worry they sometimes caused for their dear mother.

He remembered how his father kept a fifty-yard gap between them during corn-hoeing to stop them from talking. He got in trouble for bringing a book into the field.

When he saw a picture of his parents, he stared at it for a long time before speaking. “Mother was a devout woman, but fragile. Father was strict in how he lived and worked and in what he expected of others. That worsened after the battle. You must realize, it changed them. They mourned deeply, grief that lasted until their dying day. Because of one afternoon’s events, they lost two sons, a grandson, a son-in-law, and other ‘sons’ among their neighbors and friends. One never truly recovers from that.”

Ethan realized that with those words, Custer was also talking about himself. “You have to realize that it changed them."

Ethan realized he had finished his task and completed his assignment. Over the past six days, many questions had been asked and answered, and many stories had been shared. However, the last few hours revealed the truth he had been searching for. In just one afternoon, the veil was lifted, exposing the real man behind the storied legend.

Custer rose and placed the scrapbook of photographs back on the shelf. When he returned to his chair, he sat quietly for a short time. His mood had changed, and he seemed to be considering his following words quite carefully. He turned his full attention to Ethan and asked, “Will you write the article capturing my legacy, Ethan? It's a task that holds the seriousness of history mixed with personal memories.” His tone softened just a little. A slight, almost vulnerable insistence tinged his usually stern voice. A feeling of expectation filled the air, a silent plea beyond words, resting squarely on Ethan's shoulders.

"I will," Ethan responded, his voice firm and resolute. He understood the responsibility he was determined to face. The approaching anniversary of Custer's election was not just a date; it was a deadline, a nearly tangible urgency, and a silent drumbeat. "I know you are familiar with my editor, Walter Bennett. He is a man of unwavering principles, and I am confident he will handle this task with his customary integrity," Ethan affirmed, his gaze steady. "I will strive, General, with every fiber of my being, to tell the unfiltered truth, to present it as accurately, as painstakingly, as humanly possible, always aiming to create a narrative that honors both the complex, fascinating man you are and the lasting history you represent."

Custer slowly lifted his head, and a gentle peace washed over his face, as if sharing this burden had eased his long-held grief. He said, "I don't know which will endure: the public's image of me or the actual truth I lived. In your writing, I hope for the latter, capturing not just the history but also the complexity of doubt, fear, loss, and love. I can ask for nothing more." He exhaled slowly, and his shoulders noticeably relaxed as the tension in his frame evaporated. It seemed he had finally found a sense of contentment and clarity amid the noise of his storied past.

In the quiet of General Custer's study, filled with the scent of aged leather and lingering pipe smoke, Ethan carefully organized his detailed interview notes as the anticipation of departure grew, creating a vivid picture of Custer's life. An immense feeling of achievement washed over him. The idea of a compelling feature article began to take shape in his mind, forming like a masterpiece sculpted from insight and recognition.

Custer slowly rose and moved toward Ethan, lost in thought as he twirled his pipe. His eyes were fixed on the opposite wall while Ethan continued working on his notes. Then, Custer dropped his pipe again. The moment seemed to freeze, just like before; Ethan remained perfectly still, only turning the pages, and didn't react or acknowledge the slip. Custer, perhaps jolted back to the present by the familiar sound of the pipe hitting the floor, noticed Ethan's calmness without surprise. A faint, almost invisible sigh escaped him as he stooped down. He took a little longer to pick up the pipe and straighten up. Ethan saw the delay but had learned not to acknowledge Custer's pipe retrieval. Custer then took the few remaining steps back to his chair and settled himself again, the pipe now securely in his hand.

Custer said, "After you have finished writing these articles, I would like to arrange for you to return. I look forward to our discussion regarding your completed work."

Ethan agreed and felt a sense of duty to accurately portray the man before him and the many historical elements intricately linked to his extraordinary journey. This went beyond a simple assignment; it became a mission rooted in respect and honesty, a calling to shed light on the complexities of the past. He understood that history can often be an unreliable guide, usually shaped and interpreted through the perspectives of those who controlled the story: the victors, the victims, and those brave enough to speak their truth. For General Custer, it was a legacy marked by complexity, a rich tapestry of bravery, sorrow, and a longing for redemption, as reflected in the stories that would forever be connected to his name.

As the day came to an end, Ethan and Custer acknowledged the mutual understanding and respect they had built. A genuine connection had formed through their honest conversations and candid observations. This journey was meant to be more than just a trip into history; it was a true exploration of the human experience through the eyes of one remarkable individual who had lived it.

Ethan cast a quick glance at the mantel clock, mindful that he would need to end their meeting momentarily. He took a deliberate breath and reviewed his notes one last time, contemplating the important and meaningful task that lay ahead. He aimed to preserve history and communicate it with the depth, richness, and complexity it deserved, ensuring that the individual and his influence would not be overlooked.

With a firm handshake, Ethan said goodbye. However, he knew he would carry the essence of this moment inside, ensuring that General Custer's voice would remain long after their conversation ended and faded into the distance.

As Ethan turned to leave the study, the sound of his heels clicking on the smooth floorboards reverberated through the silent room, emphasizing the finality of their encounter. Just then, he noticed Custer raising a finger, steady and deliberate, as if giving one last piece of advice.

"Remember," the General said, his voice low and full, resonating with a gravitas that seemed to bridge the gap between past and present. "The genius of a great story is revealed not just by what is written but also by when it is revealed, much like a clever joke."

Ethan was momentarily taken aback and caught off guard by Custer's comments; still, he managed to produce a polite, slightly forced laugh that seemed to mask his curiosity. "Certainly, General," he replied, giving a brief but respectful nod, a gesture of acknowledgment. With that, he left the library, his mind swirling with thoughts, intrigued and still a bit puzzled by Custer's enigmatic words.

As he boarded the train, the rhythmic clattering of the rails greeted him like an old friend. This familiar sound offered little comfort amid the mental exhaustion he had accumulated from the assignment, creating a stark emotional contrast that left him unsettled. He focused on crafting the perfect opening for his article, aiming to highlight the key themes of Custer's life—his victories, struggles, and complexities—that he hoped would resonate with his readers and draw them into the detailed story he planned to tell. The last rays of sunlight poured through the window, illuminating the worn seats and emphasizing the thoughtful expressions on the faces of fellow travelers, who were absorbed in their thoughts.

The gentle conversations around him gradually grew louder, resembling the lively noise of a peaceful town waking up in spring. A quiet giggle broke out near the aisle, soon followed by another subtle note of amusement, creating an atmosphere of shared gaiety and the comforting connection that often arises among strangers in fleeting moments. Heads turned, and eyes sparkled with delight as the once-quiet buzz of chatter shifted into a wave of laughter that spread through the train car, becoming contagious with each moment and significantly raising the mood.

Confused by the increased laughter among the passengers, Ethan furrowed his brow and looked around, trying to find the cause of the unexpected amusement spreading throughout the train. When his eyes landed on a man across the aisle, he saw that the other traveler was nearly doubled over with laughter, pointing directly at him as if he were the main subject of the shared amusement. "You've been plumed!" the man shouted, his voice almost drowned out by the joyful uproar around them. The phrase hung in the air, steeped with implication and filled with the playful camaraderie that often arises in shared spaces, creating a sense of togetherness.

A middle-aged woman nearby wavered between annoyance and amusement, unable to suppress a faint smile that showed her mixed feelings about the situation. Meanwhile, a sudden wave of embarrassment crept up Ethan's neck, quickly spreading from the collar of his shirt to his scalp and tinting his cheeks with a bright color, clearly showing his discomfort in the spotlight. Confusion and curiosity twisted inside him like a tightly wound spring, sparking a flurry of questions about why the sudden laughter was directed at him, and igniting a series of thoughts about what was happening and why it was so funny.

The man across from him pointed toward his boot, and Ethan instinctively reached behind his heel, his fingers clumsily searching for what had caused this uncomfortable situation.

There it was, a perfectly white feather tucked into the seam of his polished leather boot. It looked deliberately placed, as if someone had intentionally left it there to provoke a reaction from him, testing his dignity and composure in front of others.

For a brief yet intense moment, Ethan was entirely overwhelmed by a sharp wave of embarrassment that heated his cheeks. He wished he could disappear, avoid the attention, and wipe away any sign of awkwardness. The pressure of being in the spotlight felt overwhelming, and he longed to melt into the background. Then his thoughts drifted to General Custer's bright, mischievous eyes, an image fixed in his mind, along with his parting words, which echoed "much like a clever joke."

Gradually, as the awkwardness and giggles faded, a smile broke through his unease, like sunlight piercing the clouds. It started as a grimace, a hesitant response to his unexpected situation. But as he processed the moment and its meaning, it transformed into a genuine smile that lit up his face and lifted his spirits. He remembered Custer's tale of the prank he had played at West Point.

Ethan appreciated the Custer-like cleverness of the scene, full of humor and playful irony. The seasoned general, known for his cunning, probably planned this elaborate prank from the start. Dropping the pipe on the first day as a warning to Ethan was likely a deliberate tactic to distract him with a playful tease. Each subsequent drop was another move, carefully arranged to shift Ethan's focus away from his primary goal of staying calm and dignified. The mysterious comment at the end of their talk, the unexpected appearance of the feather now perfectly nestled in his boot, and this public reveal were all key parts of a cleverly designed, fun-filled prank. Ethan's face lit up with a broad smile as a low laugh escaped him, blending with the fading laughter in the train car.

As he turned to look out the window at the scenic countryside, he was captivated by the natural beauty, its features fading as dusk settled in. Feeling connected to both the world outside and the playful spirit inside, he couldn't help but smile again. At that moment, gratitude filled him, and he silently said, "Well played, General. Very well played."

Made in the USA
Monee, IL
31 March 2026

46745122R00167